Lucía Guerra was born in Santiago, Chile. She obtained her Master's Degree in Linguistics in the US, on a Fulbright scholarship, before entering the doctoral programme in Latin American Literature at the University of Kansas. She is currently Professor of Latin American Literature at the University of California, Irvine. She has published numerous books and articles on literary criticism and her first novel *Más allá de las máscaras* (*Beyond the Masks*) was published in Mexico in 1983. She has also published an award-winning collection of short stories, *Frutos extranos* (*Strange Fruits*). *The Street of Night* is her second novel.

Chile:

An Aymará Indian word that means
'the place where the world ends'.

GARNET WORLD FICTION

The Street of Night

Lucía Guerra

Translated by Richard Cunningham and Lucía Guerra

The Street of Night

Published by
Garnet Publishing Limited
8 Southern Court, South Street
Reading, Berkshire, RG1 4QS, UK.

ISBN 1 85964 113 X

First UK Edition

British Library Cataloguing-in-Publication Data
A catalogue record for this book is available from the British Library

Jacket and book design by David Rose
Typeset by Samantha Abley

Printed in Lebanon

Foreword

In world literature today, Latin American writers have distinguished themselves by their versatility and the presentation of multiple realities in response to the geographic and ethnic diversity of their continents; history and imagination have always gone hand in hand. The history of the region has also been tainted with violence and fiction since Christopher Columbus dropped anchor in the New World. Along with their weapons, the conquistadors were armed with images of cities like El Dorado, the fountain of eternal youth, and the Kingdom of Jauja – a place where labour was unnecessary because bread ready to be eaten grew on the trees.

These dreams of golden cities, eternal youth, and utopian paradise motivated a menagerie of expeditions, many of which ended in shipwreck, foreign captivity, and horrible death. The few victors (Cortés, Pizarro, and Valdivia, most notably) did not stamp out the beliefs of their subjugated indigenous serfs which, along with the cultural repertoire of black slaves kidnapped from Africa, remain alive today as a kind of archaeological strata affecting the world view of Latin American people both in terms of their everyday relations with reality and their artistic creativity. Simultaneously, the fictional worlds created by European and North American authors flow into the estuary of Latin American literature and form a bridge leading to a limitless rainbow of unexpected colours.

One Hundred Years of Solitude by Gabriel García Márquez might well stand in the centre of this spectrum where the concrete circumstances of Latin America are woven into a tapestry of western myths, folk tales belonging to the New World, and magical events. José Arcadio and Ursula (a new version of Adam and Eve) exhibit a unique type of original sin – they are afraid they will have a child with a pig's tail as punishment for their incestuous marriage, for they are cousins. Like the pig's appendage, the novel spins with a revolving symmetry: chronological time whirls in circles with characters that are mirror images of one another throughout this extended family saga where male personages are marked by the traditional rift between body and soul. The Arcadios (symbolic of the Latin American macho archetype) resemble Dionysus, while the Aurelianos and their spiritual search through alchemy function as a modern resonance of Apollo. Women, on the other hand, serve to display a proliferation of the Feminine and its mystique: Circe and Penelope; fertility goddesses; the *femme fatale*; industrious housewives; irreproachable mothers; and the Virgin Mary (especially Remedios the Beautiful, who ascends to heaven by hitching a ride on the sheets she has recently pinned to the clothes line).

In the guise of an old story-teller seated by the hearth in a remote village in Colombia, the narrator is, as we discover at the end of the novel, the gypsy Melquíades – a sort of reincarnation of Nostradamus – whose prophecy comes true only after a hundred years of astonishing and mystical episodes occurring within and around the cruel chain of events sparked by a century of political violence in Colombia.

At another point along this spectrum, the writings of Jorge Luis Borges transmute the concepts of philosophy and physics into fiction. Yu Tsun (in *Ficciones*, for example) is a Chinese spy for the Germans during the First World War. To alert his employers to the name of the city they must attack, he crosses the garden of forking paths to kill Stephen Albert. Ironically, Stephen has devoted years to deciphering the strange novel written by Yu Tsun's grandfather in China. The novel is an allegory of the endless forking design of the universe and the infinite. Labyrinths, mirrors, dreams, the cabala, and literary classics such as *Don Quixote* and *A Thousand and One Nights* are transformed, in Borges' imagination, into pretexts whereby he challenges and fantasizes about the prevalent notions of truth, time, space, and fiction itself.

At the other extreme, Juan Rulfo presents the voices and beliefs of Mexican peasants to produce in writing not only the impression of simple human speech, but to inscribe the basic human experiences of sexual desire, hunger, vengeance, and guilt shared by men and women attached to the earth in its eternal cycles and its unpredictable disasters. Rulfo is the paramount figure in the culmination of a Latin American literary trend which, since colonial times, has searched for an identity in non-urban cultures that have remained in the margins of modernization. His novel *Pedro Páramo* is an extended chorus of the dead circling the ghost town of Comala. Their voices recall the story of the *cacique* and the Mexican Revolution to Juan Preciado who, like the Aztec mythic figure Quetzalcoatl, embarks on a quest to search for his father.

Within a similar universe of life, death, and half-seen visions, María Luisa Bombal (in *The Shrouded Woman*) sets her protagonist off on a journey to that marvellous region submerged deep in the bowels of the earth, a landscape inhabited by luminous insects, humid prairies, luscious flowers, and skeletons miraculously twisted into the shape of a foetus. Like the intermezzo at a concert, her supernatural exploration is suspended briefly while she re-emerges above ground to enter the flow of memory and to reflect on her past life as she listens to the mourners surrounding her coffin. In an eerie conjunction of the real and the fantastic, María Luisa Bombal, during the 1930s, also denounced the repression imposed on women. Her novel *The Final Mist* introduces for the first time female sexuality from a feminine perspective. In a true adventure of desire, the protagonist sinks naked into a pond and discovers the sensual beauty of her body. Later on, while standing on a street surrounded by thick fog, she encounters a man who leads her to a mysterious house where they make love. His reappearance in a ghostlike carriage, whose horses don't disturb the water as they drink from the pond, leaves us in doubt as to whether the lover is real, a dream, or an apparition. But in the foreground of this ambiguous reality, women's desire – a taboo at the time – is finally unveiled.

The Street of Night serves as a vivid adjunct to this complex literary tradition. Lucía Guerra offers us a diagram of dictatorship in Chile – her Benefactor of the Republic is a character resonant with echoes of *I, The Supreme* by Augusto Roa Bastos, *El Señor Presidente* by Angel Asturias, and *The Autumn of the Patriarch* by Gabriel García Márquez. In Guerra's novel, however, the figure of defiance to dictatorial power has been altered by the inclusion of women prostitutes, who despite their marginality conspire against a violent despot and in so doing enter history as significant protagonists.

The Street of Night thus illustrates the phenomenal role contemporary women have played in countries like Chile, Nicaragua, and Argentina. In Argentina, the mothers of the Plaza de Mayo still march in protest, demanding justice for their murdered and disappeared sons, daughters, and husbands. This refusal to remain silent has modified the traditional image of mothers, and indeed of women in general throughout Latin America. (For example, the dictator's response to their political demonstrations was to dub them with the highly revealing and bitterly cruel epithet of "Las Locas" – which means the Crazy Ones, but also signifies prostitutes in Argentina . Their humble motto, announced daily in Buenos Aires is: *Con vida los trajimos, con vida los queremos* – We gave them life, and living we want them returned.) Like Alda in *The Street of Night*, the mothers in the Plaza de Mayo use their bodies as a political weapon, bearing the photos of their loved ones pinned to their chests and shrouding their heads with white scarfs.

The world depicted in *The Street of Night* is a place where mass communication produces a host of images and clichés which are assimilated by various personalities in the novel. Songs, movies, billboards, television and radio ads – all become incorporated into the novel's world view in the same way Manuel Puig involves such stimuli in *The Kiss of the Spider Woman* and *The Buenos Aires Affair*. The Spanish title of Guerra's novel, for example, is *Muñeca Brava*, the title of a famous tango about a man who tells a prostitute that she is a sinful flower and warns her that she will quickly lose her looks and hence her way of earning a living. The singer embroiders her life with flamboyance and fashion, evoking a dance with champagne and passion. At the beginning of *The Street of Night*, this tango functions as an inspiration to Alda who, upon being initiated into the evil nature of the excesses committed under military rule, rejects the customary portrait of her profession as distilled through the lyrics of the tango and opts instead for the biblical model of Deborah the Avenger.

In the prologue to *The Kingdom of This World*, published in 1949, the Cuban novelist Alejo Carpentier asserts his view that Latin America is the continent of the *insólito* – the realm of the extraordinary event. An exuberant natural geography (full of jungles with flesh-eating plants, the eternally snow-capped Andes, and the lunar landscape of the Atacama Desert), a history of absurd and whimsical dictatorships, the juxtaposition of the Catholic religion with enduring indigenous and African beliefs – which have given rise to Santería in Cuba and the Dominican Republic, Voodoo in the Antilles, and Macumba in Brazil – have in their totality created a unique panorama of reality. In *The Street of Night*, Martina absorbs a concept of the supernatural rooted in the rituals of the Mapuche indians in the south of Chile. As a girl she encounters Doña Rosa, a *curandera* (healer) who re-emerges miraculously in the novel to furnish the spells and incantations which enable Alda to seduce Colonel Arreola and in the end permit her to spy for the Resistance. The fact that Doña Rosa manifests herself in the fire on the kitchen stove adds a supplementary dimension to Carpentier's theory that the preparation of food in Latin America is itself another source of mystery. Lucía Guerra is thereby legitimizing an important aspect of women's subculture based on the culinary arts.

During the 17th century, the Mexican nun Sor Juana Inés de la Cruz defended the validity of scientific experimentation in the kitchen, formulating what she termed the philosophy of cooking and lamenting that Aristotle lacked the skills of a chef to enrich his writings. The Chilean Nobelist Pablo Neruda inscribed odes to the artichoke, the tomato, celery, even to the lowly onion. His contemporary Pablo de Rokha, on the other hand, wrote epic poetry celebrating certain popular dishes, such as *charquicán* and seafood delights including *congrio* and *abalone*. Both poets established the aesthetic value of food and also its sensual effect on human beings. Each writer in his own way was praising the cosmic properties of simple matter, which is generally ignored as a source of the spiritual. From the viewpoint of women writers such as Gabriela Mistral, Rosario Castellanos, and Amparo Dávila, cooking is but another reflection of the oppression of women. Note the difference between the two camps. Women are relegated to the kitchen in the same way that they are marginalized in most of Latin American society. Paradoxically, the kitchen also provides a sanctuary where women encounter the freedom to express themselves, to order the world according to their own dictates.

Martina makes an art of preparing meals. Boiling vegetables, peeling potatoes, stripping celery, skimming away fat – these activities give meaning to her existence, but also provide her with a singular concept of time and a philosophy of life. The futility of her endeavours – after all, the food she has so diligently prepared and arranged around the table as an adornment is consumed almost immediately – gives her a special insight into death and human relationships in general. In the end, what makes Martina remarkable is her sense of solidarity with Alda and Meche, to whom she is also a kind of mother, carrying her burden of grief and joy much as the mothers in the Plaza de Mayo share their own untimely fate. In *The Street of Night* women not only endure, they triumph by the very act of their refusal to accept a back seat on the bus.

Lucía Guerra is the author of four works of fiction, and she has been awarded numerous prizes for the quality of her work – among them the Premio Municipal de Literatura in Chile, the Premio Casa de las Américas in Cuba, and the Letras de Oro Prize in the United States. *The Street of Night* represents the apogee of her efforts as an author to mirror the modern complexity of Latin American society in our time. Its heroines are pariahs; conversely, they are ennobled by their desire to do away with despotism. In truth, the charade of *machismo* is on its way out, and its demise is long overdue when one considers all the suffering it has forced upon its victims – who are mainly women, and who, in *The Street of Night*, hurl down the gauntlet, challenging men to act as fellow human beings. Men invented the world. They gave names to all the animals, the trees, the insects, the denizens of the deep, the very planet on which we struggle to make our way. They invented women, too. And then they went one step further and committed the cardinal sin of inventing themselves – a fabrication they have never been able to live up to. In *The Street of Night*, Lucía Guerra is pointing out that this atavistic battle between decency and the desire to dominate is nothing more than a figment of the imagination, and the solution is simple: we must at any cost resist injustice, and at the same time we must remember that we are all brothers and sisters, in the same leaky boat, on the same perilous sea.

Richard Cunningham
1997

Select Glossary

leliuquen	A plant that grows on vines.
huinllin	A type of otter.
curandera	A healer.
maqui	A black-coloured fruit that grows in the south of Chile.
cuyen	A maiden.
cuyen nuque	A pregnant woman.

(The last four words are taken from the Mapuche language.)

Part One

I am the land where the world ends.

I am the earth which extends from the hot sands of the Atacama to the desolate glaciers in the frozen south, my face to the desert sun and my feet submerged in the cold waters off Tierra del Fuego. And so I stand, swallowing the sour taste of a history written by rifles and suffering. Here, where the world ends, my long hair sways in the wind and my waist is imprisoned by thick barbed wire.

Fixed.

Paralysed.

My arms and legs anchored to metal stakes.

Crucified for more than a decade now, I can hardly turn my tortured face to the west to hear the wail of the dead rising from the sea. In this prison under the heavens (and its multiple guises), my eyes drink in the torrent of tears and blood which day and night descend from the mountains. My hair floats in the nauseous air amid the tombs of freedom while the sharp pounding of military boots grinds up my entrails and penetrates my wounded womb, sending blood flowing down my thighs to stain the snow-covered territory of the south.

Here, at the end of the world, evil stars, medals and other military badges stick in my breasts, and from my nipples sour and bloody milk flows incessantly. Day after day, the buccaneers of death strip away my skin, burning it off with edicts and proclamations, curfews and death squads. Sinister, curved knives menace my throat while my muffled voice cries for the stars of freedom which were smashed by bullets and bugles. What once were fields embroidered with all the colours of the rainbow are now long desolate stretches of land covered by the shroud of military oppression.

At this place where the world ends, I am but a handful of hair waving in the infernal steam of tyranny's cauldron, a body confined to the quarters of injustice, a mutilated despairing soul imprisoned in this region of hell which used to be the happy motherland of paradise.

The narrow street of night began in a corner of the city and ran parallel to the avenue named in honour of the country's forefathers. In the distance, the old two-storey houses resembled broken-down wooden bird cages held together with wire. Under the dim light of red electric bulbs the faded patches of paint on the doors and walls created a mosaic of irregular and grotesque designs. Behind the rusty bars of the balconies one could glimpse several silhouettes of women brushing their hair and hastily zipping up the skirts and trousers that hugged their bodies like a second skin. Other nearby shadows sat peering into a circular mirror, carefully applying make-up, some meticulously outlining the contours of their lips, others applying mascara with that incessant curling stroke like a painter; two of them were plucking their eyebrows and chin hairs with tweezers.

At eight o'clock sharp the encaged women, wearing long earrings and cheap plastic necklaces, moved to the balcony rail to exhibit themselves for the men passing through the street. Each woman had been assigned a place according to her most attractive bodily feature, a merchandising ploy devised by the owner of the house at the time the contract was signed. The most generously endowed perched on the railing sideways, profiling their hips and raised legs. Those with big bosoms stood with their stomachs pressed to the rail to enhance their lavish breasts, while those with beautiful eyes or sensual lips accentuated this choreography of bodies by changing places at the end of each bolero. The women were forbidden to speak; they were only permitted to make those gestures which advertised that fragment of the body being showcased for the nightly auction. Thus, behind the bars: legs and hips gyrated in brief sexual overtures; eyelids painted green or blue winked lewd invitations to lust; for just a second swollen breasts emerged from a low-necked blouse before their owner tucked them back in place; bright red lips mouthed kisses.

Exactly ten minutes before curfew, the women left their imprisoning display window and, after the balcony doors were locked with a heavy, dry click, there commenced a clamour of clinking glasses and voices which, in this clandestine refuge, ignored those commands issued by the dictator in the centre of the city who had assigned to himself the role of owner and forger of all destinies.

In the age-old routine of the merchandising and trafficking of female bodies, the present remained as a nocturnal and millenary flower extending its petals to erase the vortex of reigns and battles. The ancient rituals of the fornicator, hetaera and concubine dressed in purple or saffron silk were repeated each night in heterogeneous places which harked back to the aphrodisia, the floralia and bacchanals, to the pleasure galleys of Alexandria, to the temple of Isis and the brothels of Pompeii and Herculaneum. In the immaculate mirror of timeless prostitution, Hagar offering her submissive body to Abraham's lust was reincarnated in the low-class and often starving streetwalkers loitering in medieval doorways, in the famous tarts of Jack the Ripper's London, in the hard-working whores of occupied Paris – and in every woman who lies down naked on a bed to sell the use of her body.

The street of night extended beyond the exultant shouts of hope that invaded the city every six years. In that other world of ballots and slogans and fingers shaping the V of political victory, one president after another came to power: the sober teetotalling leader wearing a scarf of fine English wool, was followed by a man with good intentions who gave sewing machines to housewives. In this torrential succession of power there was also the dandy who publicly danced a samba after outlawing the Communist party, and even an old man who held up a broom at political rallies, promising that he would sweep away all the evils in the country. In the eternal cycle of sexual transactions, the red flags and joyful songs which celebrated the victory of the people were only a small inconvenience for a couple of nights when the number of customers and profits were reduced. Some time after that came the bombing of the presidential palace, the murder of President Allende, the political prisoners thrown from military planes into the sea, the soccer stadiums converted into detention camps where informers covering their faces with black hoods selected those who were to be tortured and killed, and the soldiers with black paint under their eyes guarding each corner with M-16s – but all these events transpired beyond the border of the barred balconies in the street of night.

For those women, as for the daughters of Lot, men who crossed the threshold into that world beyond the passing of time were stripped of all the vestiges of history. Behind those dilapidated doors, they lacked both a name and a political creed. In the prelude to pleasure, all men were alike; only after the rituals of sexual intercourse had started were those women able to penetrate beneath the veneer of natural and essential features, to that which secretly swarmed under the vestments of political, religious and athletic affiliations. To the eyes of those experts in the reading of the soul, man's sexual behaviour was a hieroglyph they would quickly decipher to determine whether he was generous or mean, arrogant or modest, romantic or beastly.

Nevertheless, the cyclical image of sexual transactions was about to burst into pieces, and the denizens of the street of night were to become splinters, dispersed in the dark and stormy waters of that other world revolving among moans and military orders.

On the avenue of the forefathers of the country, the Great Benefactor of the Republic entered his palace, nodding briefly to the uniformed, saluting guards who flanked his approach. With rigid military steps he walked towards one of the armchairs in his private chamber, returned the salute of his guest, removed his dark glasses, took a seat and announced with pride and satisfaction in his familiar, high-pitched, irritating voice: "Colonel Benavides, today, October eighteenth, 1985, it is with great pride and pleasure that I declare that I have finally accomplished the sacred mission of saving our Fatherland."

The Colonel, accustomed to the General's odd and stultifying rhetoric, searched uneasily for the correct response. "Yes, my General. You have saved our nation, thanks to your manly strength and your superior intelligence."

"Everything," the General intoned, "is under control. The subversive forces have finally been smashed, totally destroyed . . . All the communists who infected our national territory are either full of lead or paying for their sins in a detention camp. There is not a spot in our beloved land which is not guarded and protected by our brave military forces." He took a deep breath, puffing his chest. "Ah, our glorious Army! I have turned it into a network of vigilantes which circulate through every inch of our country: shanty towns as well as sports clubs, university campuses as well as factories . . ." He paused as though he had forgotten something.

". . . Both private and public offices," the Colonel chimed in, "medical centres, supermarkets, churches, both radio and television stations." He held up a hand and started ticking them off on his fingers. "Restaurants, libraries, cemeteries, newspaper stands, even the city dump."

"Yes!" the General agreed. "There is not a single street, highway or country road which is not under the eternal watchfulness of my alert soldiers, by God! It is for this reason that I officially declare today, October eighteenth, 1985, that we have reached the end of the most difficult phase in our admirable mission. And since we are only men, not gods of infinite strength, I believe, Colonel, that the moment has arrived for us to have a brief and well-deserved rest from our work in the valiant effort of saving the treasured pureness of our country, virgin and intact again after being violated by those dirty communists who tied it to the Marxist yoke . . . and I believe that this unique victory, although still partial, deserves a reward; modest, of course, because I have never been an ambitious man, but a reward after all. At the bottom of my heart I have always had, Colonel, the soul of a child. What I mean is that although the years have gone by and I have won the lauds and laurels of glory, I have never forgotten the hopes and aspirations of my innocent childhood."

The Colonel was puzzled but managed to conceal it. "I understand, General. Your admiration for Comte, for example."

"No," the General rebuked him. "You are wrong. I started admiring Comte when I was already eighteen years old . . . it bothered the hell out of me to watch those arsehole civilians showing off when they talked about books and weird ideas. That's why I started going to the library at the Military Academy to look for a brainy man no one talked about, preferably French. Due to the immeasurable forces of destiny, Colonel, one day I had a premonition that I would find that man in the encyclopedia, under the letter C. My hand trembled as I flipped the pages. My search ended on page 309. Comte, August, it said next to his picture . . . I was so overwhelmed by his motto: 'Love as a principle, order as a basis, and progress as the goal.' I swear to you, my eyes were wet with tears . . ." He faltered, at a loss for words.

The Colonel found them for him. ". . . I don't blame you, my General. Those words ring like a hymn. And that motto has been the illustrious idea that has guided your admirable mission of saving us all from infamous darkness. Your incomparable love for our country has led you, my General, to impose an efficient order and progress in this nation, which seemed in danger of being consumed in the maw of sin and debauchery."

The General stroked his moustache pensively, a bit piqued by his subordinate's command of phraseology. "Exactly. Anyway, as I was saying, I would like to satisfy some of the desires of my childhood in this well-deserved moment of rest. Look, Colonel, my childhood was a model of happiness. All my dreams and yearnings were totally fulfilled."

"How lucky for you, my General. A unique childhood for a unique man."

"Yes, really. How fortunate I am, I tell myself, when I turn my eyes to the past. Except for two, how can I say . . . dissatisfactions, that's it, two dissatisfactions that remain embedded in my memory and which today, as the commander-in-chief of this republic, I feel deserve to be resolved."

The Colonel held up both palms and gestured for emphasis. "You deserve everything, General, absolutely everything."

"Well, look, these are feelings that one has when still an innocent child. And I am about to make a confession which you must swear to keep strictly confidential."

"Of course, my Leader." The Colonel came to attention.

The General frowned. "At ease, man," he croaked, then leaned forward like a conspirator. "Unlike all the other children, I hated clowns. In fact, I still detest them, because childhood leaves very deep scars, as you know, Colonel. And tell me if I wasn't right: why in the hell do those shitheads paint their faces, fall all over the floor, and punch each other around, expecting children to laugh. Tell me – do you not find that outrageous?"

"Without doubt, my General," the Colonel said in astonishment. "I assure you that never before this moment did I realize how absurd clowns really are."

The General snapped his fingers. "Absurd, that's the word! Grotesque, Colonel, with those high faggoty voices which are so unsettling. When I was a child, I had terrible nightmares about those stupid clowns. Sometimes in my dreams there appeared a huge painted face grinning and laughing at me. Can you imagine – laughing at *me*? Picture that, if you can!"

The Colonel was shocked. "That, my General, I find totally unbelievable."

"It's like questioning my manhood," the General said in amazement.

"That would be unthinkable, sir!" the Colonel shouted.

"Even when I was awake, clowns hounded me. Sometimes it seemed to me that one of those painted faces – real monsters, to my eyes – was outside my window making threatening gestures. Or laughing at me during the most solemn moments of my youth, as when I won first prize in my gymnastics class."

"How awful, General. What a burden to have carried all these years!"

The General slapped his thigh with some force. "Yes, it has been an awful load, and I have never stopped hating them. Even today, while I devote my life to completing this sacred mission assigned to me by destiny, they appear in my dreams, and even during official ceremonies I sometimes hear their laughter, you will find this difficult to believe, behind the heroic chords of our national anthem. This is why I consider it time to take action. Without mentioning a single word of what I have told you, I order you to arrest every clown in our national territory and put them out of circulation for ever."

The Colonel hesitated. "Ah, all of them, my General?"

The General fixed him with a look of beady-eyed ill humour. "Every last one of them."

Still the Colonel was reluctant. "Some of them are quite famous, my General, cherished even." Realizing his mistake, he quickly added, "By children, by the ignorant and easily led, I mean."

"More famous than me?" the General demanded petulantly.

"No, of course not."

"More beloved?"

"Never."

"Then do it," the General ordered, crossing his arms to indicate that the discussion was closed.

The Colonel pulled pen and pad from his tunic and began scribbling. "As you wish, Sir. I guarantee that within five days not a single clown will be left alive in the entire country."

"Good . . . My other concern is, how can I put it, of a more intellectual nature. And I again demand your absolute confidentiality. You know well the price paid by those birds who sing too much. And I say that it is of an intellectual nature because this concern began when I was already ten years old and could read and write. As you are well aware, kids at that age speak about sinful things and, of course, I came across a stupid prick who dirtied my ears with the story of prostitutes."

The Colonel's eyes narrowed. "What story is that, General?"

"The story – it was new to me, of course – that some women lived in a house and a man could go to bed with any one of them for a couple of pesos."

The Colonel's eyes narrowed even more. "Oh! A kind of general story, my General."

"Precisely. And I with my pure soul, because I have always been pure and impeccable, Colonel, couldn't stop thinking about these filthy women who sell their bodies and indulge in obscene activities. Tell me how I, with my sensitivity, who felt myself chosen for greatness, could fail to be shocked upon learning that in our world there are women who commit such despicable sins? And every time I thought of them I was filled with nausea and repugnance. Later on, when I was older, thanks to my moral stature, I never accepted when my fellow officers invited me to visit one of these houses. But of course, Colonel, as years go by our character acquires strength, and when I was absolutely sure of my inviolable integrity, I felt at last prepared to face this horrible experience. But the result of this . . . uh, experience did not alter the profound disturbance these women caused me. Because they are very strange, very mysterious."

The Colonel tapped his temple knowingly. "A mystery, yes. No one really knows them, General. Some rarely speak, and the first thing they do is to rub their bodies against ours as if they were bitches on heat —"

The General shuddered, shoving a hand deep into his pocket, his voice rising to a whinny. "Stop it, Colonel! Don't go on like that! Such descriptions activate the unbearable repugnance that used to oppress me when I was young. Whores, excuse my language, are weird. I would daresay that they are the most indecipherable, the most impenetrable women on earth."

The Colonel bit his lip and nodded.

"That's why I believe that, during this break from our arduous task of saving the Fatherland, I can resolve this concern that started when I was ten years old, and which in my youth became real anguish. But I would like to do this by simultaneously emulating the great August Comte, thus contributing to knowledge and the betterment of humanity – and thereby killing two birds with one stone, you see? I am sure that no one, absolutely no one, has analysed and studied whores. No one. Not even the North American gringos, who have even set up laboratories to investigate rocks from the moon." The General cleared his throat and got to the heart of the matter. "Considering that our armed forces have successfully completed the immediate tasks, and that our soldiers must keep working as part of their military training, I have decided that in one of our detention camps there be installed a . . . how can I put it . . . a study centre."

The Colonel broke in excitedly. "A laboratory for experiments?"

The General turned his head to one side and patted his moustache before deciding. "That, too, in time. But first, a special headquarters to put these creatures under observation for the first time in the long history of western civilization. A centre to discover who these women really are, what they are like, how they feel, what kind of opinions they hold . . ."

"What kind of pain and pleasure they feel," the Colonel said in a dreamy voice, then, fearing he had gone too far, adding hastily, "that is, if they feel any pleasure."

"Perhaps. But that phase of the study should be carried out afterwards. Our first task will be an exploratory study based on questions and answers, a type of multiple-choice quiz, to unveil the mysteries of those sexual misfits who have devoted their lives to the malignant sins of the flesh."

"Therefore," the Colonel said, tacking into the wind, "what you so brilliantly suggest, General, is that we initiate this truly innovative operation with inquiries and questionnaires of a sociological nature?"

"Exactly. And don't forget observation."

"My Leader," the Colonel said reverently, his voice choking, "we could even use these specimens to put into practice some experimental torture methods or, better still, we could subject them to examinations to determine those parts of the female body which are the weakest, the most vulnerable, the most susceptible to pain."

Now it was the General's eyes that narrowed. "We discovered *that* a long time ago, Colonel." He shrugged, becoming magnanimous. "But who knows? Maybe more effective methods could be discovered through diligent research. We should never forget, as August Comte pointed out, that everything is perfectible, that we men can always improve our efforts . . . In any case, the officer in charge of the operation must, in essence, have the mental make-up of a scientist. He must be a man who can conduct rational research and gradually, step by step, accomplish the objectives of his studies. I must be thoroughly informed of all the details of his investigative work, and every week or so I want a report, a very detailed report, of each discovery he makes."

The Colonel made a note on his pad. "Rest assured, my General, that your orders will be carried out with devotion and to the utmost perfection."

"Very well." The General stood to dismiss him. "We must not forget for a single second that we soldiers are clean and honourable men born to worship duty and the holy concept of authority. Our sacred task is to protect the innocent, to defend purity, and to uphold the pillars of justice and law." He pointed to the door. "Now, go get those parasites. I want no more subversive laughter or illegal fucking in my domain."

With the precision of foraging ants, the soldiers invaded the street of night. Silent figures wearing brown berets ran crouching along the crumbling walls with their pistols raised; others stood guard on the two adjacent streets to prevent any possible escape; and at the four corners demarcating the attack zone sat military transport trucks, closing off all exits.

Units of five enlisted men assembled in front of the run-down doors with their peeling paint, awaiting the signal from the officer in charge of the operation. He stood to attention in the middle of the street, proud of the importance of his mission. He counted off one minute and forty seconds before raising his right arm. Each unit moved instantly into action. The night erupted with the sound of hammering on old worn-out wood and the threatening choir of voices shouting orders in unison.

"Open up! Open the door in the name of the Supreme Law of the Benefactor of the Republic!"

The continued pounding and strident voices pierced the soft atmosphere inside like a dagger, probing amid the cries and whispers of bodies entwined and rubbing against one another to the rhythm of sensual music. Bursting through the opened doors, the soldiers sprinted across each threshold with their shoulders in the straight military position while their eyes darted here and there to inspect every nook and cranny of this new battlefield.

"Everyone is under arrest!" a Lieutenant shouted. His eyes scoured the room. "Two lines," he commanded. "One for men, the other for women. I want silence and respect." He drew his pistol. "Now move it!"

Without a word, the male guests abandoned their Martinis or separated from their dance partners to stand side by side. The women, knowing themselves invulnerable, approached the officer in charge with flirtatious smiles to the clacking rhythm of their high heels on the wood floor. Meanwhile, other soldiers forced their way into the bedrooms to drag out half-dressed men and women. In front of the unmoved eyes of the Lieutenant, one woman swayed to the melody of a tango still playing on the record player; another fixed her slip, purposely offering a glimpse of her naked thighs.

The daughters of Hagar knew they had nothing to fear. Those commands and threats delivered over the barrel of a carbine belonged to that other world which was always struggling for power. A power they despised, because in bed victor and vanquished are the same: a body in movement conjuring pleasure; a child's moan at the moment of climax; and a long, heavy sigh which gives way to the languid tide of sleep. The male clients, on the other hand, were horrified because they knew they would be the victims, the sacrificial lambs offered to the altar of the dictator's constant crusade on radio and television for a holy cleansing of any subversive germs which threatened to infect the harmony of the Fatherland. The male patrons prayed in an anxious, fearful silence that the soldiers would be content with making them do callisthenics in the street while being worked over with boots – the alternatives were jail, interrogation, torture and death.

"Outside, ladies," the officer said. "Single file and keep it down."

The street of night had been transformed into a carnival of flashing bright colours as the women walked in total silence. In between the brown barriers of masculine figures, the women marching towards the military trucks created a kaleidoscope of tinted hair and exotic garments, one girl's long red hair tossing like the tail of a fox. They passed by the rigid, uniformed, drab shoulders in a soft flow of rouged cheeks, crimson lips and eyelids painted in different shades of blue and green which fluttered in amazement and fright.

After the last woman had climbed into the dark, olive-green truck, the Captain in charge of the entire sector clicked his heels together and called to his troops: "Soldiers! Our heart and our intelligence . . ."

". . . For the sake of our Fatherland!" they replied as one, a wave of passionate voices that bounced back and forth across the pavement of the street of night.

"Mount up!" the Captain ordered, turning on his heels.

Engines growled into life, headlights pierced the darkness, and the street trembled as if whipped by a sudden storm.

Roaring off, the trucks disappeared into the distance, en route to the detention camp, bearing their load of women who would be used to satisfy the most intimate concerns of the Benefactor of the Republic. In their wake, surprised and relieved, stood the transitory patrons of the street of night which, until then, had been relegated to the clandestine margins of history.

The neatly painted white cabins were spaced evenly within a square site fenced by rows of poplar trees. In the centre there was a two-storey building reserved for military offices and a lecture hall. The cabins had been especially designed for political prisoners, and each cell was equipped with a television monitor while the ceiling was made up of naked beams to facilitate torture and suicides. Before being taken away, the sleepy and tousled women were ordered to tell a clerk their age, place of birth and complete name, and an index card bearing this information was taped to the wall beside each door after it was slammed shut.

"Holy Mother of God, what are they going to do to us?" asked a tearful young girl with blonde hair and a pale complexion.

"Who the hell knows?" exclaimed a tall woman dressed in blue jeans who was giving the cell a disappointed once-over. "Maybe they've decided to modify the tradition of prostitution by adding take-out pussy."

Hands on her hips, she started on an inspection tour with a youthful, uninhibited stride. She stared at the ceiling for a moment, puzzled by the beams. Then her eyes moved down the wall to pause at the sight of one narrow cot and a double bunk-bed, all three covered by dirty grey blankets. Frowning, she said, "I must say, I've seen better working conditions . . ." Then, facing an old woman who sat on the cot with her head lowered in total indifference, she added in surprise, "Damn it, I'm definitely out of luck tonight! I can't believe this bitch is in the same cell as me."

Without looking up, and in a hoarse, angry voice, the old woman said, "My luck is worse. When I smacked the shit out of you at Josefina's place, I thought I'd never see your ugly kisser again."

The tall woman laughed. "But as Pedro Navajas says, you old hag, 'Life brings surprises, surprises bring life, ay, ay, ay'." She sang, thrusting her hips insultingly.

"Sing your silly arse off." the old woman told her. "You're all mouth, you stupid cow."

"Hey! Watch your tongue, you hear?" the tall woman threatened, moving in on the other woman.

"Don't give me orders, you bitch!" the older woman replied, folding her arms across her chest with a defiant expression.

The blonde girl held up an arm and shouted through her tears, "For God's sake, don't fight! Can't you see that we are in serious trouble?"

The tall woman spun around like a cat. "Serious, your arse! Jesus, what a worrywart . . . and in any case, who the fuck are you?"

"I am Maria de las Mercedes," the young woman said, nodding to both of her cellmates. "But please, I beg you, stop fighting, okay?" She made the sign of the cross. "Blessed Virgin Mary, who art in Heaven, illuminate us and help us to see what these soldiers are going to do with us . . . Do you think some General has planned a party, you know, maybe just as a whim? Yeah – and tomorrow they'll let us go."

The tall woman sneered. "What a silly shit we have as a room-mate, don't you think, granny?"

The older woman sat up stiffly. "I was baptized Martina, and for your information, it's the only name I have."

"That's your story. More likely your name has become as worn out as you."

The old woman's face turned red. "Shit. That's all life is, at rock bottom. I've known this since I was a *huaina*, nothing but a little girl. Even so, I won't stand for any crap from you, you dirty slut," she said, spitting a gob of phlegm that landed beside the tall woman's shoes.

The tall woman looked down at her feet in amazement. "What a fucking temper you have! Thank God I only called you granny . . . But Maria de las Mercedes is right, we shouldn't fight, not now when our butts may be on the line." She ran a hand through her dark hair. "By the way, all this heated discussion has made me forget my manners. My name is Esmeralda, like the famous ship of the national navy, although I prefer to be called Alda because it sounds more exotic." She held out a hand to the blonde-haired girl. "A pleasure to meet you."

The girl clasped both hands over Alda's palm with relief. "Likewise, both of you. Please forgive me, but I am scared to death," she said, rewarding them with a shy smile. "I've been a sissy since I was a baby. And when I'm frightened my heart starts pounding like a drum and I feel a knot in my throat. I try not to cry, but the knot feels like I'm choking on a stone."

"Don't be silly, little one," Alda told her with a motherly smile. "No need to panic."

The girl was doubtful. "But these soldiers have weapons, and who knows what they're planning to do?"

Alda laughed. "Well, there aren't too many alternatives, as I see it. Let's say they brought us here for the old in-out. As always, they will be on fire at first, jumping our bones like hungry lions. But men can't keep it up for too long, eh, granny?"

Martina again crossed her arms and said, "I told you my name. It's about time you learnt to say it."

"Okay, okay, Martina," Alda surrendered. "I don't like all this shaved-head bullshit: knocking down doors in the middle of the night and loading us like cattle for slaughter into their trucks; and that fucking road, full of bumps – I thought my kidneys would explode . . . and will someone tell me where the hell we are?" She nodded to the blonde-haired girl. "Meche is right. You don't mind if I call you Meche, do you? Why have they brought us to this shithole? What the fuck are they up to?"

Martina got up heavily, pulled down the bed cover and, patting the pillow, said, "You two can chew on that bone 'til the cows come home, but I'm going to hit the sack. This night is nearly over, and it does no good to fret about tomorrow. As I told you, life is nothing but crap, and you, girl," she fixed a baleful stare on Meche, "will regret saying it was a pleasure to meet us." She slid beneath the blanket and turned her face to the wall.

The other two women moved to the bed on the left, where they started whispering to each other.

"You don't mind if I call you Meche, right?"

"No, of course not. That's what my friends call me."

"Great. See? We're friends already."

"Uh huh. Hey, tell me why you two had a fight at Josefina's place."

Alda patted her gently on the shoulder. "That's private, honey. I'd rather not discuss it. Not now. As Martina said, it's time to hit the hay, recharge our batteries for tomorrow, huh? Who knows what's waiting for us?"

"You're right. But wouldn't it be better to sleep with our clothes on like Señora Martina?"

"It's okay with me if you want to act like a peasant. As for me, I'm going to take my jeans off, because they're cutting me in half. The clerk in the store where I bought them said they'd stretch with wear. Stretch, my arse! No matter how much I do those knee-bends, these damn blue jeans are so tight they leave marks on my waist. Look."

Meche nodded. "I know. The only ones that really stretch are those you get from the United States. A girl that works in my house bought a pair of Levi's that were fantastic. But she had to zip them up lying in bed because they were so tight she couldn't do it standing up. Can you imagine that? Then she would get up, kneel down a few times, and they moulded to her body perfectly – you know, instead of that ugly bulge at the belly that our local blue jeans make."

Alda grinned. "Like you were smuggling a string of sausages around your waist . . . But seriously, kid, I wonder what these military bastards want from us. What animals, eh? When they crashed through the door all I could think of was those movies where the Nazis rounded up the Jews. You know what I mean?"

"No. I was so afraid that all I could do was pray to the Virgin Mary."

Taken aback, Alda slapped herself on the side of the head. "Wait a minute! Do you know if the Benefactor is a devout Catholic? Shit, maybe he's decided to eradicate sin from the city. That must be it! My God, we've had it! We'll be staring at these four walls for the rest of our lives – condemned to work this house for ever!"

Meche covered her face in her hands. "Dear God, it may be worse than that, Aldita!" She began to sob. "They may be going to shoot us! I can see myself standing against a wall with a blindfold over my eyes while the bullets tear into my head!"

Alda embraced her. "Stop it, honey. Don't go apeshit on me. Listen, at times like these you have to keep cool and use your head. Whatever happens, we must save ourselves, because life is worth living in spite of all the bullshit you step in. Don't cry, Meche." She wiped the young girl's eyes with her fingers. "We'd better sleep now so that tomorrow our heads will be clear. It could be that all these shitheads want is a good screw, after all." Glancing at her wrist, she said, "What time is it, anyway? Those bastards dragged me and the guy right out of the bed, and I didn't have time to grab my watch."

"I guess it must be five in the morning."

Alda stretched and yawned with her head thrown back. "Definitely time to sleep, my little one." She looked around the room, adding, "To make things worse, they haven't even given us any water, and I always wash my make-up off before I go to bed. Otherwise I can't get to sleep."

Meche examined her face, and said, "It's because you put too much mascara on your eyes."

"Part of our job, sugar. The first rule of our profession is to look attractive, and our eyes are the kind of capital that invites investment, no?" She patted the bottom bunk. "You don't mind sleeping on top?"

"Oh, no."

Alda clapped her hands to settle the arrangement. "Great. Sleep well, then. And keep praying, Meche. In our present circumstances, we need all the help we can get. Good night."

Seated at his desk, Colonel Arreola was arranging in alphabetical order a pile of index cards containing the basic information about the prostitutes in the nearby cells, preparing to conduct the first part of the research project he had been ordered to carry out. Arreola smoothed his thin moustache and smiled to himself while he organized groups according to age, place of birth, parents' occupation, amount of education, and marital status. He felt excited at the thought of toying with all that data which, like files of troops, would soon be forming into the columns of his statistical tables.

Since childhood his hobby had been to observe everything around him, recording those similarities and differences which allowed him to group his findings into separate categories until he was able to establish the longed-for general laws which made him owner of another slice of the world. He was overwhelmed by happiness upon realizing that his systematic pursuits allowed him to establish control over the nature of things and, for this reason, while his brothers romped in the garden, he would devote his time to organizing his toys according to their shape and colour. He would measure them carefully before lining them up on the basis of size (largest at the head of the rank), and making secret bets over how many toys would fit into one of the cardboard market boxes his mother gave him at the end of each month.

As time went by, Arreola accumulated a vast collection of toy military vehicles, weapons and miniature soldiers. Every afternoon he would distribute them over the floor, creating an ever-changing tapestry of battles. When he was in the third grade, he was the only student in his class who listened with rapt attention on the morning that the teacher, having first written the title of his lecture on the blackboard, explained "The Three Kingdoms of Nature". Animal, vegetable or mineral? Arreola immediately began asking himself about each item he encountered. Questioning his father at the dinner table, he discovered that combs, which appeared at first glance to be mineral, actually belonged to the animal kingdom because they were made of whalebone. Likewise with hairbrushes, which in those days were fitted with horsehair instead of plastic.

Up to that point he had not been very popular among his classmates – a mere "hello" from one of them filled him with gratitude. Now, however, he felt a sense of power when he raised his hand and told the teacher that deep in the earth there were petrified clams which in appearance (and only in appearance) were members of the mineral kingdom, because in fact (and here he paused to impress his fellow students) they belonged as well to the animal kingdom.

One day his grandmother's canary accidentally escaped from its cage while her trembling, arthritic fingers were placing a heart of lettuce in its bowl. In spite of the efforts of the entire family, the canary flew through an open window and headed towards the roof. His father mounted a ladder and was near the top when a cat appeared from nowhere and killed the bird with a single swipe.

"We must bury the little thing," his mother said with tears in her eyes.

While his father dug a hole by the lemon tree, Arreola, holding the dead canary, wondered what exactly was inside that mass of bloody yellow feathers.

After this experience, Arreola ceased to be the lonely boy who played by himself in his room. Now, all day until twilight, he devoted his energy to hunting and killing birds with his slingshot. The first time he eviscerated one with a razor-blade his father had discarded, he found only a bloody, unrecognizable mess that slipped through his fingers like a ball of snot. But day after day he perfected his surgical methods until his skill allowed him to formulate some extraordinary conclusions – for example, that sparrows, although smaller, possess a much larger heart in proportion to their bodies than doves.

Examining a thrush one night, he overheard the forensic pathologist on his favourite television show explain that it was possible to determine what a murder victim had eaten up to eighteen hours before the time of death. It was then that Arreola decided to specialize on a precise incision to the throat and stomach.

Upon opening the still warm craw, he would find tiny seeds, half-digested worms, and ants, some incredibly still alive and moving, that he would kill meticulously with his mother's tweezers. When he found eggs in the womb of a female bird, he rubbed them in his fingertips until they disintegrated, feeling an overwhelming pleasure at the touch of the oozing, jelly-like, granular matter.

In his first year in high school, the young Arreola overheard a construction worker at a bus stop say to a companion that to make ends meet was as difficult as grabbing the balls of a mosquito. This colourful expression so profoundly inspired him that he resolved to concentrate his research exclusively on insects. After mastering the dissection of spiders, flies, cockroaches and crickets, a new field of interest suddenly seized him: the observation and categorization of people. Now, at night, he made complex sketches in his maths notebook, grouping his relatives, friends and acquaintances according to weight, height, hand size and ear shape. Arreola grew up with the conviction that he was an extraordinary individual. Through his sharp inspection of humanity he found that he was able to determine not only the degree of intelligence from a stranger's eyes, but also that he had the gift of predicting the future behaviour of all sorts of people.

Thus he had no problem choosing a wife. The wise and carefully considered reflections written in the diary his sentimental aunt had given him when he was fifteen had led him to a number of conclusions. Namely, that girls who smoked were potentially impudent and rebellious; that high heels and tight skirts signalled future adulteresses; that pearl necklaces indicated a woman fond of spending money. Excessive make-up almost always hid acne or a scar. Wide nostrils denoted, in general, an inclination to sensuality – proper in men but not in women, in whom sensuality bespoke a sinful abnormality. He knew, sight unseen, that his future wife had to wear high-necked blouses adorned with Chantilly lace, low-heeled shoes, pleated skirts and a thin golden ring with a small ruby centrestone. Her voice and gestures would correspond identically to that category he had labelled "Submissive and a Good Mother".

And he was proved right. Since their wedding night, Ester had confirmed beyond doubt his hypothesis by behaving as a woman with an inborn maternal nature, for whom sex was the sanctified means of procreation. During his fifteen years of marriage, Colonel Arreola had maintained his matrimonial bond according to the strict regulations of sobriety and moderation. He never allowed his wife to go beyond the borders of decency during sexual intercourse, which he conducted once a week – on Saturday or Wednesday, depending on the days he was on duty. On two occasions after their first wedding anniversary, Ester had suddenly started rearing her hips, but he had quickly stopped her by gripping her thighs while urgently thrusting for his own orgasm. After satisfying himself, he had felt her eyes sliding heavily over his body like the hot gaze of an animal on heat, but pretending that he hadn't noticed anything he turned over and feigned sleep. Their first child soon arrived, after which Ester underwent a transformation into a slightly obese woman with a voice as sweet and comforting as the German apple pie she always baked for teatime on Sundays. The change in Ester did not surprise Colonel Arreola; thanks to his superior analytical skills, he had foreseen its arrival a long time ago.

It was with joy and pride that he received the order to investigate the mysterious traits of the prostitutes. Moreover, he felt that he deserved the honour. After all, he had already demonstrated admirable talent in the task of supervising the interrogation of subversive thugs. He was able to determine at a glance whether the trembling voice of a prisoner being questioned was due to fear or concealed hatred, a fact of utmost importance, since, basically, political prisoners fell into two main categories: cowards who broke down and rapidly became informers, and the arseholes who would die before saying one word. With an ease that awed his fellow officers, Arreola designed in three days a statistical table that established the proper amount of voltage and exact number of minutes and seconds an electrical current should be applied to the naked bedsprings so that prisoners, sorted by height and weight, wouldn't die before confessing. It was Arreola who invented the "Butterfly", an adjustable wire noose that encircled the penis and which, if necessary, could be tightened until the organ was amputated.

Arreola had from the beginning opposed adoption of those methods of torture devised by the Brazilians, and he had often intervened to supervise any interrogation that tended toward tropical excess, which he felt dishonoured the cultural identity of his country, forged through the centuries by sober men of unsurpassed rectitude and integrity. "In this land of real men, everything must be done with scientific intelligence and without any strident excess whatsoever," he would assert incessantly at the regular meetings of those officers in charge of Defence and Purgation.

From the very first, Arreola detested those torture methods tainted by primitivism which, in his opinion, had been totally displaced by the advances of science in the modern world. The day following the military *coup d'état*, he and several fellow officers had climbed to the top of an armoury with battlements that served as gunports for artillery pieces in order to watch the soldiers below as they tortured political prisoners. Surrounded by the most finely wrought and up-to-date weaponry, the blows and insults raining on the captives with their heads covered by hoods and their hands tied with wire seemed to Arreola a barbaric and anachronistic procedure which went against the evolution of knowledge and technology, negating the modern practice of warfare as another expression of human intelligence. And it was to eliminate the crude procedure of hanging prisoners by their feet over a bucket of excrement that he created more civilized methods of torture, inspired by the precise and logical beauty of the artillery guns.

One day earlier, Colonel Benavides had paid a personal visit to Arreola to inform him that he had been placed in charge of a vitally important mission whose overall objective would be made known to him only after the operation was successfully completed. Smiling with his eyes half-closed, Colonel Benavides mentioned that the mission would contribute to the spiritual peace of the Benefactor of the Fatherland.

The possibilities of this new research project seemed extraordinary to Arreola. At long last he was going to experiment on women, which was of course a real challenge. Although he had already made some written observations dealing with the variations of torture that could be applied to the vagina, these notes were largely of a speculative nature because, since the first week after the coup, he had worked exclusively with male prisoners. But now he would have at his personal disposal and in the flesh the only valid subject for true scientific research. He was certain that new and invaluable data would grant him the status of a real pioneer in torture designed specifically for women. That same intelligence which had earned him the respect of his fellow officers would now guide him to discoveries that might even lead to international fame. Heart pounding, he imagined his name immortalized in future manuals of torture. And this time there would be no political ideology to distort his findings, no fanaticism to interfere with his working hypotheses – these individuals were apolitical and hence, in a manner of speaking, unpolluted; virgins, as it were.

He smiled at the paradox and gazed with satisfaction and anticipation at his tape recorder, his impeccable leather notebook, and his pens neatly arranged in a metal canister. Then he turned and hastily pulled from his bookcase a volume of the *Concise Encyclopedia Sopena*, a source which had in the past allowed him to shine in conversation during cocktails at the Officers Club. He opened the volume, and thereby took the first step in what he would later call the "Adventure of the Synonyms". He spent the next several hours listing a variety of definitions for the word "prostitute", underlining in red such phrases as "a woman who engages in promiscuous sexual intercourse for pay" (from the Latin *prostuere*, before, and *statuere*, to cause to stand), and copying the ancient and modern terms for the world's oldest occupation: concubine, courtesan, doxy, floozie, fornicatrix, harlot, hetaera, strumpet, dollymop, *putein*, *puta*, streetwalker, tart, whore. In other words, he decided, a low and vulgar woman.

"I'm about to pee in my pants!" Alda shouted. "Where the hell is the bathroom in this filthy hole?" She ran to the door and pounded on the iron bars with the heel of her shoe. "Guard! Guard! Will somebody please come?"

A stocky man with a dark complexion marred by measle scars on his left cheek approached and said with a sneer, "They're preparing breakfast for the ladies of the house." He bowed slightly, then spat in her face, and said menacingly, "Now stop bothering me, you slag!"

"Look, I'm not asking for food. I need to use the bathroom, and soon, because my teeth are floating. So would you be so kind as to tell me where one can take a piss in this place?"

The guard was enjoying her discomfiture. "We have a strict schedule here, with no exceptions. At ten o'clock in the morning, four in the afternoon, and eight in the evening. Those are the hours that our guests are allowed to piss. Does madame have any other questions?" Without waiting for an answer, he added, "No? Then try to hold it until ten o'clock, baby, and I'll personally help you to pass water."

Crouched and clutching her groin in pain, Alda watched the guard walk away. "*Hijo de puta.* This is the end! I can't wait any longer, so please excuse me, girls, but I'll have to do it here on the floor. There's no other way."

"Don't worry, Alda," Meche said. "We don't mind, do we, Señora Martina?"

Martina shrugged. "Whoever needs to piss, may piss. I've put up with much worse in my life than a little water on the floor."

Later, sitting in front of Colonel Arreola, Martina felt again that wave of hatred that poisoned her soul when her husband sat at the table asking for food; remembering his face, like a toad on heat, as he chased her around the kitchen; remembering his hands lifting her skirt and rubbing her while he bit her neck; remembering him pushing her against the wall and penetrating her with his dark and wrinkled prick . . .

"What is your occupation?" Arreola asked, his voice rich with authority.

Martina spat on the floor. "I don't have no occupation."

(. . . "Move your arse, bitch, or I'll feed your nipples to the pigs . . . ah, good, that's good, go on, pump, ah God, that's so *gooood*" . . . and she would close her eyes and pray for him to come. Afterwards, crying with humiliation, she would wipe away the semen staining her thighs . . .)

Arreola adjusted his tie importantly. "By occupation, I mean the way you earn your living, the type of work you do."

Martina cleared her throat insultingly, about to spit again.

(. . . "I'm quite a guy," he would boast to his cronies. "I like to fuck every day at lunch-time, for your information. Any woman on earth would fight to have a macho lover like me." Every day at noon, Martina's husband would sit at the table and play with breadcrumbs, keeping watch on her out of the corner of his eye as she placed the silverware with trembling hands and he, absent-mindedly stroking her hips, would say, "Now bring the napkins," tapping the table with his fork; and when she bent over to put the napkin at his plate he would bound up behind her and force himself into her.

Every morning at eleven o'clock she would go into the kitchen to prepare lunch. Vomiting hatred, she would give two sharp chops to the potatoes that fell sliced in four pieces into the soup pot; the incisions multiplied like splintering stars on the surface of the onion which, when minced, she would pound and crush as though it were the skin of her husband's flaccid thighs; gorged with anger she would dismember the chicken, lopping off the greasy rump; and at the sight of a wrinkled cooked carrot, she would squeeze it hard, imagining that at long last she was destroying that piece of flesh which never again would creep like a burglar between her legs. That morbid old man of fifty had taken her from her parents' house when she was only thirteen. From that time on, she had lived amid the bad smell of his breath and his wet and foamy words that never ceased. At night she was persecuted by terrible dreams in which slimy and repugnant monkeys pounced on her naked stomach and sat there staring at her with their round and inexpressive eyes while shrieking and moaning lasciviously. Like her husband, this man sitting behind his desk had the cold eyes of a lizard . . .)

"Señora," Arreola said encouragingly, "I imagine that at your age it must be rather difficult to talk about a sinful past, but we are here to prevent this kind of behaviour in the future. Any information you can give me regarding the type of work you did, I imagine quite some time ago, will be of considerable value to all the citizens of this brave and glorious republic."

Martina cleared her throat once more and sent a gob of spit near one of Arreola's shiny boots.

(. . . When the devil's lizard left for work, she would go outside and walk in the field; angry and feeling sick, she would kick the dusty weeds thriving in the hot sun and spit to keep from screaming. One afternoon, with the disgusting taste of her husband's nicotine-flavoured saliva stuck in her mouth, she found among the wild poppies a black leaf with rough edges which to her seemed poisonous. The next morning, without washing it, and feeling a strange joy, she threw it into the soup, believing that she was putting an end to her martyrdom. When nothing happened, she continued to doctor the soup, adding leaves, seeds, roots, dry flowers, even insects, but he did not even show signs of a stomach-ache.

"What I really need is a *curandera*," she said to herself one night while her husband slept placidly by her side. On the pretext of a pain in the chest, she visited the house in the *pueblo* of Señora Rosa, a *curandera* who knew how to heal with herbs. "It's not that easy to learn my trade, *huaina*, but I will teach you," said the old woman while sticking two potato slices on Martina's temples.

Thus she began to learn the secrets of herbs and poultices; very soon she could easily recognize the *chequén*, whose sap held the power to cure diseased eyes, and the fruit of the fennel, which made milk spring from the breasts of feeble mothers. She also learned to identify the *pichoa* with its white juice that exterminated warts, and the *quimai*, which cured liver ailments.

"Now I want to learn about bad herbs, Señora Rosa, herbs that kill." "No, *huainita*, no. That's witches' stuff. I only make love potions. Look. There in the mountains grows the *manoa*, a plant with big silvery leaves. Those girls who want to keep a lover for ever must take the thread from a black slip and sew two *manoa* leaves together and leave them in the morning dew for three days in a row. After this, both hearts are sewn together for ever, and your lover will never abandon you." "No. Please give me at least a herb to paralyse his legs, or a juice to blind him, anything to keep him off me." "My little *huaina*, a young woman like you shouldn't have such black thoughts. I've already told you, my witchcraft is only for curing pain. Can't you see that this world is a valley of tears, and we've only come here to suffer?"

That day Martina did not return to her house. Shielding herself from the sun with a willow branch, she walked beside the railroad tracks without any destination in mind. As the sun started to fall, the petals of the wild flowers began closing, as if they feared the darkness just as she did. Her fear stemmed from the tales her father used to tell about the bewitched mountain lion and the fox, who roamed the countryside at night together. There was also a headless man who searched for his wife, and the spirits of dead oxen which returned to earth to take vengeance on the men who had mistreated them. Suddenly she saw a bonfire glittering in the trees in the distance, and soon she came upon a small white hut, a well, and a young man who offered her bread fresh from the earthen oven . . . but that was another story . . . the only good and beautiful story in her entire life. Now, in front of this other lizard, she wished she had sulphur to throw in his eyes, to blind him before killing him . . .)

"Three photographs, all profiles," Arreola ordered a soldier who held an instamatic camera.

While the camera flashed, Martina imagined herself tied to a stake, flames devouring her arms and legs while a crowd cursed her.

Arreola's face was stern. "You must definitely change your attitude, you fucking witch! To co-operate is a sacred duty, do you hear? A sacred duty. And you will have to tell me how many men you went to bed with – when you were thirty, then forty, fifty, et cetera. Because you sold your arse, didn't you?"

For a second, Martina's eyes were piercing. She stared at his cold eyes and, spitting near his other boot, said in a raised voice, "I never sold my body or my soul!"

"Take her back to her cell," Arreola ordered a Corporal with a wave of his hand. Before departing, the Corporal handed Arreola Martina's file.

The Colonel stared at Martina's retreating, hunched back for a second, then wrote, carefully keeping to the margin of his notebook: "Deceitful character, typical of the Araucanian Indians. Dark skin and high cheek-bones indicate indigenous ancestry. It is evident that at her age she no longer practises prostitution. Investigate whether she is a go-between, an owner of a whorehouse, or . . . find out other possible activities which, up to now in our research, are unknown. Her spitting occurred approximately every minute and a half, and this dirty habit confirms her origins in the indigenous population, which refuses all our efforts to implement civilized behaviour."

"My dear God! The General beat me, Aldita!" Meche moaned, sobbing, her cheeks reddened.

"Why did he beat you? Come on, sugar, tell me."

"In the name of the Sacred Virgin of the Estuary, I swear that I don't know. I only remember that two soldiers were pushing Señora Martina out of the office, and that a guard dragged me in, and then I saw a General dressed in a very elegant uniform sitting behind a big desk full of books and pens. He ordered me to sit down in an armchair and then he asked me what type of job I did. My heart was pounding faster and faster, and I was so scared that I couldn't say a single word. Holy Mother of Christ! I felt the presence of the Devil in that room; it was as if thousands of evil eyes were glaring at me, and the General, that man had eyes like swords; they stabbed right through me. They have brought us to hell, Aldita."

Alda grabbed her by the arm. "But why did he beat you, dammit?"

"I tell you I don't know! The General, one of Satan's disciples to be sure, seemed to be asking me questions. I can only recall that his lips were moving, and that his eyes started to close, as if he were really angry, and all of a sudden he got up and began slapping me. 'For the last time, you filthy whore, confess!' he said several times, and then everything got dark and my ears started ringing . . ." She opened her blouse. "Look. He hit me so hard my breast is bruised. I knew it! I'll probably get cancer!"

Alda rolled her eyes. "Enough," she said, taking Meche's head in her lap. "Calm down. I've told you not to get hysterical."

And while Meche wept and sighed, Alda started to think about her own situation. "To save oneself, that's the only important thing in life. To survive against wind and tide," she said to herself. "The only thing that prick wants is for us to talk. And I'm sure he's not a General. He's probably a fucking second-rate Lieutenant. I don't give a shit about why he's interested in what we do for a living. He must be a dirty old man who wants to learn some new positions, or a pervert who jacks off listening to the tapes he's making. But I don't care about any of that. I will speak, I will burn his ears with a thousand stories, as many as he wants, because the only important thing is to save one's skin and escape death as long as it is possible."

After being led to the interrogation room, Alda decided to promote Arreola. "You ask me, my General, what kind of work I do?" She crossed her legs slowly. "Who am I, in fact? Because for you what one does, one is, right? In all honesty, it is very difficult to answer your question because it's the type of question only intelligent men ask." Twirling a lock of her hair, she smiled sweetly. "Who am I? I must confess that that's a hard one. The truth is, I have many names. I am called a 'bad woman' by those chaste women who wear high-necked lace blouses and spend their day fingering their rosaries. They are not of my circle, you see, my General; but it occurs to me that when they pray, being women after all, they probably imagine the priest without a cassock, bare-arsed while he dispenses the Host, or it may be that at night they dream that the good padre comes to their bed and mounts them."

Examining her nails, she darted a glance at the Colonel's face, wondering if she was scoring any points. "Oh dear, excuse me, my General, but I am wandering off the subject. As I was saying, they call me a 'bad woman', but they also call me a 'public woman', you see, by which I understand they mean a woman who belongs to all men – like the public gardens and the corner street-lights that illuminate the darkness. In contrast, you understand, to the private woman, who gets married in civil and church ceremonies, and belongs to only one man for the rest of her life. That's the legal custom. Although, and I trust you won't be offended, my General, my own personal opinion is that there is no great difference between a public and a private woman. After all, you see, their husbands feed them, shelter and clothe them in exchange for the same old pleasure, the only difference being that a private woman has to cook and wash, while in our case men pull on their pants, give us the money, and beat it." She gave her abundant dark hair a flirtatious toss. "With respect, I must tell you how much it makes me laugh when these men, who always seem to be late for an important meeting when they arrive at the house, have a quickie, zip up their pants in a hurry, and take their stained shorts to the devoted little woman, who the next day must scrub them clean with washing detergent. Don't you think it's funny? A paradox, as that handsome devil on TV would say, the one who stars in *That's Incredible*. And since they have named me a public woman, it has also occurred to them to call me a woman of the street, as if they, my betters, were women of the house, get it?"

Just then Arreola frowned and she regretted having treated him with such familiarity; but she clasped her hands over her knees, bit her lip, and continued on her course. "Well, to a certain extent they are right. I don't deny that they have a little bit of intelligence, they are accurate to an extent because some of us do work in the street. But not all of us, no, my General. I, for example, do not live in the street like a dog; on the contrary, I have a room of my own which is comfortable, and the house where I work is also a home. Not one of those traditional family homes defined by law – which I respect, of course, because laws must be respected, right? But by hook or by crook, it is a home after all, don't you agree? I find nothing wrong with the fact that we stand at the balcony to display our merchandise; businessmen do much the same thing, even those big shots who advertise their products on TV, in magazines, and in the newspapers.

"The only thing that puzzles me is why they dub me a woman who leads a bad life, yet at the same time one who follows a life of pleasure, of joy even. To link a bad life with a life of joy seems contradictory, don't you think? And supposing, because all this is only a supposition on my part, supposing that those decent women lead a good life – well, I mean, following this contradiction, what a sad and boring existence they all must have. Not for me, I confess, because I was definitely born for joy and merriment. If you only knew, my General, how much I like to dance! At the house, we start boogying at about ten at night and I . . . But excuse me, my General, I am wandering again, and the truly important thing is to answer your question.

"So, let's see, referring to those who do business in the street, other people, mostly men, call me a streetwalker. Yes, meaning by that a woman who glides up and down the avenues as if she were on roller-skates, who tramps from north to south, east to west, her heels tapping on the sidewalk until an old man beckons from a car, or a young guy with less money but a more urgent erection approaches with a beginner's shyness or the arrogance of a peacock. Ah! Because generally men are totally unpredictable, somewhat mysterious, my General, like you. At this very moment, you strike me as mysterious, and I have always been a sucker for mystery . . . Anyway, at this point it would be a good idea to summarize a bit: bad woman, public woman, streetwalker . . . sinner, because I practise the trade of sin, a trade founded by no less than a saint, Mary Magdalene, who washed the feet of Christ. Now, I don't know if she washed His feet because He was one of her clients – I won't dare voice an opinion on this matter – but the Bible says that they knew each other well, and there has to be intimacy – and even love, I would say – between two people when one of them kneels to wash the other's feet. Think of Saint Teresa cleaning the feet of her lepers. Although Christ's feet couldn't have smelled *that* bad; on the contrary, I am sure his toes gave off the odour of roses and jasmine, don't you imagine? Perhaps – who knows – if Mary Magdalene hadn't existed, our profession wouldn't have come into being either." Feeling more confident, she stretched her arms over the back of the armchair to highlight her breasts and looked straight into the Colonel's eyes. "Someone has to invent professions, the same way someone invented the steamboat, the typewriter, and the satellites in space. Saint Mary Magdalene invented the practice of placing a price on her pussy, if you'll excuse my frankness, my General, and thus she established our profession, which I'm told is one of the oldest in the world. How about that!"

Arreola was not amused. "You're speaking blasphemy."

Alda nodded. "In any case, more romantic folks, or maybe men who enjoy a good time with us, have given us a prettier name: 'companions of the night'. Isn't that a lovely description? It's my personal favourite, and, to be sincere with you, my General, I feel that I am a real companion of the night. I truly possess the tender heart of a companion of the night, because the word 'companion' has nothing to do with one-off fucking, nor with drunkards rubbing my arse, nor the commands of those insolent bastards who, without any consideration whatsoever, shout: 'Hey you, in the green dress, I'm talking to you, whore, let's do the nasty!' No. The word 'companion' implies something far more profound, a kind of friendship, even though it's usually brief . . . Oh, if you only knew, my General, how many times men enter our house with a sad face, totally depressed, the poor things, and they talk about their troubles, which are sometimes so awful and tragic that I feel like crying, and I comfort them while I dry my tears with a corner of the sheet or the bottom of my slip. I'm very sentimental, you know; I caress them with extraordinary tenderness, like those wronged women in soap operas." She locked her eyes on to his again, smiling sweetly. "What does it matter if I'll never see them again! The most important thing is to give love, don't you agree?

Yes, I am a real companion of the night, and the night fascinates me, the sky so dark, the white mountains brooding in the background, the stars, and the ever-changing moon – one night only a crescent like in those movies filmed in the Sahara desert, all you lack are the palm trees, another night it's swollen like a pregnant woman, as if it were telling us mortals, 'Here I am, and here I have been since the world was created,' full and rounded as a silver dollar, and if you examine it closely you can even see, as my grandmother pointed out to me when I was a child, the silhouettes of the Virgin Mary on a donkey and Saint Joseph seeking shelter on the night Jesus was born; and at other times it looks like a sliced lemon . . . wow, the moon is so beautiful! That's why I don't mind being called a companion of the night.

"Some years ago, one of my clients was a guy from the left, a communist or something like that . . ." She immediately regretted having mentioned the persecuted ones, and instinctively she unbuttoned her blouse, wiping her brow as if she were overheating. "Anyway, this young man, who had such wrong ideas about everything, used to say that we girls should be called the proletariat of the night, because we as labourers were exploited by the capitalist system. And an older gentleman who sometimes visits the house as a way to remember the brothels of Paris, where he spent a lot of time writing poetry in his youth, tells us that we are the vendors of nocturnal pleasures. Oh, he speaks so beautifully! I love him, although he only drinks a few glasses of wine and never goes to a room with any of us. It was he who told me once that, before Christopher Columbus came to America, the Indians of Mexico referred to us as toasted flowers of maize . . .

"So, General, sir, you must forgive me, but in this intimate confession I would prefer to omit the rude names given to us by vulgar people. With your permission, I will skip the labels pasted on to us by arseholes, such as floozie, pro, tramp, sleazebox, hothole, and so on. On the other hand, the Argentinians, who add such a poetic touch to everything they say, call us toys of passion.

As you know, they always tell such tragic stories in their tangos, like the one about the woman who leaves her lover for ever after sharing a last cup of coffee; or that lady who was so beautiful in the past and is now dying in the attic while waiting for her lover to return; or that unfortunate man who has wept by his silent accordion with his guitar still hanging in a corner since the day his sweetheart abandoned him. 'Chère madame, you who speak French,' is the first line of that tango, and the woman, the toy of passion, has long curly eyelashes, a sexy body like Raquel Welch, and she carries her purse well-stocked so she can buy drinks *à la frappé*. To tell you the truth, I have no idea what *frappé* means, but it must be French, as I'm sure a man like you knows. Naturally, the tango refers to those women from Argentina who wear a beret and a skirt slit on both sides, and who use expensive gold cigarette holders when they smoke. I love how elegant and fashionable they are! That's why the tango singer says that she struts her way through a series of fleeting illusions . . . And there's a beautiful verse, the one that tells the toy of passion that when misfortune overtakes her, she always knows how to wring laughter from her tears. How sad, isn't it, that happiness always comes to an end. 'Go on drinking champagne while you're young, my defiant little doll, flower of sin; go on drinking and laughing while the days go by. For when you reach the end of your journey, you will see the spring of youth disappear for ever.'" She had risen from her chair to recite the tango, smiling seductively with her hands on her hips. "Oh, please excuse me," she said, resuming her seat like a proper lady, "but tangos thrill my heart and soul.

"Well, of course, there are some elegant names, too. For instance, courtesan, concubine, paramour – words you often find in books. Paramour, with an o–u–r at the end, like *amour* in French, as you are no doubt aware. Hooker is an interesting word used to describe us. I don't know if it comes from those aggressive girls who used to hook a prospective client by the arm so that he couldn't get away, or if, as the old poet once told me, it originated during the American Civil War when a General named Hooker carried a contingent of ladies for his troops. The most popular name is prostitute, which I imagine has something to do with prostate, no? And to shorten things, they call me, you know, whore." She lowered her head bashfully for a second; on raising her eyes she noticed his manhood bulging against his trousers, and for the first time she adopted a defiant attitude, staring at his lips with an insinuating expression. "I am a whore, my General, that's what I am. And I am here to co-operate with you in any way you desire."

In a husky voice, Arreola said, "You may leave."

And before going back to his notes, he was surprised to find himself staring at the rounded and rolling hips of the sexy woman swaggering off on high heels as she exited the room with a soldier guarding her on either side.

Next morning, Arreola shuffled through his index cards with exhilaration. To the right side of his desk he had placed the information provided by those women who had demonstrated a willingness to collaborate; to the left were four or five reports identifying those who, through fear or rebelliousness, had refused to answer any questions. But the subversive ones presented no serious challenge. He knew they would beg to speak when they were introduced to the mouse device, his most efficient method of untying the tongues of recalcitrant women. Simple and cheap, its only necessary implement was a cup that was placed upside down over the navel, sucking tight to the skin. Then it was raised slightly, lifted just enough to allow a little mouse to wriggle under the brim. Usually, the feeling of the little creature's feet was sufficient to induce hysteria and capitulation; otherwise, an hour or so of nibbling by rodent incisors almost never failed to elicit a confession.

For Arreola, this was the most appropriate interrogation method because he was convinced that women were nothing more than womb and vagina, two sections of the body which predestined them, from the moment of birth, to be mothers or prostitutes, both equally tied to masculine pleasure, which in women led either to sublime procreation or despicable sin. How different the destiny of men seemed to Arreola! What a glorious fate handed down by the gods, who led them to become the inventors of knowledge and weapons, of all that rises straight to heaven. In Arreola's imagination there was a constant passing parade of figures erect and proud in the sunlight, of rifles raised on high, of bayonets thrusting skyward like shining, iridescent phallic symbols.

The Corporal interrupted these reflections to inform Arreola that a message officer had just arrived.

Arreola stood to button his jacket. "Show him in immediately," he ordered, waiting at attention while the Corporal ushered in a young Lieutenant. Returning his salute, Arreola enquired, "Have you come in the capacity of a message officer or a command officer?"

"Only as a message officer, Sir," the Lieutenant replied respectfully. "Therefore, as you know, Colonel, I cannot discuss the contents of this document, which comes directly from the Intelligence Service," he added, handing over an envelope and then stepping back and snapping to attention.

Arreola picked up a silver letter-opener from his desk and nodded to the younger man. "You may stay for lunch if you wish, Lieutenant."

"Thank you, sir, but I have other important messages that require immediate delivery."

Arreola shrugged, then saluted, and in a loud voice exclaimed, "Long live our Fatherland!"

"Long live our glorious nation," was the Lieutenant's response. "Adiós, Colonel," he said before doing an immaculate about-face and marching out of the room.

Arreola waited for the Corporal to shut the door before slicing open the envelope. He slipped out a typed page containing the following brief command: "Secret Document, number 1.001-09-04. Suspend current operation indefinitely. A strong subversive movement has been discovered in the South (04-LY). A new contingent of soldiers has been dispatched to your headquarters. Train them under Sight and Knife Plan."

Excited now and breathing rapidly, Arreola stowed all the indexed information on the prostitutes in his filing cabinet, which he locked. Next he shouted for the Sergeant of the Guards to report. Then, both hands on his desk, leaning forward, he told him, "Take two vans to the usual place. We need thirty subjects for one o'clock tomorrow afternoon. See to it."

As if buried in the bottom of a well, imprisoned in stagnant time, the women in their cells muttered angrily because food rations had been discontinued and the guards no longer came to escort them to the communal bathroom in the courtyard. Like bees trapped in the centre of a hive, they murmured, grumbling ill-humouredly, fighting among themselves, pounding the doors and walls of their cells as they complained about the heat, shouting for bread and water. From somewhere at the end of the narrow corridor, the desperate screams of a young girl lanced the afternoon air. "Get me out of here, you shitheads! I'm going crazy in this fucking prison! Get me out, out, OUT, godammit! I'm starving to death! I'll die from this heat! Let me out, you cocksuckers!"

Three soldiers with hard, imperturbable faces walked towards her cell amid the cries and angry insults and offensive gestures of the other women, who whistled and showered them with spit and obscene comments. Opening the young girl's cell, they dragged her out, struggling and still screaming. Those women in nearby cells could see that in frustration she had ripped open her own blouse, could see the soldiers smacking her on the side of the head, punching her in the stomach, could see two of the men slam her against a wall in the middle of the corridor, saw the third soldier remove his pistol and shoot her twice in the right temple. The shooter then turned and, with the pistol still at the ready, walked away in a military manner, fixing each small window of every cell he passed with a stern and ruthless glance while behind him the other two soldiers carried the dead body. The sight of all that blood running down the dead girl's cheeks and into her immobilized and panic-stricken mouth produced pandemonium among the other women, who rushed with horror to the corners of the cells.

"My God! Holy Virgin Mary," Meche sobbed, seeking shelter behind Alda.

"Shut the fuck up, for Christ's sake," Alda said in a trembling voice. "We must stay calm, keep our heads clear." She exchanged a look with Martina, for the first time appealing to the older woman as a friend.

Martina nodded at her and cleared her throat before whispering, "Life's a piece of shit, but there's no reason to look for death like that poor kid."

"That's it exactly, Señora Martina," Alda agreed. "The three of us must support each other. No more losing our tempers. Whatever happens, Mechita, you have to swallow your fear so that we can save ourselves. Okay, sugar?" she added, hugging Meche while the young girl stared at them with a shocked and defenceless expression.

Time stretched slowly amid the heat and muffled whispers of the women, the moonlight indifferently casting shadows and silhouettes which wavered and slid across the walls during a night that seemed endless.

Forcing herself to keep her voice down, Alda said urgently, "Let's talk about something, any kind of shit, please . . . because I'm about to explode. Let's talk, okay?"

"I'm scared to death," Meche whispered with tears in her eyes. "But maybe you're right. What should we talk about?"

"I don't know, damn . . . anything that will help kill time and keep my mind off food. Maybe we could tell how we became prostitutes."

"Oh no!" Meche exclaimed. "Why talk about something so sad?"

"You're right," Alda said. "Dumb idea. That's the favourite topic of clients who come too soon and have some time left on the clock. And so you're forced to invent one story after another so that the prick can play one-upmanship with his friends, making them think he's one of those studs who never gets out of the saddle. But we have to talk about something that will take a long, long time. Virginity, for example. That's it! You, Meche, tell us when, how, and with whom you lost your cherry."

Meche pondered the request for a moment before shaking her head in puzzlement. "Mmm. To be honest, at the time I didn't realize I was losing it."

"Well, it's only an expression," Alda said. "And what you get in return is well worth the loss. Isn't that right, Señora Martina?"

The old woman coughed. "All this fuss over a little flap of skin. Besides, you don't lose your virginity all at once. That takes time." She sighed. "Years, even, for some. When you learn what rats men are, after enough of them have ploughed your pussy like a field, and your heart is full of holes, *that's* when you ain't a virgin no more."

Alda said, "You're dead right. But let's not dwell on sadness. Come on, Meche, tell us, when was the first time a guy made love to you?"

"But it *was* sad, Aldita," Meche protested. "Besides, I didn't have a clue what virginity was – my goodness, how was I supposed to know? When the first kid threw himself on me, I was only nine years old. To make things worse, it was for a bunch of grapes."

Now it was Alda who shook her head. "Jesus, what a dummy! You mean to tell me that you gave up your *chucha* for a lousy bunch of grapes?"

"They were the ripest and most golden in the entire vineyard! And this boy, who was the son of the nightwatchman, said he would let me have them if we could play mummies and daddies. How much does a nine-year-old know about what her parents do at night? And to top it off, his aunt caught us in the act, and my mother beat the hell out of me."

Alda slapped her lightly on the shoulder. "Oh, Meche. You're too much. What a dumb story. I lost my virginity in a marvellous manner, amid bright lights and fireworks, with the only man I ever loved. But you're right, there's no use in talking about the sad times."

"No, go on," Meche said. "Why all the bright lights and firecrackers? Was it New Year's Eve?"

"No, dumb-arse, that was just a figure of speech. He was such a special man, the only really worthwhile one in this avalanche of men I've had in my life. He was a Portuguese sailor, and I met him when he was just getting off a Norwegian ship at Valparaíso. In high school, we girls used to run out after class to see the sailors coming into port. They came from all over the world, and most of them were really friendly, always laughing, although we seldom understood a word they said. There was always one who would let us have some chewing gum from the USA. This particular afternoon I was in a terrible mood because I'd had the usual fight with my mother; so, instead of joining the other girls, I stayed by myself near the dock to watch a group of sailors who were blond and had red, healthy cheeks . . . That's when a young, slender man with black eyes caught my attention. He was dark like the sailors on Greek ships, and when he got near me he stopped and smiled and said, '*Vocé é muito bonita.*'"

"Wow." Meche was spellbound. "Just like in that song by Roberto Carlos! That's *sooo* romantic . . . go on, don't stop, Aldita."

"My heart skipped a beat when he told me I was pretty. His voice was sincere, not like those stupid guys who hang around on corners and flirt with you just to show off in front of their friends, pretending to be Don Juans. Well, he kept smiling and asked me my name, and we started talking, and I offered to show him the city. So we spent the whole afternoon together! He spoke slowly so I could understand his Portuguese, and when I pointed out something of interest, he would look at me as though I were the most beautiful girl in the whole world. Boy, what a terrific feeling that was! Men somehow recreate us, make us over. Hasn't it ever happened to you: on the same night one man makes you feel sensational, half an hour later, the next arsehole in line makes you feel like trash?

"The next day, instead of going to class, I went with him to the beach. And while we were sitting on a rock, he started kissing me . . . I tell you, they were the most incredible kisses a mortal can imagine. Shit, in all my life since, no man has kissed me like that! Of course I had already had boyfriends, but João's way of kissing was so unique that I felt I was being kissed for the first time. How can I explain? He kissed me and it was as if a tidal wave were pulling against my body . . . and while we embraced he kept saying that he wanted to give me a night full of love, '*uma noite cheia de amor*'. He pronounced the 'r' in *amor* so softly, almost like a sigh, and the only thing I wanted was his lips on mine. Despite my mum's boring, once-a-day litany to protect my virginity, I went to bed with him that night. At the motel, he removed my clothes with the most intense tenderness I have ever known, covering every inch of my body with kisses. I swear, there are no words to describe what I felt, because everything was too wonderful, as if it were taking place in another world."

"What magic!" Meche exclaimed with emotion, while on Martina's wrinkled face there was a sweet expression.

"Yes, magic. I felt that João was a musician playing a torrent of constantly changing melodies on my body while I was submerged in a green lake full of fish and algae which caressed my thighs, my breasts, all of me. And suddenly I felt him enter me, anchoring me deep and shuddering inside me for the longest time."

"That's so great," Meche said in amazement. "I feel like crying."

"Well, it beats the hell out of your grapes," Martina said. Looking down at the floor, she remembered the white hut, the fresh water and the warm bread that Juan Manuel had offered her on that evening when she left her husband. He had been the only good man she had encountered in her life. She remembered that he used to take her with him to the forest where he would cut wood with great energy and skill, and then at twilight he would make up a fire under the stars. With Juan Manuel, she was no longer afraid of the darkness or of life, because he cherished and protected her under a canopy of tenderness, each morning smiling at her as if she were the sun itself.

"But happiness doesn't last in this world," Alda said with regret.

"No, sir," said Martina. "Happiness is God mocking us, like the man with three balls."

Meche was perplexed. "Three balls – who's that, Señora Martina?"

Alda rolled her eyes. "A pawnbroker, honey. A long time ago, they used to have three balls hanging over their door."

"So," Martina continued, "like a dirty old moneylender, God loans us happiness for a few days and then takes it back, and we spend the rest of our lives wondering where it went."

Meche made a quick sign of the cross. "Don't talk about God like that! God is our Father and the Creator of all things . . . hallowed be His Name!"

"Okay, okay," Alda said, patting Meche's arm. "Don't get all stressed out. After all, God is a man, that's the way He's been painted in church, although he never has a wife or lover at His side. Perhaps He doesn't function in that respect."

"What a sacrilegious thing to say!" Meche cried in outrage. "God will punish you for that, just wait and see! The Name of God is holy and must always be worshipped, and you are talking as if Lucifer himself had taken over your tongue," she declared indignantly, leaving her bed to kneel in prayer in a corner.

Alda threw up her hands in exasperation. "All right! Jesus, don't be so pious. Come here so I can get on with my story."

"Don't tell me – your happiness was over before you could spit," Martina said helpfully.

"Yes. João's ship was due to leave in five days. That last afternoon when we kissed goodbye, João held me tight and told me he'd return as soon as he could, but all I could think of was the words of that tango about Margot, the girl who wore a blue beret and a golden crucifix, who waited for ever for her lover, who chose to go back to the sea instead of staying with his beloved. 'No, my sweet *menina*,' João would insist, 'you are my heart's soul, and we were born to love each other for ever.' It's been so long that I no longer remember how he said it in Portuguese. I watched him sail away, stood on the dock for hours, motionless, as if I were dead, alone with only the image of the ship's name . . . *Ensom Sjømann*, that was its name; João had explained that in Norwegian it meant 'lonely sailor', and I remember that the '*ø*' of *Sjømann* was divided in two by a diagonal line, and with tears in my eyes and grief in my heart I felt that I also had been cut in two, and that I would never be whole again. It was awful to think that the sea had swallowed him, that he was nothing more than a dot, almost invisible, in the middle of the wide blue ocean. I felt so full and empty at the same time, hell, it was as if my body were swollen with caresses and yet encircled by some deadly wind that carried poison gas which made my arms, skull, tongue, my entire body shrivel up. I felt choked with kisses I could no longer give back, because he was gone."

"How awful," Meche said, wiping her eyes. "That reminds me of a girl from my village. She had a baby who died at birth, and because the poor girl was giving milk, the midwife bound her breasts with a strip of cloth. I still remember how she howled with pain."

"I know how she felt," Alda said. "I was about to go crazy, and the only thing I wanted was to die. I went to school like a robot. After class I stopped at the soda fountain to play the jukebox. Always the same song, the bolero that says 'I can't go on without you' . . . remember the words? 'And to think that you'll never be beside me again.' The owner was a good old Italian gentleman who treated me with kindness. Every time Los Panchos sang the part that goes 'It's useless to live without you, as useless as trying to forget you,' I would break down in tears, and the owner – he was always behind the cash register – would pat the air with his palm as if he were trying to comfort me. The second time I came in, he told me, 'The sun always appears after a storm,' but for me the sun and happiness no longer existed.

"It wasn't long before those girls appeared who give bad advice with good intentions, thinking they're doing you a favour. They started telling me that men were worthless, and they convinced me to go with them to a bar where there was dancing every night. I guess it was the devil inside me that gave me the idea that the only way to forget João was to get involved with another man. 'Good,' said those well-intentioned bitches, 'the king is dead; long live the king,' and I started going from man to man. To make things worse, my mother, who was all over my arse because I went out every night, started calling me a whore. She threatened to tell my father so that he would beat the shit out of me. But my old man was such a kind person, one day he asked me, 'What's going on, daughter?' and I who loved him so much said, 'I'm in love, papa.' I was about to tell him everything when he turned away from me and said, 'Ah, if it's love, don't worry, honey, anything is allowed in love.' I should have expected as much – he was always in love with another woman.

"One night a man in his forties approached me and asked, 'How much do you charge, kid?' and out of sheer spite I told him, 'Four thousand pesos.' 'Done,' he agreed, and after he screwed me he gave me the money . . . and that's the way I started as a prostitute. It happened just when I was about to finish high school. I don't know, maybe I could have studied to become a secretary, or taken some other decent job, but I guess it was fate, what else? I believe that somewhere everything is already written. But enough of this – tell us, who was the first man who made love to you, Señora Martina?"

"Ain't no use talking 'bout the first," the old woman replied, wetting her lips. "When you get a few more miles on you, you'll realize that the most important man in your life is not the first one, but the last. And I think you're right, Alda, our fate must be scribbled somewhere. I was born a long way from here, in the south, among country folk, cows and rain, and you can bet your life that my mother never dreamed that one day I would earn my keep by peddling my arse. You wouldn't know to look at me now, but I was quite a pretty little *huaina*; in the houses where I worked I collected the most steady customers and made the most money. I was proud when I looked at myself in the mirror, at this really knockout body and those eyes black as charcoal that conquered them all . . . but old age is a different story, another one of God's little jokes – your mouth withers like a dried poppy, wrinkles fan out across your face like empty river beds, and even your tits sag like over-ripe fruit on a tree. So when a man notices you again, it's like a miracle, like rain in the desert. That's why I clobbered you that time, Alda."

"Mario Alberto was the last one, huh?" Alda asked contritely. "Forgive me, Señora Martina. How was I to know? Besides, I was just a young bitch and I enjoyed snatching men from the other girls, I don't know why. But the bastard wasn't worth a damn, I assure you, and he soon lost interest in me and took off for the south with Tina, the youngest girl in the house. Tell me, why the hell do men go to pieces?"

"What on earth are you talking about, Aldita?" asked Meche.

"Just what I said," Alda replied. "They break. Have you seen those glass angels you hang from the branches of a Christmas tree? It's the same thing with men. In the beginning they're shiny and perfect, and you're full of illusions, thinking that at long last you've found happiness – and once again you believe in God, you know . . . but no way. When you least expect it, they dump you like a bag of trash – the pigs can be so cruel – and they go to pieces, break up like a glass thrown against a wall, because for them politics or a soccer game are far more important than love, and there's no difference for them, really, between a boxing match, a heroic battle and a political rally."

At that moment they heard a squeal of brakes outside, followed by the rhythmic thud of boots landing on the ground. A hoarse voice shouted a series of commands, and after a moment of silence came the chorus of men crying out in unison as they advanced across the training field:

Hup, two, three, four,
This is the motto of the military corps:
Manliness, Bravery,
Duty, *Pundonor*!
For my Nation, this I swear:
Sacrifice, Denial
Faith in the power to dare!

Hup, two, three, four,
This is the motto of the military corps:
Manliness, Bravery,
Duty, *Pundonor*!

For my Country,
All my Strength!
Though hungry or cold,
My heart will be bold,
And I will defend You to the end!

The following morning Colonel Arreola addressed a group of thirty recruits and several newly commissioned officers assembled on the parade ground. After saluting his adjutant, he gave the men "at-ease" and cleared his throat.

"Soldiers of the Republic," he began, "we are gathered together today to conduct an exercise designed to prepare you to deal with our enemies. As you know, despite our holy crusade to exterminate these vermin, there are still a sizeable number of good-for-nothings who infect our land. Yes, I use the word 'infect' because they are diseased, carriers of filth, like rats bearing the plague. Therefore, in our treatment of them we will show no pity, no weakness of will, no display of sympathy when we encounter such dangerous animals. You must steel yourself against such tendencies. Remember your sworn allegiance to our glorious leader's goal of ridding our country of evil. Remember as well that, for those who deviate from our code of conduct, the punishment will be swift and severe.

"Discipline is the foundation of any military organization. An army does not march on its stomach, as the gringos are so fond of saying, but on command. And the backbone of this command is discipline, instilled through training, such as the drill which you are going to engage in this afternoon. You may question its wisdom, you may be taken aback by its crudeness, you may even be repelled by the viciousness it demands, but you will carry out the prescribed manoeuvre because it will demonstrate your resolve, your commitment to our cause, and your faith in our Supreme Leader."

He held up one hand, palm out, and shrugged. "Also because," he flashed a bright smile, "if you refuse your orders, you will be shot."

An hour later one of the prostitutes, a young girl called Lily with large breasts and black curly hair, managed to persuade one of the guards to let her use the bathroom. He was a thick-set man with hard eyes, and she felt his gaze measuring her body before he unlocked the door.

"Only you," he said, waving the other women away.

When she came out of the bathroom, the guard took her up a flight of stairs.

"What are you going to do?" she asked.

He put a finger to his lips. "No talking. And don't worry, señorita, all I want is a service you are quite familiar with. Afterwards, I'll return you to your cell."

They went through a door and on to a railed balcony where the guard led her to a corner behind a column, shoved her to her knees, and unzipped his trousers. Holding her head with both hands, he rammed his organ into her mouth and she sucked until his fingers tightened on her hair and he came with a groan. She looked up at him, stretching himself and smiling contentedly until she spat the semen at his fly.

"Shit!" he hissed. "You filthy *puta*!" He yanked her to her feet.

"It was an accident," she told him. "I can't swallow it. Some girls can, not me; it makes me sick."

He slapped her. "Shut the fuck up." Then he jerked her forward until his face was an inch away. "Stay here. Sit down and don't move. I'm going to clean this shit off." He slammed her against the wall and pointed to the floor. "I'll be back in five minutes. If you so much as cross your legs, I'll cut your tits off."

She nodded, rubbing her cheek as he closed the door. Spreading her legs, she spat in his direction and gave a mock salute. "From one cocksucker to another, you miserable piece of *mierda*."

Suddenly she froze as shouted military commands split the quiet afternoon, followed by the clatter of soldiers running in the court below. Creeping to the railing, she crouched down and stared in open-mouthed wonder at the scene unfolding before her.

There were two large military vans parked near the soldiers, who had formed a semicircle close to a grove of trees that bordered the parade ground. Each soldier held in his hand what looked to Lily like a slice of raw meat. Colonel Arreola stood off to one side with his hands locked behind his back. At that moment Arreola said something to his adjutant, who snapped to attention and yelled, "Release the targets!"

The rear doors to both vans swung open and, to Lily's consternation, dogs began spilling out – dogs of all sizes, colours and breeds, mangy, collarless mutts by the look of them. And angry, it was obvious, as several fights immediately broke out. She had no way of knowing they were strays who were regularly collected off the city streets and starved for three days before they were packed into the vans. With growing amazement, Lily watched as the animals caught scent of the meat and scrambled in a frenzy towards the soldiers waiting in front of the trees.

Her gaze fixed on a young soldier with the face of an actor who knelt to pat a little black dog as it gobbled the meat, its stump of a tail wiggling comically; and then the adjutant blew a whistle whose shrillness carried across the field like an eagle's cry, and the handsome youth grabbed the little dog by the scruff of the neck and lifted it, with his free hand pulling from a sheath on his left side a long serrated knife nearly as big as a bayonet. Swinging the now howling, thrashing, outraged black ball of fur around and up he drove the knife into its neck, ripping it sideways in the classic military manner; and then the day exploded with screams of pain, a choking, strident, mortally wounded choir of creatures whose agony sounded almost human, whose blood, urine and faeces spurted everywhere, on to the grass and into the air, spattering the hands, faces and uniforms of the soldiers, who were themselves growling like dogs and who, in a kind of primitive *coup de grâce*, proceeded to batter the convulsing bodies against the nearest tree trunk until even the twitching ceased.

Arrcola came to attention and saluted the troops. "*Bien*," he said. "*Muy bien*." He gestured to his adjutant, who saluted, turned to the men, and said, "Operation Sight and Knife is now completed. Soldiers, this is how we will treat our nation's enemies – without mercy, no quarter asked nor given. Officers, form the men into ranks and return to your barracks."

"Dear God," Lily said. She sat slumped against the railing, staring through her tears at the door through which the guard had disappeared while the rough voices, beating out the rhythm, faded away into the distance:

> Hup, two, three, four,
> This is the motto of the military corps:
> Manliness, Bravery,
> Duty *Pundonor*! . . .

At three o'clock the next morning, the metallic roar of military vehicles approaching the camp resounded once more.

"All the whores are to evacuate this place immediately!" shouted a Corporal while other soldiers, smiling maliciously, threw open the cell doors. "This time you'll have to hoof it, my dears," the Corporal taunted them.

The hollow-eyed women walked quickly down the corridor without a word, most of them trying to arrange their dishevelled hair and straighten their clothing. Once outside, they encountered a group of male prisoners guarded by a squad of soldiers with their rifles at the ready. Most of them were young men wearing cotton shirts and sober expressions, eyes defiant and jaws firmly elevated. Walking past them, the women sensed that the air surrounding the prisoners was pregnant with a strange mixture of fear and strength.

"Comrade, please," whispered a young man with a short beard, handing Alda a small piece of paper which she quickly hid in the pocket of her jeans.

After a long march, having been told nothing of their destination, the women finally came to a set of railroad tracks, which they followed for two hours before reaching a train station guarded by another group of armed soldiers, who leered at them as they climbed on to the platform. Another Corporal, one with a cunning face, informed them that the train to the capital was about to arrive.

"But, sir, we don't have money enough to pay our fare," a fat girl with defenceless eyes dared to say, expecting some compassion from the Corporal.

"The government does not provide free transportation, chubby," he said.

"So be prepared to pay with your jewels, or maybe the conductor will settle for a blow job," another soldier said, slapping the fat girl on the behind.

And so the women, dirty, hungry and sweaty, boarded the train without knowing at which station the conductor would force them off, while a pair of helicopters hovered overhead like vultures who feed on the dead.

Part Two

I am the land where the world ends . . .

My body, which is also a valley covered by shrubs and weeping willows, has been invaded by the dark forces of a tyranny that has poisoned my sweetness, the sweetness of wheat and honey. Years ago, when the star of freedom shed its light on my skin, gallant horses used to gallop over me and yokes of oxen slowly knitted each twilight with care. During the day, peasants with loving and patient hands drew horizontal tattoos on me to deposit their seeds that made all my pores flower in a ceremony of love under the clear blue sky. Roots trembled inside me, filling me with lightning bolts that burst in greenness, and the sun mounted me like a feverish lover, covering my body with petals and buds. A symphony of bees buzzed around me, and I, a pregnant bride, smiled in my altar of pollen, ready to give birth to green and rounded fruit. In the heat of summer I would lie, lazing under the weight of my children, each second growing and ripening with bounty. In a birthing ceremony of harps and guitars, other patient and loving hands came to harvest my joyful offspring, and afterwards the cyclical rituals of life began anew.

But today my body is also inhabited by rotten corpses, their bones covered by mud, a grimace of terror still fixed on their worm-eaten jaws. In the tidepool of my roots, arms without flesh now erupt, wrists bound and fingers clasped in posthumous supplication, and my womb now gives shelter to the ashes of hearts and long hair. In the darkness I tremble upon hearing the shrieking brakes of armoured cars and military trucks which arrive after midnight, the best time to discard their seeds of death. Doors spring open and on the surface of my skin fall a number of bodies illuminated by headlights and the shiny reflection of so many polished weapons in the hands of men in uniform. After deploying in the correct manner, the soldiers disperse to wound me with their picks and shovels while an officer struts up and down with steps that seem to echo from the grave. Bathed in a moonlight that is now foreign to me, I receive in anguish the avalanche of bleeding bodies which tumble into my violated womb, and then cold steel pounds me with my own shovelled entrails, sent flying by harsh commands which crack the silence of the night. They stomp on me vigorously to hide all traces before escaping like criminals in the early morning fog.

And at midday, when a peasant caresses me with his slowly moving plough, believing me unchanged, the same ancestral mother, his blade carves a path over my nocturnal wounds. My skin opens with intense pain to receive his seeds, which will now germinate inside the caverns and cells of perforated skulls.

Like birds confused by an early spring, little by little the women returned to their shelters in the street of night.

After leaving the detention camp, Alda, Meche and Martina united as sisters on an uncertain itinerary in which the only fixed goal was to obtain transportation to the capital, where on one of its thoroughfares stood the houses of patched walls and high balconies.

Once on the train, the hungry and dishevelled group of women started fanning out through the various cars, but these three kept together in one corner of a second-class carriage, cementing that bond which had been formed in the net of the fear of death. On the piece of paper the young prisoner had passed to Alda as they were being taken away was written one name and an address. Putting their heads together, they decided that it might be the name of a person the young man wished to warn.

"Maybe if this guy gets the message in time, he'll hurry up and save that poor young man," Meche said in a serious but optimistic tone.

"Stop dreaming," Martina said, wrapping herself deeper into her shawl. "You're always looking for a saviour, girl."

Meche's smile was tight. "Maybe, but we should deliver the note, don't you agree, Aldita?"

"Yeah, it won't cost us anything," Alda answered, remembering the young man's bright eyes and urgent voice.

Some thirty minutes later, while they were crossing a green valley that extended to the foot of the Andes, a conductor dressed in a black uniform came into the carriage. Without looking at them, he held out his hand in a ceremonial gesture, waiting for their tickets. Martina gave a long sigh of resignation while Meche fixed her frightened eyes on the man's hand.

"Forgive us, inspector, sir, but we don't have tickets," Alda told him with a grin that she hoped was humble enough.

The conductor snapped his hand back efficiently and frowned. "You can buy tickets now or get off at the next station, and be thankful that because of my good heart I don't charge you a fine. What a day! I've lost count of how many women there are on this train without tickets. Who do they think they are, royalty?"

"But we're broke," Meche exclaimed. "Would you believe that they yanked us out of our house at midnight—"

"Señor inspector, please," Alda interrupted, pointing at Martina. "What she means is that our mother, this poor woman, is terribly ill and has to be treated by a specialist in the capital; but my sister and I have used up so much money on medicine that we don't have one red cent left."

Martina took her cue and moaned. "This damned pain is so bad I'd be better off dead." Taking Alda's hand, she gave the conductor a sorrowful look. "I'm ashamed at how much trouble I've caused my girls."

"If you don't help us, sir," Meche pleaded, "my poor mama will surely die. In the name of God the Father, the Merciful, and the Holy Virgin Mary, who ascended to heaven to watch over us, I beg you, help us."

"All right, all right!" the conductor said, backing away. "But after three more stops, your luck may run out. That's when I'm replaced by another conductor who will not be moved by your story. He's a hard man – we call him the Hyena."

As they approached the third station, the three women saw several weather-beaten tents on stony ground beside a river-bank.

"Let's ask the gypsies for help," Martina suggested. "They always know what to do when a Christian is in need."

It took them an hour to walk to the encampment. They stood outside the group of tents while a fat gypsy walked towards them, looking at them with mistrust. He nodded his head in greeting, wearing an enigmatic smile and stroking his thick moustache. "You've come to have your fortune told, my ladies?" he asked. "The three of you together resemble the Three Marias in the night sky." He swept an arm in invitation. "Come in, stars of heaven, and my wife will read your fortune for the modest price of two hundred pesos."

"No, *paisano*," Martina told him. "We've had our fill of misery lately, and if there's any more bad luck in our futures, we don't care to know about it. The truth is, we need help."

A few minutes later, seated in one of the tents, surrounded by the fat gypsy and a dozen children, together with a like number of women dressed in colourful silk garments, the three women related what had happened to them since the night they had been taken to the detention camp.

The gypsy's face was grave. "This was once a pretty good country. The authorities were tolerant, and the people treated gypsies better than anywhere in South America. In fact, we have much in common. Like us, they are great believers in superstition. In spite of their fine universities and beneath the veneer of civilization, they inherited a whole system of witchcraft from the Indians, especially in the south. And like us, they enjoyed laughter, the guitar, and they were full of life. But now, death is everywhere. I go to fetch water in the morning and see bodies floating down the river, turning in the current like logs. And in every village plaza uniformed men walk around with machine guns.

"Death surrounds us, *paisanas*. Only three weeks ago, two of the children from our tribe went to explore a cave and found a pile of half-burned human bones. My father and I wanted to report it to the police, but what for? Most likely we'd have ended up in jail, blamed for the death of those poor devils. Besides, I doubt they'd even listen to us. 'Gypsies' stories,' they'd have said. Or, more likely, they already knew about it, were even part of it, because many of them cover up the massacres ordered by the Benefactor, who knows how to use death to his advantage. One of our band travelling in the north told us that now the soldiers burn their victims' bodies in order to kill the smell and to keep dogs from digging them up. Life is getting tough here, especially for gypsies. The soldiers accuse us of hiding subversives. They come into our camp in the middle of the night and tear it apart. They interrogate us with rifle butts. A number of our young men have been arrested. Two have disappeared. As you know, we gypsies are no strangers to persecution or suffering. We don't forget that in Europe the Nazis turned half a million gypsies into ashes. We carry that memory wherever we go. I was a child in Romania during that time, and these soldiers look more and more like those Nazis who turned my homeland into a cemetery."

By now a small crowd had gathered. A young gypsy man who was staring at Meche with considerable interest offered them cigarettes and muttered some words which brought laughter from the other men. With a cordial smile, he snapped his fingers and a few moments later a woman with blonde braids brought out three bowls of hot rice, a platter of boiled vegetables, and bread. The three women ate in silence, enjoying each mouthful, surrounded by a tide of foreign words and gestures full of warmth and friendship.

"I know it's an abuse of your kindness, my dear *paisano*," Alda said, "but we need a little money to help us get back to the city."

At that moment an ancient gypsy woman who had been staring at Alda with her old eyes half-closed scratched her breasts, causing the coins on her wrist and the charms on her necklace to jangle before she spoke in the loud tone of an oracle making a prediction: "A rich and powerful man desires your body! But his heart is as cold as a tomb!"

The other gypsy women began to moan, a brief lament punctuated by strange ritual movements of their hands. The fat gypsy spoke sharply to them, then stood and raised his arms as he addressed his three guests. "Normally I would send you on your way with some flowery excuse of which I have many in stock. But these are not normal times. Though hate is abundant and money is short, let us not allow generosity to be scarce as well. Don't worry, you are guests, we will help you."

The following day Alda, Meche and Martina boarded a rickety bus that crawled down the gravelled roads and wheezed asthmatically each time it stopped at the bridges guarded by soldiers with arrogant eyes and olive-green camouflage uniforms the colour of thick jungle vegetation. At every stop an officer commanded the passengers to get off and wait in line for a luggage search. Without fail, four soldiers (no more, no less) would order the driver to open the hood in search of hidden weapons before they entered the bus to check everything on board, opening beaten-up handbags, cardboard boxes tied with string and cheap twine, and old canvas bags that had more miles on the clock than the bus. At military outposts set up in the larger villages, the soldiers marched with their weapons at "present-arms", growling orders and wearing savage grins on their stern faces. It was at one such post that the three women saw four handcuffed men stumbling along with an escort of eight soldiers, who used their rifle butts to make the prisoners keep pace. Panting, carrying their heads low, the prisoners passed by a news-stand where a woman came out and started running after them with a blanket clutched in her arms.

"Poor lady," one of the male passengers remarked. "She's wasting her time. Blankets do not warm the dead."

Hearing him, Alda remembered again the eyes of the young prisoner at the camp. She saw them fixed and lost in nothingness but still shining with the determination of invulnerable courage, like two red-hot coals floating in the river of death, and she had the urgent sensation that his life was in her hands. To Meche she whispered, "As soon as we get to the city, if we ever get there, we must look up that guy whose address is on the note."

During the long and seemingly interminable journey, the three women found themselves growing closer; that bond, born in fear and confusion now growing in strength, was knit tighter by their experience of impotence in the face of injustice. The bus driver's voice trembling each time he was stopped on the road, and the anger of the passengers upon finding their clothes strewn all over the floor and muddied by military boots seemed, like the incidents at the detention camp, but pale reflections of an immense, sinister mill that never ceased turning, grinding away the lives of so many innocent men and women.

When at last the lighted valley of the city appeared in the distance, Alda proposed that the three of them take up work in the same house.

"It took me bloody ages to establish myself," Alda told them, "and now Doña Carolina, the owner of the house, treats me as if I were her only heir, and I bet she does leave it to me when she dies – if I don't croak first, you never know – but I guarantee you respect, good food, a fair work schedule, and as much comfort as you will find in a whorehouse. Martina, you can work in the kitchen. You and I, Meche, will continue playing the same old game, making men happy, which is what they pay for."

But the street of night had ceased to be what it had always been, and when Alda, Meche and Martina finally arrived at Doña Carolina's house, they were surprised to find that the other women now listened intently to the news on the radio, and that at eight o'clock in the evening, the hour when they began preparing to receive their clients, they would dress and apply their make-up in front of a television set that they had demanded from Doña Carolina, claiming that the circumstances of the military raid made it imperative for them to keep informed of both national and international political events. And that Sunday they succeeded in getting a night off, thanks to the leadership of Patoja, who had been a close friend of the girl who had been killed in cold blood in front of their eyes in the narrow corridor between the cells of the detention camp.

Early on Sunday morning, Patoja stopped by each house to hand out a flyer instructing the women to dress in black, cover their heads with a white veil, and take a red rose and a burning candle with them to the symbolic burial. At seven that evening, the women left their houses in silence and walked slowly towards the tallest and oldest building on the street of night. Once everyone was assembled, Patoja climbed a stepladder and began to read the following litany: "Deborah, you who were assassinated with us as witnesses will now be our sacred spirit. Friend and true companion, you who died at the hands of injustice will from now on protect us, make miracles for all of us, who will never forget you."

While the choir of women prayed devoutly, Patoja took a brush soaked with red paint and in huge letters printed on the wall behind her:

DEBORAH
WE DON'T KNOW WHERE
YOUR BODY IS,
BUT HERE IS YOUR SOUL

Walking in line by two's, the women came to the wall and, after making the sign of the cross, each placed a red rose and a flaming candle on the pavement. Soon there was a half-moon of fire at the foot of the epitaph.

"Saint Deborah, you who art in heaven, protect us from evil and misfortune!" exclaimed a tall girl named Alicia, stepping over the flames from the candles. She turned to face the others, pointing at the inscription Patoja had painted on the wall. "You who in the Old Testament arose among the weak to defeat the powerful!"

Each woman made a sign of the cross upon hearing her words, which opened for them a portal to a sacred and remote past.

"The Bible tells us, comrades," the tall girl continued, "that thousands of years ago there was a prophetess who, with a woman's hand, liberated her enslaved people. Braver than any man, she ambushed the enemy and made them bite the dust. Mother among all mothers in Israel, she was more intelligent and astute than the powerful ones who ruled. And after returning from battle, she said . . . allow me to read for you, comrades, what valiant Deborah said." Leafing through a book with old and ragged binding, she found the passage and read in a solemn voice: "Hear, O ye Kings; give ear, O ye Princes. Deserted were the villages, defenceless until I arose, mother in Israel . . . Then the weak defeated the strong. The people of Yahweh prevailed against the powerful."

"But our poor Deborah is already dead, comrade!" Patoja told the tall girl, bursting into tears. "All the Deborahs of this world are dead, for ever!"

A wave of murmurs arose among the women, shattering their moment of faith.

"The body dies, but not the soul," the tall girl protested.

"You don't kill soldiers with the soul," Alda asserted. "Our Deborah here will protect us because she died like a saint and a martyr, but the powerful, those shit-eating soldiers, will go on telling us what to do."

Patoja knelt on the pavement. "Let us pray, comrades," she said, "let us pray."

And the street of night filled with voices in supplication, their call to God ascending past the deserted balconies and disappearing over the huddled roof tiles, bathed in an opaque glow under the full moon.

After a while, the women returned slowly to their various dwellings, drying their tears, mumbling insults against the military and the Benefactor of the Republic, who in an official edict had just declared over radio and television that the country would remain in a state of emergency for another six months.

Martina had already taken charge of her duties in the kitchen. She was peeling several pounds of potatoes to prepare the *charquicán* that Doña Carolina had ordered her to cook. A bad mood invariably overtook her when she had to prepare a dish she didn't like. While she grumbled softly, it seemed to her that the wind blowing outside was the same wind that had blown on her hair on other late summer afternoons, as when she had crossed the fields to reach the house of Señora Rosa, the healer, who had taught her the art of good herbs.

Remembering with a grimace of disgust those days when cooking was a sour ritual and the perverse preamble to her husband's sexual aggression, she slammed the ground meat in the pan and started slicing an onion with the same anger she used to feel in those faraway days. "Stop it, Martina! Don't be stupid," she said to herself when she felt that strange constriction in her throat, like a huge snake trying to cut off her breath. With rancour in her heart, she stirred the meat and onions as they fried over a low fire, adding four cloves of minced garlic, a dash of oregano, another pinch of cumin, and three bay leaves. Waiting for the onions to turn golden brown, she ran her wooden spoon through the thick hash; and just as she was about to pour in a little boiling water she heard a strange noise that seemed to emanate from the pan, a sound not unlike a human sigh. "Godammit! I know I'm old, but I can't be cracking up," she told herself, tilting the kettle and pouring a spout of water into the frying mixture, from which a thick cloud of steam arose. "All I need now," she mumbled bitterly, "is to lose my marbles! Shit. Everything turns to crap." She continued grumbling to herself, experienced a weird sensation that someone nearby was observing her with enquiring eyes. On the pan's thin surface of oil, tiny volcanoes began to erupt, signalling to her that it was time to toss in the potatoes cut in fours; but at the precise moment she turned towards the kitchen counter where the dish of white chunks waited, she heard again the sighing voice, which now whispered, "How fast the years go by, *huaina*, faster than a mountain lion on the move . . ."

Amazed, Martina let the spoon drop. "Dear God, is that you, Señora Rosa?" she asked in a low voice, bending over the pan so close that the fragrant steam bathed her cheeks.

"Yes, it's me who's come to see you, *huainita*, but my God, you're so old, almost as long in the tooth as I was when I taught you the good spells of love."

"Which didn't help me a damn," Martina said in a voice heavy with reproach.

"That's because your husband put the evil eye on you, and it will go with you to your grave," replied the voice hidden in the dark, boiling pool of ground meat and onions which was spitting little drops of oil on the stove top.

"That's a lie!" Martina exclaimed. "I did meet a good man who truly loved me!"

"I know, I know. No need to tell me more, because I see everything. Hmph. I saw you many, many times at night in that white hut. There in my bed I would close my eyes to go to sleep, and I'd see you snuggling with that man who loved you as if you were a princess. But the tree that crushed him was sent by the evil eye, the curse your husband, that lynx, put on you."

Martina wiped the sweat from her forehead and continued to contemplate with a stoic expression the little volcanoes bubbling in the pan where she now seemed to recognize Señora Rosa's eyes. Tears ran down her wrinkled cheeks, falling into the steaming food. "And life gets worse every day, señora."

"Yes, I know. These aren't the days for love enchantments. That's why I've come, to teach you those other spells, the ones that will go right through those walls built by the devil."

For several days some of the women in the house whispered in awe among themselves that Martina spoke to the spirits while she cooked; out of malice, others who did not believe in ghosts attributed her mutterings to the typical hallucinations and manias of old age. It wasn't long, however, before all the women in Doña Carolina's house grew accustomed to entering the kitchen and seeing Martina bent over a pot as if she were listening to words uttered by an invisible shadow which lived in the bottom of boiling dishes. Many times they caught her gesticulating in front of the stove while in a low and irate tone she told the details of an unfortunate event – because Martina confided in Señora Rosa the suffering of her life as if the old healer were her mother, come to visit from the realm of the dead.

In the street of night, which was also now the street of miraculous spirits, other strange events would soon occur. These occurrences radically modified the ancestral image of the merchandising of bodies reflected throughout all time. The women of the street no longer reverted to the figure of Hagar in the arms of Abraham. It was as if the mirror which over the centuries had revealed the ancient, repetitive profiles of concubines and courtesans was now shattered. Among its splinters there appeared a dark void which prevented any bond with the circles of the cyclical and eternal. And yet the void gave birth to an idea, an attitude that lodged itself in the horizontal and unrepeatable tide of history. The Benefactor's whim, his positivist project of contributing to the advances of civilization by establishing a research centre where the peculiar traits of prostitutes could be analysed, had interrupted the marginal, seasonal flow of time and channelled it into the dangerous currents of historical events, whose waters were beating back and forth against the walls of a dam erected by the dictatorship.

As they passed through the front door of an old-fashioned residence on Cathedral Street, Alda and Meche eyed the bronze plaque with the name JUAN BAUTISTA ALBORNOZ, and under this the announcement GENERAL MEDICINE. A dark young woman had opened the door and, ignoring their question as to whether they could see Doctor Albornoz, confined herself to guiding them down a glass corridor which opened into a small receiving room.

A tall old lady of distinguished appearance said to them, "Come in, please, and have a seat."

"Is the doctor in?" Alda enquired.

"He'll be home from the hospital soon to see his private patients," the woman told them. "For what time this evening did you make your appointment?"

"I don't have an appointment, madam, but . . . I must see him, I feel very sick," Alda said hurriedly, hoping to ward off the old lady's inevitable arguments about the inconvenience this would cause.

But instead, the lady opened the appointment book and said in a friendly tone, "The doctor can see you at eight-thirty."

"What a pretty Friar Escobero you have!" Meche said impulsively, forgetting the seriousness of their mission. "Where did you buy it? When I was a small girl, my mother kept a Friar Escobero on a shelf in the dining room, and she always claimed that he protected us against all illnesses and saw to it that there was bread and food on the table."

"Your mother was correct, señorita," the lady agreed, moving to the table where the little plaster of Paris statue stood. "He is one of the most generous and kind-hearted saints our Lord sent to earth. There is only one requirement for receiving his generosity: one must always place flowers and four copper coins at his feet."

While Meche and the lady prattled on about saints, Alda examined the bookshelves, trying to decide on the most discreet method of passing the message to the doctor. "*Manual of Pathology*," she thought to herself. "Shit, maybe the best thing to do is simply hand him the piece of paper and beat it. No, one of the patients might get suspicious if I leave so quickly. I guess I'll have to invent an illness . . . *Treatise of Surgical Pathology* – what kind of frigging title is that? Harrison . . . no, that's not a title, you stupid bitch; my heart aches so much, doctor – no, what an idiotic thing to say; besides, it sounds like a corny love song. I'd better tell him there's something wrong with my liver . . . *Clinical Exploration of the Heart*. That's it, the heart! Who cares if it sounds melodramatic, maybe he specializes in the heart. But I have no idea of what symptoms a person feels when he has a heart condition . . . *Atlas of Surgical Techniques*, bah! I thought an atlas was just for maps. Okay, I'll say that my stomach hurts, that I keep throwing up after I eat, that I have diarrhoea in the morning, et cetera, et cetera, and so on and so forth . . . and when he starts to examine me, I can hand him the note without saying a word – yes, it will be less dangerous if I don't say anything, first because the military arseholes may have installed a bug in the light fixture like the Russians did in that movie I saw with Angélica, and second, because we might be completely off base, we women who are so good at imagining that people are kind . . . But it could very well be that the young man at the detention camp was twice betrayed, and that this Doctor Albornoz is really an evil double agent who works for the secret police, or maybe a counter-spy or whatever they're called . . ."

"You may go in now," the old lady said before she joined Meche on a couch to resume their conversation.

Alda went into a small examination room that contained a hospital bed along one wall where a strange-looking glass tube was hanging next to a wooden panel that held what looked like a huge thermometer filled with some kind of silver fluid. She greeted the doctor, a tall man with dark hair wearing a long white jacket, and felt her heart jump – whether out of fear or because he was so incredibly handsome, she didn't know.

"Please, sit here," he said, pulling out a chair by his desk. "You haven't been feeling well lately? My mother told me that you came to my clinic without making an appointment in advance."

"Yes, doctor. I can't bear these stomach-aches any longer. They're so awful, I throw up the entire night. Blood comes out, and yellow stuff that must be pus, and this constant diarrhoea, all day and night, so that I don't have one single minute of peace. And here, on my right side, I feel a terrible pain, as if someone were beating me with a huge hammer, one of those—"

"Lay down on the examination table," Doctor Albornoz said with a smile that, to Alda, seemed to doubt her.

She could not take her eyes off his face as he examined her with firm but reassuring gestures. He asked her to breathe deeply while he moved a small metal sphere down her back. When he pressed different areas on her stomach, asking her each time if she felt any pain, she noticed that there were small wrinkles around his eyes which formed a kind of design such as those created by the rays of the sun. "He has the wrinkles kind people have," she thought. "People who love and laugh. He can't be a traitor, counter-spy, or whatever it's called, and, Jesus, he's so handsome . . ."

"Avoid fried food for five days, and four times a day take the pills I'm going to prescribe," the doctor was saying when she quickly put her hand in her pocket and slipped the small piece of paper into his long fingers with their carefully trimmed nails. "Yes. In a couple of days you'll be good as new again," the doctor went on, stroking her arm as he helped her down from the bed. "On your way out, tell my mother that the visit is already paid. And please do not forget to give her your address and telephone number."

Alda and Meche went out into the cool night air feeling that they had accomplished a very important mission. They walked gaily past the tall trees now turning green again with new leaves, laughing and discussing each detail of their adventure.

"I swear, Meche, it's really beautiful to get involved in something. I feel great. It doesn't matter if we never know why that young man sent the message to the doctor, who is *sooo* attractive. You would have fallen on your arse if you'd seen him. A real movie star. And he must be terribly intelligent."

"The message will save a life, Aldita, I just know it will," Meche promised with a smile. "It wouldn't be exaggerating to say that we have been messengers sent by our Lord. And his mother, Señora Leonora, is so elegant and friendly. I haven't had anyone to talk about God with for such a long time. Listen to this: she told me about the group she works with at her church, and she even took my telephone number because she's going to invite me to go with her to the special services for the Virgin Mary."

Alda's smile was buoyant. "I tell you, honey, I'm convinced that the most wonderful thing in life is to *do* things, to feel that one has *moved* something, even if it's only a grain of sand. Don't you feel that way, Meche? In Doña Carolina's house one never changes anything . . . the guys go into the room, drop their pants, pull out some bills, and take off without leaving a trace of anything, even when they say goodbye – if they take the time to say goodbye, that is. You know, I think our job is exactly like the work of housewives, who spend their entire day cleaning and dusting and making beds. For what? To do it all over again the next day. Women don't change the world, baby, they just keep it clean."

"Yuk," Meche said. "It must be so boring to be a housewife. And to top it all off, when their husbands make love to them, it's so old and familiar, like watching the same movie for the twentieth time."

"But at bottom, they live the same kind of life we live," Alda said. "Attending to our chores, the same thing over and over, mending underwear or choosing the right shade of rouge. Can you imagine how great it must be to cure a sick person? Never mind building a bridge or inventing something like . . . the telephone or an airplane."

"That's why we are so happy now," Meche said enthusiastically. "We have saved a life, Aldita!"

"I wouldn't be so sure of that, Meche. You always get so optimistic over the smallest thing. We may have done much less than that, but anyway, the important thing is to feel that we have given a little shove to this world, which isn't that bad after all, so stuff the soldiers and that frigging old goat who appears on television every day."

Four days later, the women of the house were having lunch at the long table headed by Doña Carolina, who always saw to it that her girls ate fresh vegetables rich in vitamins and iron which, according to her, were essential nutrients that guaranteed a good performance at night.

"I don't think I can give you permission, Meche dear, to go to church tonight," the owner of the house said in that motherly, soothing tone she always used when she issued a command decision.

"Good!" Alda broke in. "We whores must not mix with decent ladies."

"But Aldita," Meche protested, "you know very well that Señora Leonora is a very special lady, so different from other women."

"Different, my arse," Alda said scornfully. "As soon as she learns you're a hooker—"

"But she already knows!" Meche exclaimed. "Yesterday when we talked over the phone, I told her what I did for a living, and she said it didn't matter, that she was coming by at six to pick me up." She pointed a finger at Alda. "And she said it was very important for you to go, too."

One of the other whores burst out laughing. "Shit! Either that old bitch is crazy, or she thinks you can help her get laid."

"Or else she wants to play the saint," another woman chipped in, raising her eyes to heaven, "redeeming whores like a good Christian!"

Adela, the most elegant and best-dressed girl in the house, said in a disdainful voice, "I believe this granny would like you to explain what it is to be a whore, confess the most intimate details of our profession, kneeling before the image of the Virgin Mary."

Lighting a cigarette, Alda shook the match at Adela. "As if it made any sense to describe what it's like to be a whore. How can anyone understand what it means to go to bed with so many men who've had too much to drink, who don't smell good, who can't get it up, who pass out on top of you, with so many arseholes who come in less than two minutes. Men march through us exactly like those fucking soldiers parading through the street on Independence Day: lots of noise, an impressive show of good looks, but not one drop of heart, my sweet. Nobody, absolutely nobody, knows who and what we are."

"True," a middle-aged woman next to Meche said in a deep voice. "I think men keep asking us why and how we became whores because they think it's that simple. They don't even suspect what the real story is, the one that happens here every night. Bah! You end up bored to death with so many men who want the same thing, with so many beginnings and always the same end. You're right, Alda – no one knows who we are. Nobody cares, either."

Adela gestured with her palm and said reasonably, "We don't even exist. The only time a man makes love to me with real desire, it's because he's thinking of another woman."

"What does anyone know about what it means to be a whore!" exclaimed a girl with sad eyes. "Even with those nice guys who offer you a friendly drink, you're still the same thing – a body without a soul!"

Another woman roused herself from silence and clapped her hands in mockery. "You're full of more crap than those soap operas you watch every day."

Alda shook her head emphatically. "But she's right. All those bastards treat us as if were mannequins, like god-damned dummies in a store window, disposable; just throw the skin and bones in the trash after the show's over. Big smile, a couple of dances to rub their bellies, and then the shitheads empty their load inside us. Afterwards, we turn into vermin, like dirty cockroaches in a corner. If you really think about it, ladies, this job is pure humiliation! When I see some arsehole in bed puffing smoke towards the ceiling, pretending he's a fucking professor with serious thoughts, this after he's been slobbering on my tits like a wolf with rabies, I get so . . . fucking . . . *mad*! I say to myself, the son of a bitch has already killed you, Alda. I used to ask silly questions, say stupid things, to make them speak, so that I could feel like a real person again. But I knocked that off after a while, and now I figure, go ahead, kill me every night, you cocksuckers, and I rehook my bra, feeling like garbage, like some disgusting insect, because they cross us out as real people, they even forget our arse – after using it, of course."

Yet another whore joined the conversation. "Christ, what a stupid fuck you are! Why in God's name do you expect to be treated as a person? Look, sweetheart, I decided a long time ago that if I'm just a piece of meat for them, all they are for me is a stack of dollars on the dresser."

A voice said, "And what do people know about the smells one has to put up with! Men sweat over us, dripping stuff into our eyes, everywhere; not to mention those clods who come in fresh off the farm after a bath of cheap cologne that would kill every mosquito in the room."

Another voice complained, "And to make things worse, we are despised! Talk about ingratitude, my God! As that actress says on that record Doña Carolina likes so much, 'A whore is a crazy doll, sailing on a sea of alcohol.' And what about the one that goes, 'filthy traders in human flesh', or the one that says we carry 'the infection of sin' . . . What kind of shit is that? Even in that tango about blonde Mireya, they treat us badly. The first line says we are loyal lovers with a great heart, but how do we end up in the song, eh? Like old, dirty beggars dragging our scabby legs along the street, our bodies full of sores and pus, payment for the sin of having been prostitutes."

"And every night the same shit!" yet another voice declared. "I would give everything I own if just once a man invited me to the movies, gave me red roses, and spent a month courting me, the way they do with other women. All they leave behind are cigarette butts, not love stories."

Alda sighed audibly. "And the real love stories are so beautiful! I would sell my soul to the Devil just to see myself once more walking towards a bench in the park where my lover sits feeding pigeons, waiting for me."

"Yes!" Adela said, leaning back in her chair. "When I imagine beautiful things, I picture myself dressed in a black gown made of silk, wearing long white gloves and walking along an avenue full of modern skyscrapers, those huge ones with all that glass reflecting the sky. My heels tap out a rhythm on the pavement, and I see in the distance the back of a tall, elegant man who is waiting for me near a fountain spouting columns of water into the air."

"What a way to make a living!" a voice bewailed. "No man will ever give us his heart."

"That's enough, girls," Doña Carolina said firmly. "At least you have a job. Which is quite an advantage in this country, where people are starving to death. Now, going back to the original subject—"

"Please, Doña Carolina," Meche pleaded, "please allow me to go."

"I'm sorry, dear, but I think Alda is right. It isn't a good idea for you to go out with one of those ladies."

Meche was near tears. "But she told me she was going downtown early this morning, and from there she was coming straight here to pick me up. I don't have any way to let her know I can't go."

"Good," Alda said. "I always wanted to see a scandalized matron surrounded by whores. That'll be worth something."

But Señora Leonora wasn't at all scandalized when she arrived at the house. Smiling politely, she sat in an armchair and told Meche that she needed to talk to Alda about something urgent.

As Alda came down the stairs, she assumed an air of open aggressiveness. "You'd better go, señora. This is a whorehouse, and decent ladies like yourself don't belong here."

Señora Leonora sighed. "My dear girl, these are not the times to be quibbling about moral distinctions. What importance does morality have when death rules over us? Now," she said, nodding at both of them, "get dressed quickly and let's go to the procession. We have important matters to discuss."

"But señora," Alda persisted, "don't you understand what I'm saying?"

"Of course I understand. You earn your living as prostitutes, and thus, according to traditional moral guidelines, you commit a multitude of sins every night. But we should never forget that the laws of morality were made by men, and not by women. And as a woman, I tell you that I don't mind the fact that you are prostitutes, especially now when all of us must join in the struggle for life and freedom." She touched Alda's arm. "Come on, dear, go comb your hair. I want to be at the church before the procession starts."

Dressed in flowing white silk and wearing a diamond crown on her curly hair, the statue of the Virgin Mary advanced down the street on a wooden platform carried on the shoulders of six young men. Behind and on both sides of the street, a long and orderly procession, mainly of women and children, walked with burning candles held aloft, their voices raised in fervent adoration: "All of us have come today, to bring flowers to Mary, the mother of Christ." The choir of voices floated up and around the sacred figure as She swayed on Her human vehicle.

Walking between Alda and Meche, Señora Leonora broke off singing to whisper, "Awful crimes are taking place in our country. The dictator uses the secret police to spy on everyone. Soldiers assault houses at midnight, killing parents in front of their children . . ."

". . . Ave, Ave, *Aveee Mariiia* . . ."

". . . That man has sold his soul to the devil. That's why he has so much power . . ."

". . . Holiest of women, thou . . ."

". . . Two years ago, my youngest son was arrested and taken to prison. He died while he was being tortured. A medical colleague of Juan Bautista's who works at the morgue managed to let him know that his brother was dead, and my poor son spent the whole night at the morgue, trying to fix his little brother's face so that I would not suffer so much when I saw it. I don't know if the wounds were worse to look upon than the stitches. I only know that I fainted at the sight. And these monsters, who finally allowed me to recover his body, forbade me to hold a funeral service . . ."

". . . Santa Maria, mother of God, pray for us now . . ."

". . . The only reason they gave back my son was to warn us, the entire family, all our friends and neighbours – imagine, what is normally an act of mercy became a threat, a form of chastisement, a kind of blackmail. My poor son's eyes were swollen shut, his face bloated, and his lips were black where they had burned them, a boy who never in his life failed to make things brighter with his smile . . ."

". . . Blessed be thou among women, and blessed be the fruit of thy womb, Jesus . . ."

". . . At least they granted us permission to bury him privately. Other people are not so fortunate. My son's friend told him that hundreds of dead people have arrived at the morgue with their fingers hacked off, to prevent identification . . ."

". . . Pray for us here on earth as well as in heaven . . ."

". . . God must be kept too busy to put an end to so much evil, that's why you two must continue helping us . . ."

A priest's voice was heard in the distance over a loudspeaker: "*Ave María Purísima* . . ." Señora Leonora's voice joined with the choir in the procession as they replied, "Conceived with no sin . . ." She paused and turned to Alda. "Our country is becoming a river of blood, daughters, and you must join us in the resistance."

That night they said goodbye in front of the altar dedicated to the Virgin Mary, now illuminated by hundreds of votive candles. Meche and Alda agreed to receive messages from an old man named Jairo, an organ grinder who would stop by once a week to play his instrument at the corner in front of their house. "Jairo is also a fortune-teller," Señora Leonora explained, "and the first time you meet him you must ask, 'Señor, are we going to be lucky in love?' He will write his reply on a slip of paper. Don't laugh – the military have infiltrated the mail system and most of the telephones, and we must use our imagination when it comes to communications, no matter how absurd it may seem. Keep the slips. We will send a courier, a young man who will visit your house pretending to be a client."

Since childhood, Alda had considered the figure of the Virgin Mary, adorned with flowers and glittering tinsel, as an artificially elegant lady, a queen like those drawn in fairy tales, whose beauty and heavy clothing were part of some disguise that set her apart from all other women. After Señora Leonora left them with a friendly bow of her head, Alda remained at the altar staring at the Virgin's eyes, made of shining glass yet oddly indifferent, devoid of all expression, their glow but the reflection of burning candles. Remembering that other figure of the Holy Mother, the *mater dolorosa*, the suffering one, covered from head to toe in a dark robe, weeping tears of sorrow for her crucified son, Alda imagined that for Señora Leonora, no tears were sufficient to mitigate the grief produced by the death of a son that no power, neither angelic nor satanic, would ever resurrect from the grave. But Señora Leonora had gone beyond the tears of the *mater dolorosa*, choosing to oppose death by protecting life, by devoting all her efforts and strength to saving other human beings from the clutches of the dictator, with an obstinacy and fervour that were almost religious.

As one twilight succeeded another in the street of night, the symbolic grave of the murdered Deborah piled up with flowers and wreaths of natural herbs. Josefa had tacked a photograph of the martyred girl to the wall, before which, each evening, the inhabitants in this quarter lit candles and prayed before embarking on their nocturnal occupation. It wasn't long before the epitaph painted in red on the wall gave birth to a progeny of voices that denounced the dictator's injustices, systematically cloaked in optimistic military reports and punctuated by sinister incidents of torture. That first night, under the letters Patoja had printed as an epitaph for Deborah, a woman wrote in small, rounded letters enclosed within brackets: (You were murdered in cold blood!) During the following afternoon, while most of the women were taking a nap or washing their underwear, another woman went to the altar, erased the curved line which closed the parenthesis, and added: "by the military monsters".

It was as if Deborah's spirit had been transformed into a uterus undergoing multiple and angry childbirths – the epitaph began to grow, spawning words written in uneven and ominous hands which filled the washed-out furrows on the wall: "evil, bastard soldiers", "fucking dictator", "you are meaner than a jackal", "you are more deadly than hemlock", "you would kill your mother if she were a communist".

No one ever knew who the first woman was who decided to inscribe her protest with fine-pointed lipstick instead of a pen, but in no time few women went to pray to Deborah without first stuffing her pocket or purse with a tube of Max Factor, Elizabeth Arden or D'Albert Lorenz. Day after day, words were erased and replaced by others which denounced the truth in an even more open and violent manner; day after day, the insults were supplanted by blasphemies and curses which made the wall a representation of hell in various shades of red, fuchsia and orange. "You are the Demon of the Dark", said one inscription; "From Hell you come, and to Hell you will return," said another. In one corner of the wall there first appeared this pronouncement: "For each death you will pay with blood and fire". Other hands predicted additional payment: ". . . with whips of red-hot wire", ". . . with shit up to your neck", ". . . with needles piercing your eyes", ". . . with burning coals on the soles of your feet", ". . . and a crooked stick rammed up your arse", and finally, "You'll die hanging by your prick". The rubbed-out and written-over, blurred and blemished letters printed in lipstick formed the design of a fantastic tapestry, letters seemingly written in blood, pulsating in the candle glow like a placenta, both mocking and defying death, a kind of inversion of the menstrual flow towards birth, at once terrifying and intense.

There was an afternoon of *sopaipillas*, little scones, and Martina was kneading the mixture of flour and cooked pumpkin, little by little pouring the drops of melted lard and hot, salted water on to the mound of dough. "I don't know what Meche and Alda are up to, señora, but they've got me as worried as a wino at closing time. This old lady they claim is so high up has asked them to pass on messages to help in the struggle against the army and that devil who calls himself the Benefactor." She hammered the warm dough, which breathed, giving off the sound of soapy water, and she added, "Yeah, I'm worried as hell. I keep telling them that if they get caught, they're going to be killed, the same as Deborah."

"Let them help," the voice of Señora Rosa suggested. "Do you remember, *huaina*, the forests of the south? The red flowers of the *quintral* vine? Those are wicked flowers, Martina, *por Dios*. They stick to the trees and grow like weeds, suffocating the strong trunks until they kill them. The General and his soldiers are like these flowers of death, and if good Christians don't do something to defend themselves against them, they will continue drowning our country in blood until the only thing left will be a pile of bones. No land deserves such a fate."

Martina was moved by Señora Rosa's tearful voice. "But what can two women do against a whole army?" she asked as she finished cutting the dough into pieces which she rolled into balls that afterwards she would flatten with a rolling pin so that they resembled little pancakes with three small holes in the shape of a triangle on the surface.

"You'll see . . . you'll see. Listen, tomorrow night a young man is going to come by to pick up the messages."

"You don't say! Want me to tell Alda so she'll be ready?"

"No. Tell Meche, 'cause this young man is very handsome and he'll look for her. Tell the little *huaina* to pretty herself up."

On the following evening Martina went into Meche's room to make certain she had followed Señora Rosa's instructions to the letter. Her initial reaction was admiration. "Oh, what a beautiful dress, little one! You're as pretty as a rose opening up in the morning light." Coming closer, her voice changed. "Let me see . . . why the hell did you put so much powder on your face, girl? You look like a mouse in a flour mill."

Meche put her face in her hands. "I'm so nervous, Señora Martina."

"Don't be. The señora says it's okay for you to deliver messages, so that the power of the *quintral* flowers loses its strength."

"But that isn't why I'm nervous. I know I'm silly, but I can't stop imagining that this young man who Doña Rosa says is so handsome is going to fall in love with me, just like in a serial movie they showed in my village on Sunday afternoons. The girl in the movie was blind and she begged for money in a square in Paris, and the young man came every afternoon on his bicycle to pick up the messages that the Resistance fighters pressed in her palm along with the coins. And when at long last he declared his love for her and kissed her, you could hear far-off violin music which sounded as if all the birds in the city were celebrating."

"Again with your famous movies, *niña*! When are you going to learn that all those stories are just make- believe?"

"But then, why did Señora Rosa say I should make myself so pretty?"

"Who knows?" Martina said. "If the living crack up as they get older, why not the dead? Lord knows, their world is more strange and weird than ours. And don't forget, Señora Rosa is over a hundred years old."

"*Santa María Purísima*!" Meche exclaimed in wonder. "Are you saying that even the dead can lose their mind?"

Martina wasn't certain. "Well, this business of wandering around in life and death must be very tough on ghosts. They're bound to get a little loony, after all."

Around midnight a young man with fine features and a black beard came into the salon. There was a certain air about him, the kind of bearing found in men who are quite sure of themselves. He sat in a corner of the room near the bar, joining in quickly with the conversations and laughter of the other clients. When she saw him, Meche felt her heart leap, and at the first opportunity she beckoned to Alda and went to the bathroom.

Alda was severe. "This is serious, Meche. Don't give your feelings away. We don't want anyone to get suspicious. Why the hell they decided to send him to you, a little fool who drops her drawers for any pretty face, is a mystery to me. If they'd chosen me, everything would have gone off without a hitch."

"Señora Rosa said he's already predestined for me," Meche protested. "And he's so attractive – Robert Redford in person, but with dark hair," she added, adjusting her skirt.

"Shut up, you fuckwit! Someone will hear you! Besides, who knows if he's the person we're waiting for?" She caught Meche's arm. "Listen, honey, pay attention: when he invites you to dance, as he's supposed to, he must say that he has an uncle who lives in the north, where the sun rises earlier—"

"I know! I know that I have to tell him that I've never been to the north. How could I forget Señora Leonora's instructions? I know I'm a bit dreamy, but I'm not stupid."

"Yeah, yeah," Alda agreed reluctantly. "But all the same, don't forget. If he doesn't say those exact words, don't give him the messages. This is serious shit, Meche. Please don't fuck things up, for God's sake."

"I won't, I promise you. In the name of my mother, and of God the Father who is on his Sacred Throne!"

Alda gave her a long look. "Okay. Now go out there and act natural. Keep your tongue out of his ear, and your arse out of his face, at least until he approaches *you*." She gave Meche a shove, whispering after her, "And don't dig our graves, you hear?"

Alda looked at her image in the mirror. Then, opening a box of rouge, she started colouring her cheeks with a tiny brush, all the while grumbling to herself with increasing anger. "Shit! I'm so nervous my hand is shaking. How could it occur to Señora Leonora to send this young guy to meet Meche not me – when I am the one who knows how to deal with situations like this? And he's a real fox! God knows I wouldn't kick him out of bed!" She moved the brush hastily, dabbing her cheek-bones with the red powder, then paused, inspecting the small wrinkles under her dark eyes. Shrugging her shoulders in resignation she turned away from the mirror, still talking to herself as she left the bathroom. "What the hell, Meche is young like him . . . and at thirty-two, Alda, you're already over the hill."

Once the ritualized prologue of the message exchange had been observed, Meche led the young man into her bedroom where, revealing his true nature, he stood by the bed with a shy smile on his face.

"Excuse me, señorita," he said in a soft voice, "but this is the first time I have visited one of these houses, and to be honest with you, I'm nervous. Out there with the other men, it was easy to talk and make jokes and laugh. But here . . ."

Despite her attraction to him, Meche felt a stab of maternal concern. "It's all right. There's nothing to worry about. Please sit down."

"How long does one usually . . . stay with a woman? I mean, how long am I—"

"Half an hour," Meche said, immediately regretting having chosen such a brief time. "Although . . . it would be better if you stayed a whole hour, so that no one becomes suspicious."

"Very well," he agreed in a low voice. "I don't suppose people talk very much in these bedrooms. Maybe we'd better not say anything."

"No, no," Meche shook her head. "Sometimes men talk a lot, especially after . . ."

"What is your name?"

"Maria de las Mercedes, at your service."

"What a beautiful name. It sounds like the name of a patron saint of a village in Spain."

"And you? What's your name?"

He gave her a friendly smile. "Roberto. You don't know how grateful I am to you and your friend for your help. I thank you in the name of all of us in the Resistance. And now, perhaps we'd better be silent for a half hour or so, no?"

"If you wish," Meche said doubtfully. "But when the talking stops, usually it gets kind of noisy, if you know what I mean."

"I guess that's true," he said, looking down as if recalling a memory.

Meche felt a tenderness for him when she realized that his confident behaviour in the salon had only been pretence. He was not joyful or loud; on the contrary, there was in him something that evoked pity and compassion. Without knowing why, she began to pray to herself.

They let the time go by without a word, smiling at each other now and then. At one point Meche opened the drawer of her night table and withdrew the card on which Jairo had written her fortune. As she turned, Roberto moved close and said softly, "Please forgive me for not touching you. Don't be offended. You are very pretty, but I haven't made love to a woman since they killed my girlfriend."

Meche's eyes opened wide in surprise. "The soldiers killed her?"

"Yes. Now: how much money should I leave?"

"Don't leave any money. Sometimes Doña Carolina is kind enough to allow us not to charge, when the client is a special friend."

"But this is my first time here. She would suspect something if I don't pay."

Meche nodded her head. "You're right. In that case, leave two thousand pesos. But you'll come back, won't you?"

"Yes, of course. My instructions are to fall in love with you."

Meche closed her eyes at the thought. Just as Señora Rosa had said . . .

"Maybe you should start talking about our romance with the other ladies?"

"Don't worry, I will," Meche said breathlessly. "And after two or three more visits, you won't have to pay anything."

They came out of the bedroom arm in arm. At the front door, aware that several clients and the other girls were watching them, Roberto embraced her and kissed her passionately.

Some hours later, while the rays of the sun splashed across the roofs of the houses in the street of night, Meche remembered Roberto's words and smiled at the possibility of taking part, at long last, in a love story – even if it was only a masquerade to ward off suspicion of her participation in the Resistance. With nostalgia she recalled her grandmother in their village, sitting on her tall chair made of woven willow branches. The old lady would sigh while listening to those romantic songs played every night at nine on her favourite radio programme *Melodies of the Heart*. As though performing an almost sacred ritual, she would dry her withered hands on her apron after cleaning the dishes, then ask Meche to turn the dial to number forty-four, and with an excited and enigmatic smile she would arrange the pleats of her skirt before sitting down. And there she would stay for the next hour, silent, hands crossed on her lap, wearing a pleased expression as the melancholic notes danced throughout the room, closing her eyes when a guitar went into a mournful solo which seemed to echo deeply both in her heart and from the throat of the mountains waiting like patient lovers in the darkness. She only spoke during the commercials read by people with happy, energetic voices, cautioning Meche that love was always sad, as sad as a red rose that soon withers and fades away, because Fate never intended for human beings to be happy for ever.

"Love is like a morning star, Mercedita. It shines for a brief moment and then disappears, leaving without a word. It is as if love started out to brighten our lives and then abruptly changed its mind. One suffers terribly for love, girl, that's what the songs tell us. But the misfortune that most grieves me is that the star of love never shined for me, not even for one day in my life. My parents made me marry, out of pure convenience, a man who was not made for love because he was born with a heart as dry as the dead branch of a tree, whereas I was created by God with the ripe flesh of the grapevines, which were born to live and be loved." She would at times shake her fist at Meche to emphasize her emotions. "Love! I have lived all this time yearning for love!" When the commercial ended and another song began, Meche's grandmother would again lapse into silence and cross her hands, old wrinkled hands, clutching not only the grey skirt but also the ghost of her unrequited dreams.

When she was a child, Meche never imagined that her destiny would likewise be never to know love. "I should have become a nun," she used to say after her two sisters were married, remembering her grandmother combing her sparse white hair each morning with bright eyes, as though that very day she would at long last encounter love. Every evening after putting on her nightgown, her grandmother would carefully remove her false hair, and place individual strands of her real hair meticulously on the night table next to the plaster figure of St Anthony, the patron saint of lovers, creating a circle of curling ends, a white nest that increased in size with her advancing baldness, for if during the day she discovered a filament of her real hair on her blouse or skirt, she would pluck it up and run to deposit it on her night table. "You have to treat your hair as if it were spun gold, Mercedita. No man on earth is interested in a bald woman." Later she would braid her real hair into the wig. She never lost sight of the illusion that some day the star of love would shine for her. Until the day of her death she continued to collect her fallen hair, forming a bun that she would pin to the back of her head.

"If I had been a nun, I would have married God and He would have been my true love," Meche used to say to herself each New Year's Eve on realizing that the yellow panties she had painstakingly cut out and sewn, following popular folklore, had once again failed to bring her a boyfriend.

Meche had never told anyone why she was a prostitute because people would have laughed at her, the same way Alda had laughed that day when she described how she had lost her virginity for a bunch of grapes. She knew no one would understand that she had followed Rafael because he reminded her of the male lead in that strange movie *Hiroshima, Mon Amour*. They had shown it in the theatre by the main square in her village. She had just turned seventeen and some of the scenes were blurred from overuse. Each time the image faded to flickering white lines the peasants in the gallery whistled and shouted, demanding their money back. She didn't quite understand the movie; it struck her as strange for the lovers to be kissing while the young woman whispered about Hiroshima, which was apparently a place and not a person. She did, however, understand that the man loved the woman deeply, for he kept begging her to stay and surrender to their love, which he called a bond between the soul and the skin. The lovers said farewell several times, only to meet again on a corner or at a bar. The man kept imploring her not to part from him, but she would reply by talking about other things. Then, embracing him but looking at the sky, she would leave.

Biting the handkerchief that she always took with her to the movies, Meche found herself begging the girl not to abandon the man, so obviously smitten with love; at times she concentrated on the girl's face, ignoring the subtitles, whispering advice, telling the girl to stop being foolish, not to let the chance for love slip by. Suddenly the lovers appeared together in what resembled an airport, seated at a table, between them an old woman with slitty almond eyes who reminded Meche of her grandmother. "Please stay, don't leave, don't reject love, it is a true gift of God," she implored the young woman in the movie as she recalled the moment of her grandmother's death and the sounds coming from her throat, so like the cooing of doves caressing each other in the nests perched in the tower of the old church in her village. But of course the girl in the movie couldn't understand a word because she spoke a different language. And in the end the girl deserted her lover, breaking his heart.

Although she was not in love with Rafael, Meche followed him because he begged her to escape with him with the same fervour, the same devotion that the young man in the movie had shown. Maybe she had said yes to Rafael as a way of altering the end of the love story in the movie. She knew she had always been naive, and she agreed with her mother, who never ceased warning her that people would always deceive and take advantage of her. It was precisely this naivety that prevented her from realizing that the place where Rafael left her was a whorehouse. "Stay with my aunt for a couple of weeks, *mi amor*, while I look for a job," he had told her once they reached the capital city. "Be very obedient, and do whatever she says."

Aunt Amanda was a loving lady who nightly received several gentlemen as guests, at which time her other nieces put on low-cut dresses to act as hostesses while Meche kept to her room, since she had been advised to get acquainted with city ways before participating in the festivities downstairs. Then one afternoon Aunt Amanda came to her room and in the friendliest of voices said, "You'll have to help us, sweetheart, with our guests this evening." She patted Meche's shoulder encouragingly. "Sometimes they drink a little too much, and wine makes them more affectionate, but they are so nice that we must do our best to please them." A week later Meche awoke to find Aunt Amanda sitting by her bed, wearing a stern expression, her eyes hard as she explained that if Meche wanted to continue living in her house she had to allow those gentlemen to make love to her. "Don't expect Rafael to come back for you," she sneered. "He makes his living by bringing young village girls to the city for people in our business." Left with little alternative, Meche accepted Amanda's terms: to be clothed and fed in exchange for performing the act of love with the clients downstairs. She resigned herself without protest to her fate, that of passing through this life without experiencing that love her grandmother had so longed for. From the very first night, labouring under the first client, Meche realized that all those men who entered her bedroom would be nothing but faded stars, barren gardens, joyless as abandoned carousels in a ghost city. Which was why Roberto's visit to the house had seemed to her an event as wondrous as an *aromo* tree blooming with yellow flowers in the rain. As the days went by, she frequently caught herself smiling, feeling that her heart was now a thick coil of petals uncurling at dawn. The sadness Roberto seemed to carry with such stoic fortitude produced in Meche an immense compassion and tenderness. Like that young man in the movie which had reduced her to tears, Roberto had also lost his beloved, but not because she had decided to fly to another country. She imagined Roberto's girlfriend on her knees before an arrogant man dressed in a military uniform who beat her and tortured her with electric wires for hours before pausing so that she could be gang-raped by a group of recruits especially selected for such duty. Afterwards she was dragged to a cell exactly like the one Meche had shared with Alda and Martina; there Roberto's girlfriend, her body now covered with bruises and blood, had probably fallen into that swamp of static, dead time before some devil of a General pronounced her death sentence.

"I love Roberto as much as you loved him," Meche whispered one morning upon awakening, and she felt that sharing her love with a dead woman somehow ennobled her, that every minute of happiness she gave to Roberto would also ensure the unfortunate girl's happiness wherever she now dwelt, in life after death, the only region devoid of all evil. Meche knew that her feelings for Roberto would never be reciprocated, but deep in her heart she didn't mind, because now she was in love she perceived that the morning star her grandmother used to talk about was not only the beloved man himself but also the light he projected on the woman he loved. Within a month all the women in the house referred to Roberto as Meche's boyfriend, that handsome young devil who only came by once a week because he was a law student, no less, and had to spend most of his nights studying huge, important books. Like curious mothers faced with their daughter's first romance, the women in the house kept pestering Meche for details of what happened between her and Roberto. Somehow, the fact that they believed her stories made them true, and she now saw herself as the protagonist of a wonderful love story with one central recurring scene: as soon as she and Roberto entered her bedroom, he would pick her up and spin around and around while repeating that he loved her.

Only Alda and Martina knew that Roberto was still in love with the girl who had been killed in prison, which did not trouble Meche: they were her best friends and, as Alda had once said, they would always be united like the water, the moon and the earth, and for that reason there should always be nothing but the truth between them. Whenever he visited, Roberto would usually remain silent, making brief comments with a warm smile. Meche sat beside him, feeling the presence of his dead girlfriend, which produced in Meche a profound emotion of almost overwhelming love. One night she asked Roberto about the details of her death. He made a gesture with his hand like someone too weak to wave goodbye, as though he no longer had the strength to remember anything so painful.

"All of us," he said, "carry on our backs the cross of suffering. You too, right? When this nightmare of military power is finally ended, Meche, I am going to invite you to go to the movies, and I'm going to buy you lots of popcorn and candy," he added, caressing her arm. "Then we'll have a night on the town."

As winter descended on the city, the street of night acquired several habits which became part of a new routine. Every morning, Patoja swept the sidewalk in front of Deborah's tomb, which at twilight was always covered by prayers and burning candles. Under the epitaph, the wall was still growing with insulting remarks about the dictator, the condemnations written in lipstick and flowing like rivers on a map. It was not strange to see a woman reading them aloud for those companions who were illiterate. Also, by now the women in Doña Carolina's house were no longer surprised to come upon Martina talking aloud to no one in the kitchen, gesturing with her hands as she walked up and down among the pots and pans. In fact, several of the women had begun sending messages to Señora Rosa through Martina, asking her to help them, to protect them from the world of the dead. And every Friday night at ten o'clock Doña Carolina gave Meche a one-hour break to be with Roberto, explaining that she, too, had once in her youth had a boyfriend as handsome as Roberto.

Every Wednesday afternoon the women in the street of night peeked through their windows to watch for the arrival of Jairo and his music grinder. They were all anxious to buy a ticket telling their fortune because they had, by and large, become convinced that Jairo's predictions were indispensable in helping them to deal successfully with the events of each week. Jairo always announced his arrival with the sweet and joyful melody that began, "Ay, Josefina, if you only knew / That last night when you came into view . . ." Jairo wore a peaceful smile as the women made a circle around him. He turned the organ handle energetically while working the cymbals which flooded the street with the sounds of chirping birds that sang, "A divided heart is not for me / If I ever give mine, it will be completely, ay, ay, ay!" Then he swung into a plaintive tango that went, "Where are you my heart? I can hear you pounding deep, but my pain is so immense that I cannot weep . . . I want to cry but I have no tears left; I loved her so much and she left . . . never to return again . . ." Before leaving, Jairo played a comic song from the 1920s designed to make the women laugh: "Isabel, our life can't continue like this / I beg you not to behave in this sort / Consider that I'm your husband / before God and the Municipal Court!"

Alda was in charge of receiving the messages every week. Jairo always gave her a small gift, usually a paper flower wrapped in colourful tissue paper because, according to his provincial mind, she looked like that American singer who was often on the magazine covers, accompanied by a series of different millionaires.

One afternoon when the winter cold was settling in over the city and the Andes wore a white blanket of fresh snow, Alda and

Meche invited Jairo to come into the house for a cup of coffee and brandy.

"To warm your bones, Jairo," Alda told him, gesturing for him to take a seat. "At your age you shouldn't be working when it's so cold out."

"Although you may not believe me, I'm not that old, really. I turned fifty-two on January the first. I was forty when the great bastard killed our president. Those were better times . . . the university kids spent their spare time painting murals on the street walls, and often they hired us to play at those nice festivals they organized for the common people, with theatre performances and all sorts of music. They used to say that we were the creators of the most authentic aspect of culture – popular culture. Ah! In those times one earned one's bread with joy. I danced while playing the drums in . . . well, I shouldn't bore you with stories of the past."

"Tell us, Jairo," the women of the house urged. "Please, go on."

"*Bueno*, as I was telling you, I was a dancer. As soon as my *compadre* Pancho hit the first tune on his music box, I slapped the pavement three times with the heels of my shoes and then I started sliding, moving from side to side like an excited bumble-bee drawn towards my mate enclosed in the music box, *larilará, larilará, larilará*. Then, moving cool as one of those negro entertainers, using both hands, I pounded the drum on my back, put my left foot forward like this for balance and dragged my right foot slowly to pull on the cord tied to my shoe and connected to the cymbals on top of the drum, one-two-three, one-two-three, increasing the rhythm each time, making it faster and faster in order to infuse passion and emotion in my dance. A lady who once interviewed me for a newspaper wrote something very beautiful and poetic about me. Would you like to hear it?" He paused solemnly and recited with his eyes closed. "An entire orchestra of dreams, the dancer carries on his back, with no other intention, than bread and music."

"That is lovely, Jairo," a woman marvelled. "How can there be people so intelligent?"

Jairo smiled at the woman. "That's right, señorita. There are people who are born with the brains of God. This bright lady later published the poem in a magazine next to my photograph. I appeared wearing a yellow sweater and the same brown hat I wore every time I performed my dance in the streets. One of these days I'll bring the magazine so that you can see how I looked. An orchestra of dreams on my back, *chin*, *chirín*, *chinchín*, I played the cymbals and they sounded like a huge wave breaking on the sand, like green water and white foam flowing over the dark sound of the drum, *poompoom*, *poompoom*, like a tiny rhythmic volcanic eruption. Then I spun around on the edge of my shoe, stared for a brief moment at Pancho's music box with the passionate look of a lover, and started to whirl, beating the big drum and at the same time pulling on the cord tied to the cymbals as if I were a huge bird displaying his feathers in order to conquer a beloved female."

"Aaay!" Meche exclaimed, clapping her hands. "Dance for us, Jairo. I'm dying to see you dance!"

Jairo smiled bitterly and shook his head. He pulled up the turn-up of his trousers and showed them his deformed and swollen ankle bulging inside the sock. "I can no longer dance. After the coup, they put me in prison because I created popular culture. The soldiers broke my ankles with their rifle butts; others had their fingers smashed so they could never play the guitar again. Anyway, I came out alive, and that's the only thing that counts, although the bread I earn is no longer joyful. When I was a child my father always told me that he had chosen my name from a story in the Bible which tells of a man named Jairo who was a witness to the miracles of Jesus Christ. 'You must never lose your faith, my son, even when other men have felled you like a tree,' he used to tell me, because like all fathers he loved to give advice. And now that my ankles are ruined, I tell my father – since I'm sure he can hear me in the land of the dead – that I am a broken tree that will never grow straight and tall because I can no longer dance like any creature in love. But I still have my faith . . .

"Once, my dear friends, I was the owner of my cymbals and my drum, and I felt like the owner of the world. I could turn around and around at will, marking my own rhythm . . . but nowadays, as you are well aware, all of us must march to the beat of only one baton, only one cadence, terrible and pitiless."

Meche was close to tears. "But as you say, Jairo, the important thing is that you are alive."

"Yes, Jairo, and now you bring happiness to all of us," Alda said, smiling at him with affection. "Don't you think it's marvellous that each week you fill our entire street with joy?"

Adela didn't agree. "It all depends, though. Look, Jairo, for the last three weeks you have given me slips with very negative predictions. Shit, I feel as if a witch had put a curse on me."

"You must be patient, Adelita," Jairo advised her. "Your luck will get better soon."

"That's what I like to hear!" Adela said. "Next Wednesday I'll be waiting at the corner, and I'll be the first in line to buy a fortune slip."

"And I will be second," Alda said quickly. "Don't forget, Jairo, we'll be waiting."

Jairo held up his hands to silence them. "How can you doubt that I'll show up, when it's such a pleasure to see all of you every week?"

But the following Wednesday it was Meche, not Alda, who picked up Jairo's message. Earlier that day, as Martina was setting the table for lunch, two well-dressed men appeared at the front door and demanded to see the owner of the house. Doña Carolina led them into her private sitting-room; and after several minutes she called for Alda.

"My dear," she said to Alda, "these gentlemen have come for you. They say they have orders to take you to a very important government office."

Alda glared at the two men, putting her hands on her hips. "Fuck you and your orders! You're not taking me anywhere!"

"Please, don't put up any resistance," one of the men said quietly, showing her a card stamped with sinister-looking seals. "You may have cause to regret it."

Meche burst into the room. Through her tears she cried, "In God's name, please, señores! She is the kindest person on earth! She doesn't deserve to be harmed, in any way, by anyone!"

The man with the stamped identity card smiled deprecatingly at Meche. "No one has brought any charges against her."

The other man took Alda by the arm, and said, "For your own sake, come with us, now."

Alarmed, Meche ran to tell Martina, whose bedroom was in the rear patio. Martina nodded and then, walking with a purpose in her stride, went to the kitchen and, removing the lid from the pot containing *pantrucas* – a cheap dish made of left-over tortillas and pieces of meat – said loudly, her voice carrying a reproach, "Hey, Señora Rosa, why the hell didn't you tell me that those guys were planning to pick up Alda? Meche says they looked like cops dressed as civilians, the type of bastards who work for the Benefactor. You realize that they could very well kill her? What's going on, Señora Rosa of my heart, cause the only reason for two of those pricks to come for Alda is to put her in prison, the same way they dumped all of us in a cell, remember? Come on, tell me who they are, and why they took Alda. Shit! You're not gonna answer? Come on, speak up, stop playing deaf and dumb. Well, it's up to you if you don't wanna talk, but . . . I swear I will not speak to you for the rest of my life, and then you won't have anyone to entertain you in death. All right, all right, don't say nothing about the cops who took Alda, if that's your game, but at least tell me if she's in danger, I beg you, for God's sake and in the name of my grandmother, rest her soul. Enough, already, stop playing with me, especially when things are so fucking difficult."

Martina leaned over the counter and lowered her head in her hands, listening. "Shit! You're becoming so damned selfish. Say something! This is not the time, señora, to bite your lip." Martina hit the pans in rage and opened all the drawers in search of Rosa, but not a word was spoken. Replacing the lid on the *pantrucas*, she complained sarcastically, "Don't tell me – you want boneless chicken breasts with mushroom sauce or some other delicate shit before you'll open your mouth for a friend, huh?" And slamming the ladle into the stove top, she left the kitchen in a huff, muttering to herself and slicing the air over her head with the wooden spoon.

Alda followed the two men to a black automobile with tinted windows. They seated her between them in the back seat while the driver started the engine and signalled for a right turn. After passing the second street-light one of the men grabbed her arms and pinned them to her sides. His companion pushed her head down and tied a blindfold over her eyes. After they released her, she leaned back into the seat thinking, "Jesus, I fucked up! These arseholes *are* going to kill me, godammit! Somehow they found out that I was the one taking the messages from Jairo. I wonder if they have put Roberto in prison, or maybe poor Señora Leonora was captured and they tortured her. At her age, she wouldn't be able to take much beating, so she gave them all the information she had . . . No, I don't think she told them anything, she's such a strong woman. Although . . . yeah, it was probably Señora Leonora; otherwise, it means they caught Roberto. Oh my God, Meche will die if they've nabbed Roberto, she will have a heart attack or slash her wrists, and even if I try to save her . . . but how do you save someone who has sliced her veins with a razor? Ah, now I remember, you have to tie a handkerchief around the wrist, tight, to stop the bleeding. Blood . . . these fucking brutes are going to kill me! No! Before killing me they are going to beat the shit out of me. Take that, you bitch, you fuck, you worthless parasite! Spill the beans, you filthy whore! I'm going to be bleeding like a butchered pig when these cocksuckers kill me. What can I do, my God, what? Jesus, did I blow it. Let's face it, I'm a fucked-up whore, not just some common whore like Meche, Patoja, and Eliana; not just a regular whore like Martina was once, or a whore like Deborah, may her soul rest in peace, but I mean Fucked-Up with capital letters! Christ, whores don't harm anybody, all they do is offer a little pleasure, while in this fucked-up country the real whores, the most degraded *putas*, are those posturing arseholes who dress up in military uniforms and impose injustice on an entire nation, killing whoever they want to at their will, on a whim, for having the wrong last name. Attention! Ready, aim, FIRE! I'll bet they shoot me while I'm wearing this same fucking blindfold, because the lazy pricks are in such a hurry to kill somebody; so, the same blindfold, my back against a wall or a pile of sandbags if they want to make it public, and my body, from which I've earned my living, will be as full of holes as a colander, like that tin one my mother kept in her kitchen, the one made by Ferriloza, that's what it said on the rim, yes, and just under the letters Ferri there was a black indentation that filled with wet flour when my mother made spaghetti, because it was such a cheap and economical meal. You old bitch! I swear I will not think of you when they put me against the wall, in front of the firing squad. And why not? Because you were always delivering orders, because you were in love with power, and how you enjoyed making me submit to your authority, the same way that dirty old bastard enjoys intimidating all of us in this nation whenever he appears on television. 'Fellow Citizens,' he always says, in that high-pitched, old woman's voice, his face the face of power before the weak, wearing a look of contempt, as though he were about to spit on the camera. I detest his voice, cracked and whiny, like an old queer in an alley begging for a blow job. 'I've told you several times, and I again repeat, because it's always useful to repeat one's thoughts:

in this country, everyone must maintain good behaviour and irreproachable conduct, and woe to those who disobey! Because I will personally take care of these malcontents and see to it that they are sent straight to prison, condemned to bread and water for a few months. Who do they think they are, those who dare to disobey the legal government? Those who, for any reason, bad influences or inborn perversions are planning subversion, shall receive the punishment they deserve. And I repeat, fellow citizens, because, as the admirable genius August Comte once said, one must know to anticipate, and one must anticipate in order to take action. You must all recognize that you now live in a Fatherland that I intend to rule with a firm hand in order to keep it pure and immaculate, free from all sin. I shall be implacable with those who do not follow my orders . . .' Big deal! It's easy to be implacable when one has a huge military force armed to the teeth. All these fucking soldiers: instead of raising their rifles they should be raising their pricks to make women happy. João, I will think of you when I face death; I'll also remember my father because he was always kind. It's true that he didn't pay much attention to his family, that he preferred to spend his time with other women, drinking wine in the bars, but at the bottom of his heart there was much kindness . . . They're going to kill you, Alda, holy shit! And you won't even have a decent grave – although it makes no sense to worry about a grave when you're dead. No one will bring flowers to my grave, I'll bet. No, that's not true, Meche and Martina would bring flowers, that's if I have a grave, if they don't throw me into the ocean like they do the disappeared. Poor Meche, she would come to my grave crying like a baby, and Martina would swallow her tears trying to be strong. I'm going to die, I'm going to die because, God forgive me, I fucked up."

Alda heard the men in the car talking about a soccer game. "I'm gonna take my kids so they can get some sun. If you want, we could meet at the bus stop, go together" . . . "I don't know . . . shit, my old lady has been on my arse lately to take her to a movie" . . . "Well, think about it and let me know tomorrow, huh? It's gonna be a bitch of a game, Colo Colo over Palestino for sure" . . . "I wouldn't be so sure, you never know. Look, we're almost there. Park in the back, champ."

They pulled Alda out of the car and walked on either side of her along a path of pebbles that cracked and popped under her patent leather heels.

"Watch your step, bitch!" the one on her right warned, leading her to a flight of steps. "We don't want you to trip and damage that pretty nose."

Looking down through a gap between the cloth material and her cheek, she saw a marble surface, then made out the dark design of an old parquet floor. They halted her, opened a door, and pushed her forward until her knees bumped against what seemed to be a bed.

"Take your time, sugar, you'll have to wait a bit," the football enthusiast said, turning her around and forcing her to sit by pressing on her shoulders. Then to his companion he said, "Forget your old woman, *hombre*, and come to the game with me. I tell you, it's gonna be a riot." A few moments later Alda heard the door slamming shut.

Digging her nails into her palms, Alda waited. Through the tiny slit she could see the same parquet pattern on the floor, and a cigarette butt which to her seemed utterly ludicrous. "I suppose it's God's will that I die," she mused to herself. "After all, we were all born to die some day, but never in my wildest nightmare did I dream that I would be shot to death by a group of fucking soldiers. 'What was the last thing she saw?' the narrator asked during that soap opera called *Rose of the Swamps* or something equally ridiculous; well, she saw a miserable cigarette butt. No filter, of course: macho arseholes consider filters a sign of weakness. I guess it's my fate to die such a cheap death, without a normal grave, without even a wooden cross to mark where my bones are." She closed her eyes and concentrated on the ticking of a clock somewhere nearby, its steady little patter almost like rain dripping from a hole in the ceiling, or like a chant: "One-two-three-four, that's all she wrote, you're fucked my girl, you're doomed you whore, one-two-three-four."

Suddenly she heard steps outside the door, then the creaking of the hinges. The steps came nearer and she saw the shiny tips of two black boots. Her heart started pounding louder than the clock, and she felt like a young deer facing the twin barrels of a shotgun in a jungle clearing. A hand caressed her hair, and in the silence she wondered if this slight touch was due to timidity or the perverted gentleness of a sadist, her wonder increasing as she felt trembling fingertips sliding down both cheeks, descending to her throat and then on without pause until they reached the cleavage of her breasts. The mattress sank as someone sat beside her, and now she sensed the excited breathing of another body from which came a long sigh, and then the fingers began to unbutton her blouse and then unhook her bra and then a set of lips was suckling her nipples while the hands, heavy now, went exploring under her skirt . . . and suddenly the laboured breathing enveloped her like some malignant ocean tide, swelling, about to burst, pushing her down hard on her back and ripping off her skirt and her panties, flinging them to the floor along with her shoes. Frenzied now, the hands travelled her body, squeezing her waist and pinching her breasts while that malodorous tide came to momentary rest on her neck. She could hear, feel, one hand working urgently on the zipper to set free the stony bulge that had been grinding against her pubis, and then hard, cruel fingers pried her vagina open, holding the lips apart as a large male organ penetrated her with a vicious thrust.

A series of tremors erupted inside her, sending shock waves that splintered against the innermost recess of her womb. Her thighs were stinging from the feverish rubbing of the cloth of his trousers. In the darkness beneath the blindfold Alda seemed to see two bright eyes glowing amid the steam of a cooking dish, and a voice she wasn't certain was her own whispered, "Make him feel he is a real stud and he will spare your life," and summoning strength from the words, Alda began to move her hips, to moan, pretending that she was in the throes of a gigantic orgasm. The man's body tensed suddenly, then shuddered in the spasms of climax, and finally collapsed on her for a few minutes, after which he breathed deeply, sighed, slipped out of her, and jumped out of bed to land on his feet like a gymnast. Lying on her back, Alda heard the dry, sawing sound of a zipper and the metallic clink of buttons being manipulated in haste, the door slamming once more, and the rhythmic echo of boots receding in the hallway.

Trembling, Alda turned on her side and used the corner of the blanket to clean the mess from her wet pubic hair. Raising up to lean on her left elbow, she was surprised to detect a slight deviation in the regular monotonous tick-tock, tick-tock of the clock, as if the hands had skipped a beat, stumbled slightly, before resuming their normal rhythm with renewed vigour. In the distance she again heard footsteps approaching. The door opened and the footsteps stopped by the bed. She could just see the toes of two brown shoes, which brought to mind an absurd commercial in which a recently shined shoe winked one of its rounded eyes and declared that "Nugget shoe polish guarantees a bright and shiny life!"

Two sets of hands lifted her by the armpits and clumsily dressed her. Afterwards they guided her along the same parquet floor which ended at the same marble steps that led to the car. Once inside, they removed the blindfold, and the bald man sitting on her right patted her softly on the thigh. "You saved your arse only because you're good in bed, doll." The other man chuckled and said, "Which means, bitch, that you're still breathing because you have a golden pussy." The bald man was smiling when he gripped Alda's bicep and squeezed until she gasped. "Let me give you some friendly advice, bitch. Keep your mouth shut about what happened today."

Torn by astonishment and fear, Alda frowned and replied, "Don't worry, sir, I swear I won't say a word."

They let her out of the car five blocks from the street of night. When at last she saw the iron balconies of Doña Carolina's house, Alda felt like a caged beast set free by accident.

The women welcomed her with joyful shouts and clapping.

"Where did those horrible men take you, sweetheart?" Doña Carolina asked. "All this time we've been praying to Deborah so that she would protect you."

"They took me to a house," Alda told them. "But nothing bad happened to me," she added.

"Did they beat you, dear Aldita?" Meche wanted to know as she caressed Alda's arm.

"No. But I need a bath," Alda said, feeling as if she were going to vomit.

"Go, my precious, go," Doña Carolina told her in a loving tone. "And if you don't feel up to it, forget about working tonight."

In Martina's bedroom, sitting in the shadow of a large grapevine that grew outside the window, Alda burst into tears, not knowing if she wept because she had been violated or for that heavy body that, after its brief shuddering climax, had left her with the sensation of profound loneliness, of a barren desert which lay parched and silent under a burning sun.

"I wonder who the son of a bitch was that raped me," she said aloud. "That bastard has never been happy like a normal person, and all I can remember about him is the repugnance I felt."

"Why, Aldita? Did he stink?" Meche asked, stroking Alda's hand.

"No. In fact it just occurs to me that he didn't smell at all. But of all the men who have ever fucked me, he is the only one who makes me feel like throwing up; it's worse than if he had poured his dirty semen down my throat. You know, when he came I knew he was a man who has never experienced true joy."

Martina cleared her throat nervously, remembering how her husband used to rape her. Embracing Alda, she counselled, "You'd better get some sleep, my girl. Don't work tonight, it'd only make things worse."

The maternal tone in Martina's voice soothed Alda's grief. That evening she fell asleep imagining that she was sinking into a soft warm lap made of fuchsias growing like a colourful nest under the shade of southern trees.

Alda had not completely recovered by the next Wednesday when, at the same hour as before, the two men in the black car showed up at Doña Carolina's door. This time there was no preamble; they asked for Alda and greeted her by taking her arms, the bald one whispering an obscene expression in her ear and informing her that she had been requested to "fulfil the duty assigned by the High Command". Alda walked between them with lowered eyes, experiencing that strange sensation of repugnance and compassion that washed over her whenever she remembered that nameless rapist and his desolate orgasm. She told herself as she got into the car, "As soon as they bring me back, I'll pack my stuff and go to another city, even though it means my fees will have to be much lower. Later on, maybe Martina and Meche can join me."

It was as if the bald one had read her mind. "Don't think about flying the coop, little chicken," he warned her as he tied the blindfold over her eyes. "The guys from Intelligence would find you in a matter of days, and that would be the end for you, golden pussy and all."

"I'm not planning to go anywhere, sir," she told him, looking in his direction and noticing that the blindfold was looser than the last time. If she raised her chin slightly, she could make out the bottom half of people walking along the street.

"Smart girl," the other man congratulated her, rubbing her thigh as he continued. "Anyway, behave yourself today, eh? One more screw won't do you any harm."

The bald one laughed. “Control yourself, *compadre*. We both know that this whore is reserved for thoroughbreds, not pack animals like you and me.” He patted Alda on the head. “Relax, kid. Just do a good job. Work that magic snatch on the man. Okay?”

Alda rode the rest of the way in silence. Leaning back from time to time, she was able to distinguish the main streets on their itinerary. After leaving the house, they had headed downtown, as she could tell by the open stores and crowds of people carrying shopping bags. She also recognized the garden in front of that small church next to the luxurious hotel built for tourists. Then the car turned around one side of the Plaza Baquedano and headed for the main avenue which ran parallel to the river. Gradually the houses grew less expensive, and then they were passing abandoned gardens full of weeds until the car finally stopped in front of a house that was obviously on the outskirts of the city.

Meanwhile, Martina was trying to calm Meche, who lay face down on the bed in tears.

“This time they will kill her, Martina, I’m sure of it, they are going to kill her, my God,” she kept repeating as she trembled with fear.

Leaving Meche in the care of two women, Martina ran to the kitchen to make a cup of tea.

“With her left hand Alda must make three crosses on his back at the moment he is most inflamed,” whispered the old woman who inhabited the pots and pans.

“Is that you at last, Señora Rosa?” Martina whispered back as she heard that long sigh that gave a cobalt blue colour to the burning jets of gas. “So you finally decided to open your trap again. Aren’t you ashamed? How come you didn’t appear the other day when we needed you? That whole damned afternoon Meche was on her knees praying to God and the Virgin Mary, and I had a big pain in my liver—”

“I know, I know. How many times do I have to tell you, I know everything.”

"If you know so damn much, why the hell did you pretend to disappear that afternoon, and why didn't you let me know that Alda was gonna come back to the house safe and sound? Answer me, godammit!" Martina commanded, smacking the hanging kettle over the stove.

"She must make three crosses on his back," repeated the voice from the front burner.

Martina's face turned red with anger. "What the fuck have you got up your sleeve?"

"Nothing, *huaina*. I'm dealing from the top. I only want to help a little in this battle against the *wecufu* and its evil forces. She must make three crosses on his back at the moment he's about to come, and when midnight falls, you and I will cast the spell."

Martina was astonished. "What spell? What the devil are you talking about, Rosa?"

"The enchantment that will bond that man for ever."

"Look, who is that son of a bitch who spends his Wednesdays raping Alda?" Martina asked, putting her face close to the lighted burner.

"Ah! You'll find that out when we make the spell."

Martina said impatiently, "Knock off the mystery, Doña. You're much too old for such crazy games, and in the meantime that arsehole might kill poor Alda."

"He's not going to kill her. Following my instructions, the girl is at this moment about to draw the three crosses with the index finger of her left hand, and in a short while the man will leave the room with his heart enchanted and the rest of the organs of his body ready to be subdued by our conjuring. When the clock strikes twelve midnight, come to the kitchen, close the door tightly, and turn off the light. Don't forget to bring a piece of red yarn. I will provide the rest of the necessary stuff. And we will seal the enchantment at the break of dawn."

At the appointed hour, while Doña Carolina's girls regaled the clients with the customary provocative smiles, the two old women in the darkness of the kitchen were preparing to perform the incantations that would engender the love spell.

"*Huacanquis*, *Huacanquis*," murmured Doña Rosa while Martina turned on the left burner. "Night with a full moon, hear this conjuration. Repeat with me, *huaina*: the three hundred joints in his body will become one thousand and three hundred ropes around his red heart. Sacred moon, pour your enchanted water on him, flood his entire body so that through his veins runs this thick potion of *latué*, so that he is made mad with love and his skin is that of a man in heat longing desperately for the maiden's flesh."

The words uttered in a hoarse whisper created a woven braid which was the umbilical cord feeding the spell in its universe of pots, pans and serving bowls made of clay which lurked in the darkness like sombre satellites. And in the refuge of these circular shadows, the spell pulsated, beating like the heart of an embryo and growing with the resounding echo of each phrase:

> You shall be the vine of the *leliuquen*,
> always embracing the trunk of the laurel tree.
> You shall be the *huinllin*,
> always running after his mate.
> You shall be a thirsty beast,
> a forsaken bird,
> a star without light,
> a body without blood,
> and a plant without air,
> when you're not with her.

Following the whispered instructions, Martina tied a piece of red yarn around the tuber of a potato, making a cross before each of the three knots. Immediately after, she tossed a handful of salt on the flame, closed her eyes for a second, and started burning a bunch of oregano while, in the distance, she heard the sound of a *cultrún*, the drum of the Araucanian witch Machi, amid the resonance of seeds and pebbles rattling around inside the gourd of a dry pumpkin. By now the kitchen was impregnated with earthy aromas, and in the cauldron of supplications and enchantments, the spell threatened to burst the walls of the room, searching for an opening wherein to give birth to itself. Suddenly the full moon appeared through the small window, throwing its light on the plates, which reflected and duplicated its white face while the pots and pans appeared as circular craters, some looking like silent planets. The moon rays also fell on the sharpened edges of knives, which flashed with menacing reflections.

With a shudder Martina saw the cold brightness of remembered lizard eyes, and she felt like spitting.

Señora Rosa's whisper broke her reverie. "Soon that man you already know will desire Alda in other positions. He is going to remove the blindfold from her eyes because a man crazy in love needs to stare, needs to submerge himself, in the eyes of his beloved. Martina, you must instruct the maiden that, as soon as the occasion presents itself, she must draw with her middle finger the initial of her name, passing her finger three times over his erect organ to form the letter A. And, three weeks later, at night, she must collect his semen on a white handkerchief and burn it with the flame of a candle when the clock strikes eleven."

Overwhelmed, Martina stood in silence, waiting for Rosa to continue. For fifteen minutes she waited, arranging the plates and glasses in the cupboard, not daring to speak, not wanting to rupture the moment with sound nor disturb the old spirit who knew everything. Finally, she whispered respectfully, "Is that all, Señora Rosa?" Receiving no reply, she left the kitchen, going over and over in her mind the instructions she had been ordered to give Alda.

Colonel Arreola woke up startled; turning around in bed, he instinctively bent his knees into the foetal position as he used to do in childhood when he awaited with excitement the gifts he was about to receive for his birthday. Now, many years later, a host of songbirds seemed to lighten his heart, filling him with hope and an acute anticipation that produced in him an unusual sense of joy. He did not know why he felt such an intense desire to possess that woman, nor did the reason matter. During a lull from that recent round-up of subversive elements, he had caught himself more than once recalling the woman who had sung a tango at the interrogation. He could remember her disrespectful and defiant attitude, could still picture her full breasts, could still see her rounded lush hips straining to be free of those tight blue jeans.

It was at the moment when Captain Orellana commanded the firing squad to execute the last group of rebels that he felt the urge to make her his, just once, and then send her to solitary confinement in one of the special one-by-three-metre containers they reserved for political prisoners. Closing his eyes as the volley rang out, he thought it would be both brutal and beautiful to penetrate her and to possess her completely on some quiet afternoon and then imprison her in a box until she starved to death.

Several months earlier, after a meeting in which they had discussed conducting torchlight ceremonies throughout the entire country, one of the personal advisers to the Benefactor of the Republic had furnished him with research documents the Nazis had compiled while making a detailed study and description of starvation in certain detention camps. It was in this manner that Arreola learned that screams, uncontrolled weeping and stomach-aches were the first symptoms of the generally long process of starvation. One Jewish subject had declared that he felt a knot of pebbles burning constantly in his throat. For Arreola this was a somewhat useless poetic image; he was far more interested in the Nazis' precise data concerning the manner in which, once the stomach had shrunk, sinking away to a tiny sack, the bones of the subject began to protrude against the skin, transforming the body into a skeleton covered by a thin, diaphanous membrane. In a kind of bizarre mockery, the nails and hair continued to grow, taking nourishment from the withering cells. This biological phenomenon caused the victims to have luxuriant hair and at the same time accelerated the speed of dying. In the documents, which Arreola considered to be a most valuable contribution to science, there appeared the astonishing fact that all of the prisoners had acquired an opaque cast to their eyes and that, a few days before dying, they broke out into laughter. Arreola regretted that the war had ended before the Nazis could investigate more thoroughly this strange behaviour and establish a precise scientific cause for such a paradox among those doomed individuals.

But when that woman, there in one of the private homes reserved for torture, had started to moan in the paroxysm of sexual pleasure, Colonel Arreola for the first time in his life experienced power as a mystical force, superior and more enjoyable than anything he had ever known. It was far more gratifying than the admiration of his family and relations when, as a young schoolboy, he used to recite the list of abbreviations of symbols for the chemical elements; far more exciting than all the memorable steps that marked him as a rising star in the military. Her screams of rejoicing, so different from those shouted commands that rang out in the barracks in detention camps, had made him feel the sole owner of both the world and himself, as if he had risen to the incredible rank of an omnipotent divinity. Nothing like this had ever happened to him with Ester, nor with the other three or four women he had possessed in his life. "You are so quick, it must be your sensitivity, honey," his wife had told him once during the first year of their marriage, making an indirect insinuation to which he paid no attention. But now, with that woman, he had discovered that he was not only capable of staying inside a woman for more than an hour, but also that, while producing multiple orgasms, it was possible to ascend to the sacred sphere of ecstasy, of absolute domination.

Imagining himself as a biblical king surrounded by ripe fruit and exotic women, Colonel Arreola dozed off in the sway of his fantasy. Then suddenly he heard the distant roar of tanks approaching, their tracks grinding on the street. He sat up quickly in alarm as he felt the first jolt which shook the window panes and set the crystal clinking like chimes, the hanging lamps swinging around crazily while, outside, the howling of dogs could be heard, a terrified counterpoint to this cosmic outrage.

"Earthquake! Earthquake!" Ester screamed, jumping out of bed.

In another quarter of the city, half-naked men and women ran out of the houses in the street of night, horrified by the second seismic wrench which rocked the trees and dwellings and sent a flight of rats shrieking up the electric light poles that were swaying like palm trees in a gale. The wall at Deborah's tomb suddenly fractured in several spots, as if it had been struck by lightning, the lipstick-painted insults blurring, disintegrating. Her photograph crashed to the pavement, and the women huddled nearby began to scream that Deborah's soul had abandoned them. From the top of the hill crowned by the white statue of the Virgin Mary, gigantic stones broke loose and toppled on to the roofs of houses below. Hundreds of miles away in the south, several volcanoes vomited a river of molten lava which left a trail of fire and ashes before hissing into the sea.

Part Three

On my wounded body the rain increases in intensity, overflowing the rivers which carry rounded stones and cadavers down the valleys. The angry wind whips my long hair against ruined roofs and half-mast flags which are moistened by the rain and the torrent of my tears. The rain moans, as if an open wound could speak, falling on avenues and public squares with a rhythm not unlike the concentration of rifle fire; implacable, eroding hills and sown fields with its flood, dragging along the surface of my skin the putrefied remains of so much ruined flesh.

I close my eyes to block this scene of endless desolation that has invaded my territory, where the world ends, and I sink into a lethargy of suffering.

I know not how long I remain immersed in darkness, but all of a sudden I am awakened by a bizarre silence which seems to be the calm stillness of a graveyard. I open my eyes slowly, see through my waterlogged hair a subtle mist which has enveloped my body in a benevolent shroud. I stare at the design formed by the streets of the city, and I see men and women defeated by impotence, walking with their heads down, seemingly resigned irrevocably to the evil forces of the dictator and the armed men who menace each corner, sentinels who have become part of monotonous everyday life, a sad repetition of days that pass at a regular pace which is a kind of fateful replica of the incessant rain of destruction. Abruptly from the grey mass of men and women a young girl with defiant, rapid steps tosses small pieces of paper at intervals on to the pavement, which carry on their pure white surface the printed message demanding the death of the dictator. From the terrace of a tall building, pamphlets fall among the pedestrians like white birds of freedom descending. And sitting on a bench in the main square, a man sings a protest song, his voice rising with the urgent strumming of his guitar.

I foresee the light.

Smiling, I turn my head towards the mountains, and I see the eternal snow where the first rays of the sun have started to shine.

Before falling asleep, the Benefactor of the Republic rejoiced in the images of his superb and unquestioned power. With his eyes closed and his right arm across his chest, he pictured the highways and the country roads which ran like fixed rivers to the city. There, streets and avenues formed an intricate labyrinth, at the centre of which stood the heavily guarded doors of his palace. The thoroughfares were like geometrical cement lines that he had paved with blood and gunpowder, with gags and bound hands, so necessary in order to complete the cleansing process after the infamous bacchanal of the communist government.

He had personally devised the most effective methods of carrying out to perfection even the most trivial details of this sacred purgation. From start to finish, it had been his intelligence that provided the guiding light: during the first phase, which required meticulous tracing and searching for those to blame in the subversive rebellions, to the final task of creating various plans to hide the corpses. In the beginning, when real ingenuity was required, he had decided to bury the corpses under the lion cages in the zoo, his reasoning being that such an end was appropriate for those barbarian reds with their animal hearts. Soon, however, his soldiers had informed him that there was no space left to dispose of the despicable bodies. Owing to his prodigious tactical mind, he had needed only a few seconds to solve this problem by ordering that the vermin be thrown down abandoned mine-shafts or buried in uncultivated fields in the countryside. At that time, of course, he had not taken into account the dog factor, a totally unforeseeable variable under the circumstances; after all, one could not think of everything at once. Naturally, the ravenous wild dogs had unearthed the graves and dragged out the dead in search of their own kind, because commies were nothing but a bunch of mangy, scab-ridden dogs whose deaths were well deserved for having rebelled against his government of order and progress. The symbolic flame of progress had in fact inspired him to instruct his soldiers to burn the dead prisoners, thus purifying even the smallest cell of those bodies contaminated by treason.

The Benefactor started to drift into a dream wherein he saw himself surrounded by the silent glow of torches which illuminated him, sanctifying him as the sole redeemer of the Fatherland. He envisioned himself standing on the summit of a tall mountain, a figure divine and gigantic who controlled the destiny of every citizen in this land. Breathing hard now with satisfaction, he dreamed of himself sliding down a thick web of rope and braided metal, which he, having become some indefatigable kind of spider, never ceased to weave.

But already the protective armour of his woven trap had been pierced by protests and popular resistance, which had given birth to the first unified voices demanding freedom.

Annoyed, the dictator was forced to accept a petition from the High Command of his armed forces, which insisted upon an emergency meeting. He waited for them in the high armchair which in the past was reserved for the democratically elected presidents of the republic. A grimace of disgust distorted his face as he heard the drumming of boots, their heels clacking in rhythm as his visitors approached the salon through the hallway. Serious, imperturbable, he saluted the dozens of uniforms ornamented with stars, ribbons and medals.

"Our most respectful apologies, my General, for interrupting your much-deserved rest," a General of the air force said at attention.

The Benefactor was not mollified. "Let's dispense with the preambles here. What's the situation?"

"The situation is difficult, my General."

"In what way? Speak up."

The air force General smoothed his collar nervously. "Well, for example, the relatives of those political prisoners who have been executed have now started to voice resentment. They are complaining—"

"Complaints? From that vermin? How absurd! I have stated again and again, on radio and television, that to be addicted to the communist philosophy constitutes, legally speaking, an act of treason, of treachery against the Fatherland. And treason against our beloved nation is punished by a sentence of death. How many times have I told them this? But, like wilful children, they don't seem to learn. As a good father, because I am a good father, I've advised them over and over to stay away from the leftist rabble, because if they don't, we will crush them like a stampede of horses on the pampas. How exasperating this is! How often must I repeat myself?"

The General in charge of the national police, a round little man with a thick moustache, nodded his head furiously. "Exasperating indeed, General. My thoughts exactly. But these people refuse to listen to reason. During the last few months, they have not only demanded the bodies of the dead, they have also asked for a written report stating in detail the charges against each of the executed and the exact manner and place of their deaths."

The Supreme Commander brushed this aside with a gloved hand. "Just invent a trial and a sentence, exactly as we have done so often in the past."

The General of police was anxious to appear as efficient as possible. "*Bueno*, the first ten years of confusion have passed, General. I'm afraid they are beginning to channel their individual efforts at resistance into an organized group ready for action."

"Bah!" the Benefactor blurted out. "What are you afraid of? I won't have our glorious rule threatened by a handful of pettifoggers who go around waving useless pieces of paper. Besides, there is always the oldest recourse of all, the emergency War Time Law of Escape that I enacted publicly on September eleventh, 1973. Shoot them. By all means, shoot them. And then send a brief announcement to the press that on the way to one detention camp or another, the prisoners jumped from the vehicle and tried to escape; that in spite of the fact that the guards shouted for them to stop, the escapees persisted in running away; and that, faced with this alarming predicament, the soldiers of our army proceeded to open fire, killing them. Now, General Muñoz, tell us – has this procedure continued to be implemented regularly?"

Muñoz seemed reluctant to speak. "Yes, your Excellency. But if you'll allow me to offer a private opinion, that particular story has been cited as the basis for so many executions that it is no longer believed. In this instance, Excellency, with all due respect, we have gone to the well once too often."

The Benefactor smiled like an indulgent father. "Then find another well, Muñoz."

Muñoz's reluctance caused him to look down. "You must also know, then, that many women relatives, mothers, sisters of the dead, have started to protest by chaining themselves to the iron fence surrounding the garden of what used to be the National Congress."

The Benefactor cocked his head, giving Muñoz a look. "I know, I've read about it. But, *hombre*, when have we ever paid attention to women when it comes to serious matters?"

A General of the army wanted to be noticed. "I totally agree, your Excellency. Let them cackle like hens. They're only good for laying eggs, anyway."

Muñoz began speaking before the general laughter died down. "Still, the problem now is that the relatives of the executed have support from several foreign groups, and these groups are attempting to initiate legal actions in the name of what they call 'Human Rights', which, as you may have noticed, they write in capital letters."

"There's an easy solution to that problem," the General said. "All you need to do is publish abroad the captured rebel documents our Intelligence Service has on file, particularly those outlining their plans to attack a police headquarters and kill its staff as well as those policemen's sons who were more than eight years of age. Send this kind of information to news agencies abroad, and these foreign groups will soon withdraw their help. Now, any other problems?"

"No, my General," Muñoz said.

"Good. Let's get on, then, with our sacred task of restoring order. Don't hesitate for one second to implement whatever measures you deem necessary to suffocate any sign of seditious insurrection." The Benefactor stood up smiling and held up his arm in a salute reminiscent of the Third Reich. "You may leave."

The street of night had been given a facelift. After the earthquake, broken bricks and missing roof tiles were replaced with new material. During the first few days a great confusion had reigned, then workmen appeared and the usually silent daytime street rang with the sounds of shovels scraping, pails being filled and emptied of debris, the metallic chinking of trowels tapping bricks, the squeaks of screws being tightened, the steady whump-whump of cement mixers turning over and over in the once-drowsy afternoons. Laughing, whistling and flirting with the women, the carpenters and bricklayers dressed in white overalls marched down the street from house to house, mending holes and cracks in the pavement with sand, cement and tar. The sharp ping of nails being driven home accompanied the reinforcement of beams and cornices and sagging steps, the job of restoration was generally finished by bracing the wrought-iron fences and replacing broken wooden screen doors.

In the backyard of Doña Carolina's house, the grapevines were already heavy with bunches of grapes covered by summer dust. Night fell as the last preparations to receive customers went on amid the chirping of sparrows and thrushes returning to their nests in the nearby poplar trees.

"My aching arse," Martina complained as she entered her bedroom. "What's this life coming to?" As was her custom, she had left on the kitchen counter several platters of fried *empanadas* and a punch made from white wine and fresh peaches. Rolling a cigarette with corn leaves she had dried in the oven, she meditated, puffing away until she reached the conclusion that, since that night the military men had taken all of them to prison, life had started to unravel as if it were a kind of demented *chamal* – a piece of tapestry that had abruptly sprung from the four wooden boards of its loom to stagger off by itself in unpredictable directions. "I don't know why in hell there are so many things happening just when I'm about to kick the bucket," she grumbled. "That's all I need – especially now! And tell me, where do I get the strength to put up with so much shit? Me, who never harmed anybody. No sir, not a mean bone in my body. The least I deserve is a few years of peace before I pack it all in."

During her entire life she had seen nothing but sour moments; it was as if she had been born under the sign of a bad-luck star that never stopped shining its evil light on her until it changed her into a poor old woman with sunken cheeks, wrinkled skin and a hunched back. Only then had she been able to live in peace for a few years, amid the piercing aroma of fruit and the bubbling of hot oil, amid the colourful textures of meat and vegetables which while cooking smothered her in continuously different steam, from the white mist of chicken stew to the thick brown vapour of beef steaks frying on a high flame that charred the surface and sealed in the pink and juicy meat. There in the kitchen, for the first time in her life, a life made so grey with adversity, she had felt like a master of time because while cooking she could make time stretch, lazily prolonging itself as she cleaned the beans and lentils, taking out the dirt and small pebbles before leaving them to soak in water for the entire night; then advancing the clock, making time speed up as she cheerfully sliced cabbages for a salad on the chopping board, the knife knocking against the wood like rain falling noisily on the roof. She could even make it stand still by peeling the celery stalks strip by strip by strip, or by softly plucking the yellow and white silky tassels from the pulpy ears of corn.

It had also been there – in her world of pots and pans – that Martina had finally liberated herself, like a ship discharging ballast, from the cumbersome weight of happiness and misfortune. Because in her kitchen, where everything was cut, cooked and steamed, joy and sadness were like the fleeting clouds of a summer afternoon. The happiness that overwhelmed her while slicing a heavy round tomato only lasted until the moment she adorned it with parsley and carried the salad tray into the dining-room. And the uneasiness that clams produced in her was also transitory. She hated those cunning creatures which stubbornly sealed themselves in at the slightest touch of a knife, and when at long last she caught them off guard and opened their shells to the base, they stuck out their dirty tongues and twisted them in a kind of gross reprimand. But she only had to drop them in boiling water to put a stop to those bad moments. In that other world inhabited by human beings, though, Martina had always hoped that happiness would last for ever, yet each of her sufferings only served to add more venom to an everlasting rancour which during her youth had settled in her heart like a scorpion.

Many times she had said to herself that to experience happiness and anger, without the sting of hate or the childish hope that joy was eternal, would make her life as clean and shiny as a brand-new silver tray. She would then remember her mother telling her that she would live a long life because her umbilical cord had foretold it, and Martina would smile beatifically, imagining that many years would pass before death came for her, probably at the moment she was slicing a golden brown sirloin roast surrounded by baked potatoes.

"But all these weirdos, these noisy good-for-nothings, came into my life like ghosts, to strip me of my well-deserved peace," she would say as she pounded her fist in protest. "No bloody need for them to appear. They just come to disturb me, to stir things up and make a mess." She had had such scary moments with uninvited visitors who appeared unexpectedly – her hair standing on end when Señora Rosa appeared for the first time – and she somehow gained strength to stay calm only because at that moment she'd remembered her grandmother saying that one should never frighten spirits because the dead as well as the living were capable of the cruellest revenge if they were startled. But amid that entangled ball of unravelled yarn that was her life, the apparition of the old *curandera* had been the least disturbing event, a blessing in fact, because Señora Rosa continued to treat her as if she were still a young girl, with the same tenderness she used on that day Martina had gone to ask her for poisonous plants to kill the beast who was her husband. Since the first time she had entered the old *curandera*'s hut, Martina felt that Rosa loved her as if she were her own mother.

"Your eyes are as black as the *maqui*, and you have the body of a *cuyen*, of a gorgeous maiden sent by the Moon herself," she had told her one afternoon while both of them were grinding *copihue* seeds to prepare a love potion. "But my heart tells me that you will never be a *cuyen nuque*, that your limbs will never open to give birth to a cub," she had added, closing her eyes. And when Martina was about to say goodbye that same afternoon, Señora Rosa rose from her wicker chair, gave her a long embrace, and kept repeating that she would always be around to listen to all those misfortunes that would cause Martina so much suffering throughout her life. At that time, out of respect, Martina had never spoken to Rosa about her husband's cruel lust, nor had she told of his repugnant body which made her mouth so bitter that she had to go to the fields and spit on the grass to feel clean; but now, amid the steaming pots, she had revealed everything while Señora Rosa, overwhelmed by compassion, consoled her like a mother lulling her child against her breast.

But since even the saintliest soul had defects and strange whims, Señora Rosa had come up with the weird idea of sticking her nose into what was going on between Alda and the man with lizard eyes. That night of the spell had been a real scare because, apart from the strange things the *curandera* was saying, Martina never stopped fearing that the military would suddenly appear in the kitchen and chop off their heads with a single blow, so that blood would spray the walls and stain the dishes she had washed just before midnight. "I can't see why you have to butt into this mess, señora," Martina told her two days later, when she could finally speak to Señora Rosa without fear.

"I already explained," the old lady answered, "to help out a little."

"Does that mean," Martina enquired, "that once the soldier is bewitched, all the other flat-tops are going to be defeated?"

"Not so fast, *huaina*," Señora Rosa cautioned, "my power is very limited, and it's not easy to beat those devils. As I told you, one can only fight skirmishes against an entire army of men marching back and forth across this earth."

And Martina never again questioned Señora Rosa's power, because she had indeed saved Alda from death, and the man bewitched by the love spell would never attempt to kill her, since it would be like putting a dagger into his own heart.

Some weeks later, Martina noticed that Alda had undergone a kind of transformation, acquiring a lovely brightness in her eyes, a lustre which Martina did not understand. They were not the eyes of a woman in love, the look one now saw on Meche's face since the young man had started visiting the house regularly. No, these were a pair of eyes which seemed to gleam like deep water in dark moonlight, where the current is full of algae. Alda even walked in a different way, as if her provocative and insolent strut had somehow been transformed into a firm and dignified carriage.

"Alda has become a beautiful woman, señora, a real head-turner," she would comment to the old *curandera*, who smiled with deep satisfaction as Martina added, "She's like one of those strong dahlias that bloom even in the shade."

And all of this thanks to Señora Rosa, the only worthwhile person among all the other apparitions, because the others . . . they weren't worth spit! The useless spirit of Deborah, for example, with her newly restored tomb and even a small marble tombstone which the girls had paid for after taking a collection from all the houses in the street. That lazy bitch! She didn't move a finger for anyone; all she did was piss and moan. Every single morning, at the first cock-a-doodle-doo, Deborah woke everybody with her screams, which continued until Patoja or another girl washed the pavement and put fresh flowers on her tomb.

"Poor little thing; she's crying for all the dead," Patoja kept saying.

Martina was the only one who paid no attention. "You have spoiled her with all this hullabaloo," Martina grumbled. But no one listened.

"And the way things are going, Señora Martina, all of us will soon turn into moaning souls," Alda said one day, staring at her with those heavy, molten eyes. Pretending to ignore her, Martina had spun around and walked off, because she was so fed up with all the other people who had appeared unexpectedly.

She didn't even want to think about Julieta, who only knew how to be noisy. Meche had told Martina that Julieta had appeared on the street at midday wearing long hair and a skirt that fell to her ankles. Looking neither right nor left, she had advanced to the middle of the street and, raising her arms as if she were announcing some famous TV show, she had begun to harangue in her hoarse, shrill voice, like a diligent town crier.

"*Compañeras*, Julieta is my name. I earn my living on my feet, not on my back, and I have a distinguished diploma in hairdressing and the most modern strategies to enhance women's beauty. Whoever is interested in obtaining my specialized services should come closer and pay attention, because I am known as the Hair Magician."

"Then why don't you curl that grass growing on top of your own head, you arsehole," said one of the nearby women, giving Julieta a withering look.

"Ah, a sceptic!" Julieta replied. She gave a sarcastic little snort and arched her eyebrows. "I can't believe you are so ignorant of the miracles of my art. You, *compañera*, come here and touch my silky hair, which even angels in heaven envy. Come and touch, behold the wonder, and tell those who know nothing what a beautiful sensation your hands are experiencing at this moment." She held up both hands. "Egg yolks are the secret, along with an infusion of rare and practically unknown herbs that I always bring with me."

Little by little the women started to form a circle around Julieta, who, smiling and purring with confidence, began removing from her pockets an endless series of boxes and packets of herbs which quickly brought exclamations of wonder from the assembled women.

"Cream of avocado for dry skin," Julieta informed them. "Concentrated strawberries which give to our lips that natural red colour all of us secretly wish for. Coconut oil for that stubborn hair which is so hard to curl." She turned to the woman who had called her an arsehole, who had come nearer but who still stared at her with hostility. "And here, especially for you, my dear new friend, I have *quillay* powder, which, in less than a week, will transform those drab, colourless locks of yours into the most amazing blonde in the entire barrio."

Later on, when there was a long line of women waiting patiently for a turn to have their hair fixed, Julieta had mentioned that she came from the north. Then, more sure of herself now, she had started to sing loudly in that hoarse, cracking voice which resounded down the street like a distant woodsaw:

> The Negro José shakes his hips,
> His skin like the colour of night,
> He turns like a great bird in flight,
> He dances with joy, the happiest boy,
> My friend the Negro José.

From then on, not even the devil could shut her up, because her mouth, like her pockets, was chock-full of a seemingly never-ending supply of things – in this case songs which she sang poorly but with great enthusiasm. And the other fools put up with her because she managed skilfully to reward each of them with a personal list of beauty tips which she supplemented with sweet compliments, making them believe that her own brand of junk would enhance a "latent beauty", they had never before seen in themselves. "You remind me of my suffering land, Señora Martina," Julieta had said one day while trying to solicit Martina's friendship. But Martina would have none of it; she cut Julieta off by taking the dustbins outside. Why would she want to be friends with that big mouth, whose piercing voice kept everyone from their siestas!

"When I journeyed to the pampas," Julieta sang in that horrible voice every afternoon, usually from a balcony where she was drying the hair of several girls, a captive audience with their heads full of pins and curling rolls. "When I saw the rooms of the miners in the north," she would practically shout, tapping out a rhythm on the metal railing with a pair of scissors, her screams seeming to shake the dishes in Martina's kitchen. "And the sun burning high above!" It seemed she would never end with this annoying song. And when the spirit took her, she would lean over the balcony, stamping her heels in rhythm and bawling like a stuck pig:

The lines of shanty houses stuck together row by row,
sí, señor!
The lines of women waiting for a turn at the only water
pump,
Each with an empty bucket and a face full of affliction,
And the sun burning high above!

Julieta took to stopping by at twilight, when all the girls had got dressed to receive the clients, bustling in like a bawdy crow, her bag full of stuff to impart that magical finishing touch – which was nothing more than a bunch of pencils and brushes for darkening eyelids and reddening cheeks and lips. And talking all the bloody time. She told the girls an endless collection of stories about terrible suffering, deaths, and acts of injustice; strikes and demonstrations the army ended by shooting the miners with bullets; women and children starved to death or forced to escape on bare feet across the scorching sand of the Atacama desert . . . "This is not the first time, *compañeras*, that our country has fallen into the claws of military men," she would declare as soon as she noticed that one of the women was wiping her tears away. ("I sing to the pampas, the sad land / Reprobate land of an evil curse.") "Open your eyes wider, my sweet, so I can make those dark lines that will turn you into an irresistible nymph." ("A land that never turns green, not even in springtime.") "Now, turn your head to the left so I can paint a mole on your cheek. This song was written by a miner after the massacre in the Escuela Santa Maria in 1908, do you realize that, comrades? 1908! We have been forced to live through centuries of injustice in our country! Whose turn is it now? Ah, Martita! Pretty Martita, who else? Please sit down, honey, for today I am going to outline your lips with this dark wine-coloured pencil, or, as it says here on the label, cherry burgundy." (Listen to the next lines: "Year after year, through the salty earth / Of the desolate Tamarugal / Slowly crossing it, they go by the thousands / The sad pariahs of wealth.") "Close your eyes, 'cause I want to make your eyelashes as luxuriant as the eyelashes of a doll." (Pariahs of wealth, shit, that's what we have always been. Listen to this stanza, which is the saddest of all: "Bitter sweat on their foreheads / Tears in their eyes / Blood on their feet / The unfortunate workers are gathering / Piles of gold for the bourgeoisie.")

Who could find a moment of peace with those fucking foghorn mouths of Deborah and Julieta! To top it off, some very strange things were also happening in the other streets: it appeared that, all of a sudden, goblins had arrived and turned off all the lights at the same time. On the eleventh day of each month, according to what the girls explained to Martina (who for years had paid no attention to calendars), the goblins carried out "a wake as a protest" – anyway, that's what they said it was called. Late at night and quite unexpectedly (for it happened at different times), the lights went out in every house in the city, and in the darkness there resounded whistles and pots and pans being beaten together, as if the ghosts were howling while dragging their chains. Who could expect to find a quiet moment amidst such a confusion of noises and apparitions? No, the only thing Martina could expect was that death would come barging into her room like a loudmouth intruder and not as that peaceful sentinel she had expected for so long, coming to take her politely, waiting until she removed from her oven the platter containing a sirloin roast surrounded by steaming potatoes. It seemed that she, whose life had been full of suffering and humiliation, must resign herself to spending her last days on earth in a lunatic asylum, caught like a fish on a hook, submerged in a sea of screaming voices more frightening than hell itself.

"I am finally giving my body its appropriate due, its only true use,"Alda thought as she crossed the gates of the cemetery carrying a large bunch of chrysanthemums like a cradled child. She advanced through the main avenue thinking that her legs, which one day would lie stiff and enclosed in a tomb, had at long last acquired a reason to bounce, to be alive. Her breasts, which she always knew how to advertise, choosing with care the appropriate bra and the most daring low-cut dresses, would turn to dust with dignity, she decided. Lowering her head, she imagined herself lying in a coffin, and she smiled at the thought that she would not be buried as a worthless prostitute who had left no trace, no meaningful monument, of her journey through life. "Because these hips, which one day will crumble in the earth, knew how to set a trap for the man who is responsible for so many deaths, knew how to roll in rhythm to those little moans of pain and pleasure which in the end saved my life," she reasoned to herself with conviction.

Looking to her right, she remembered Arreola's naked body wedged between her legs and it dawned on her that her body, once used only for making a living, now also served to protect and aid the persecuted. As Señora Rosa foretold, the three crosses she had drawn on the Colonel's back while he was in the throes of orgasm had unleashed a passion which intensified to a kind of madness as she carried out the other ceremonials specified by the old *curandera.*

Alda paused for a moment at the mausoleum of one of the heroes of the nation, and she imagined that, once the dictator perished, it would once again be possible to see noisy and happy crowds marching down the avenues in complete freedom, once more carrying the national flag with pride. Daydreaming, she visualized her grave somewhere in the centre of the cemetery, receiving as years went by the written messages of people young and old, posthumous testimonials to her bravery. A cat jumped suddenly from behind a headstone, sending her back to reality with a start, and she laughed at herself for such exaggerated wishfulness.

Her gaze took in the people scattered among the paths between the lines of tombs and then fell on a tall statue which represented a woman overwhelmed by suffering. She remembered the day she learned of her father's death. It was late evening and she was all dressed up to receive clients. She was wearing her low-cut blue dress and was putting the finishing touches to her face when she saw Don Gabriel, a kind man who was a friend of her family, enter the house.

"Excuse me for interrupting your work, Alda, but Señora Maria told me you lived in this street, and since I was coming to the city to visit my brothers, I thought I should stop by to let you know that your father died two months ago," he informed her in a compassionate voice. She received the news dolled up in that stupid party dress, bursting into tears and feeling an empty pit widening beneath her feet. Although she hadn't seen her father in years, he had remained a real mooring post, the one fixed point in her life. Lost and in pain, she wept as she leant against a wall, eyes closed, seeing herself tumbling down a hill covered with sharp rocks. "Clean up your mascara, dearie," Doña Carolina had instructed her, handing over a paper napkin. And like a defenceless child, she had obeyed. Standing before the dining-room mirror, she started to wipe off the black stains dripping down her cheeks and her reflection seemed to her absurd, a mime's mask of death, the only certainty in life. She cleaned the black tears like an automaton, applying fresh make-up and rouge to her suddenly pale face, trying to choke back the sobs caught in her throat.

As absurd as her face was the abrupt realization that she had wasted countless hours of her life in the empty routine of painting it in order to seduce a meaningless throng of unknown men who had briefly enjoyed her without giving any pleasure in return. And following the rules of this game in which her body was simply part of a financial transaction, not once, not for one single evening had she failed to stand in front of the mirror and paint her lips and her eyes before devoting several minutes to curling her eyelashes, afterwards thickening them with a heavy black liquid, stroke after stroke, sliding the mascara brush slowly upward. But that evening, when Don Gabriel brought the news of her father's death, was the first time it occurred to her that make-up was but one part of an empty game, the preliminary, this masking of her face before the ritual of the flesh, a boisterous carnival which sought through its obscene antics to ignore death.

She had seen her father only once after abandoning her home. Now, walking along the tomb-lined gravel path, she recalled how strange was her family home. Her father always had love affairs – even the neighbours knew about them – but her mother, instead of confronting him, used to vent her fury on Alda, insulting her and hitting her as if this form of violence was her only means of survival. Since the day Alda began to menstruate, her mother set in motion a strict surveillance of her comings and goings, never ceasing to repeat the same long stories about innocent girls who had been deceived and ruined by men. If by chance Alda arrived from school a few minutes late, her mother would be waiting at the front door, where she grabbed Alda's hair and smacked her with a broomstick, shouting that she had been born a prostitute, that she was on heat like her damned father. Now she realized that she ran away with João not only because of the intense love she felt for him, but also as an act of rebellion against her mother and the strict, puritanical morality she was trying to impose on her.

After she had started having sex with men, she used to accept her mother's insults and blows with defiance. And when she began taking money for her favours, she used to go downtown and buy clothes with the deep satisfaction that she no longer depended on anyone to survive, nor did she have to obey anyone's orders. Her mother soon became suspicious. An efficient snoop, she inspected the entire house until she found two of the new dresses Alda had hidden in the bottom drawer of an old dresser. Enraged and using a belt, she had forced Alda to confess the truth and then, scandalized, she had demanded that her father send Alda packing.

"Daughter, it's my belief that all of us have the right to decide what we do with our life, but I think you're making a big mistake, if it's true what your mother has told me. I don't want any more fighting in this house – Lord knows we've had enough arguments to last us a lifetime. You are an adult, Aldita, and if this is the road you've chosen, you'd better travel it far away from this house," he had told her with kindness in his voice.

One day she had met him unexpectedly outside a bar. He greeted her with somewhat distant affection, saying goodbye quickly, looking away to tell her that he was late and had to catch the train to Valparaíso. She watched him walk away and felt like running after him to tell him that she had never stopped loving him, that she remembered with immense tenderness his nicotine-stained teeth and his laugh, which to her so resembled a flock of birds flying through the trees. But just as she was about to give way to the urge, his figure, one more man hurrying among the host of pedestrians, lost the aura of authority and respect he had possessed in her child's eyes as he crossed the threshold of his home, becoming at once and for ever after, a kind of stranger. "He's spent all his salary with other women. It doesn't bother him at all that his family must now spend the rest of the month with little to eat," her mother used to complain through tears while Alda's youngest sister, who was their mother's confidante, listened with an air of understanding and compassion. And as her father turned the corner and disappeared, Alda for the first time understood her mother's complaints and felt like catching the train herself, if only to commiserate with her mother.

She didn't know if she postponed (and kept postponing) the visit because she was afraid or ashamed, but in any case she never went back home. At times she hoped her mother would look her up to ask for money, so that both of them could have a tearful and permanent reconciliation. But she had never gone home again, and there had been no tear-filled truce. Now, walking in the cemetery, she thought it quite possible that her mother was also dead. "Why the hell does anyone put off expressing their feelings as if life had no end, as if it were an eternal soap opera," she wondered, and remembering her absurd mime's face in the mirror she decided that both of her parents would be proud to know that her life was no longer limited to dealing with images reflected off glass, as if the only card in the deck of her existence was her physical appearance. To set a trap for Arreola had meant the beginning of a new life for her, one based on a human solidarity which sprouted and grew as a challenge to the dictatorship.

At that moment a coffin appeared, riding high on the shoulders of the pall-bearers. Looking around, Alda realized that the dictator, like so many others of his ilk before him, had made the cemetery the busiest place in town. A woman kneeling on the gravel polished the bronze decorations on a tombstone; further on, two men planted a rose bush next to an epitaph which in its centre had the framed photograph of a young boy. Walking along a concrete wall of tombs in tiers, rising one above the other with the symmetry of a chessboard for the dead, she saw behind the glass windows various items: cards, confirmation medals, the tiny figures of saints, favourite toys – a motley collection of mementoes, each tomb a heartbreaking testimonial to the power of love. "And here we are, worshipping our dead in this country where life is no longer valued because of the dictator and his followers, including Arreola, although it's hard for me to call him what he is: a murderer."

Against her will, she was overwhelmed by the passion of his caresses. Even though they met three times a week, not once had he failed to fix those devoted, illuminated eyes on her, as if she were a shining star and he a mariner come suddenly out of the fog. Like a man breathless before discovered gold, he came to her haltingly, removing her clothes slowly to prolong his pleasure, whispering words of endearment as he kissed her neck, and she like a virgin remained in silence until he entered her. Only then, under the weight of his feverish body, did Alda perceive an agony which rose in synchronization with his orgasm, an agony which stemmed not from pleasure but from some kind of painful inner confrontation with himself. She could not hate him or despise him, although he actively participated in the dictator's countless murders; for her, the Colonel was a man forsaken, exiled from happiness and imprisoned in an intense vanity which was, in essence, a profound weakness and insecurity. Alda had come to feel a strange tenderness for the Colonel, a form of compassion mixed with the lancing darts of desire. She no longer knew if her caresses and moans were part of the role she had been assigned to perform, or if they were an authentic expression of her true self.

She had reached a line of crosses planted in the ground, and when she found the epitaph she had been searching for, she stood before it with her head bowed. Appearing quickly from one side, a young man carrying a water bucket for her flowers came to her side. She handed him a tip and, still looking down, told him the message Jairo had passed to her.

Before her next encounter with Arreola, the one immediately after she had burned the white handkerchief she'd used to wipe off his semen, the men who collected Alda did not blindfold her. She pretended to ignore this change in procedure, forcing herself to look straight ahead lest they catch her trying to memorize their route. And once they left her alone in the bedroom of an old house, she sat on the bed to await her rapist's entrance, his sharp purposeful stride that of a commander plotting a campaign. But this time when Arreola came into the room, he stopped inside the door to give her a look of affection, the slow smile of an overheated lover, sighing as he walked over to her, saying over and over in a hoarse voice, "My little whore, my little whore." He undressed her slowly, as if performing some secret military ritual. "You remember me, yes?" he asked, to which Alda nodded, throwing her arms around his neck and smiling at the knowledge that he could no longer live without her.

Each succeeding liaison lasted longer than Arreola had planned, because his desire for her now exhausted him; after climax he collapsed, burying his face in her breasts while she caressed his back and asked him questions about his life. "Now that's a woman you can really talk to," he kept repeating as he drove to his house afterwards. "You are so bright," she would tell him, "I've never met anyone as intelligent as you are." And beyond the open lips of her vagina, which ushered him to those mystical heights of maximum power he had always dreamed of, Arreola also found in her the pillar of that identity he had tried to construct for himself since childhood, when he'd declared in front of his classmates that the fossilized snails and clams, apparently mineral, actually belonged to the animal kingdom. Alda's praises inflamed him as much as her pendulous breasts and the rocking movement of her hips. He would listen to her compliments for a time and then, laughing with satisfied vanity, he would grab her roughly and kiss her, ramming his penis into her with the urgency of a teenager while she closed her eyes and moaned in a kind of muted choral accompaniment to his crescendo.

Colonel Arreola never suspected that treason hid behind those open encouraging lips and fluttering eyelids.

Once a week while kneeling in prayer, Alda told Señora Leonora the exact addresses of the different houses where she met with Arreola, pointing out the most familiar landmarks along each route. Later on, after becoming Arreola's confidante, she was also able to pass on details about the raids the soldiers of Military Intelligence were planning to conduct.

"You are going to end up saving all of us, Aldita," Señora Leonora told her one day as they were coming out of church.

"I hope so," Alda whispered. "Although I won't be able to discover more information until Arreola returns from the north. He wanted to take me with him, but he's going to be with other officers inspecting those cities I told you about."

"Yes," Señora Leonora said, taking Alda's arm. "It's all right. Besides, you deserve a break." She smiled and kissed Alda's cheek. "You've been going to too many churches and houses of torture."

Alda jerked her arm away. “No, Señora Leonora. I want to go on. I have to help, it doesn’t matter how,” she protested, certain that if she ceased participating in the resistance, her life would lose its meaning.

“I know, my dear, but it might be better to wait until Arreola returns. One of our rules is, stay out of sight if you can. The more visibility you have, the more danger you face.”

“I know, you’re right. But there must be something I can do. Maybe I could meet a client in the house and—”

“Ah! You wish to fall in love like Meche.” Señora Leonora gave a little laugh. “It seems she’s having quite a romance.”

“Not really. But Meche is happy. Imagine, this is the first time she’s been in love! She talks about Roberto all day long. She’s had her head in the clouds since that night they kissed each other by the front door. Hasn’t she told you about it?”

“She mentioned it without going into details. It’s so beautiful. That young man has suffered so much; he deserves to find love again.”

Alda nodded, taking the older woman’s hand. “I think he loves Meche, although he doesn’t know it. And they haven’t made love, yet.”

“Poor Roberto. He loved his fiancée so completely, and he hasn’t recovered from the pain of losing her.”

“Anyway, forget about Roberto. Tell me how I can help.”

Señora Leonora sighed in surrender. “Perhaps, for a couple of weeks, no more, you could be in charge of taking provisions to our comrades in the country. But I need to arrange this with the people I take orders from. Let’s get together tomorrow at three at the Lourdes Chapel and I’ll let you know.”

Two days later, Alda took a bus which travelled to a small village perched above a valley at the foot of the mountains. She got off at the one and only bus stop, weighed down by two heavy bags of food. Following Señora Leonora's instructions, she turned left at the end of the main street and went along a country path until she came to a cornfield on her right. She waded into the field, bitching every time her heels caught against a corn stalk and almost breaking into tears when one of the sacks tore open. Twenty minutes later she arrived at a small forest of eucalyptus trees within which she made out an old country house which had that run-down look of abandonment. She left the bags on the porch and, walking softly, went down a corridor and looked into a room which seemed to have been a drawing-room in better days. Crossing the room, she came to a patio where she stopped short, seeing a small boy and an old man standing on their hands, their heels braced against an old adobe wall.

"Sunflowers under the sun?" she asked as she had been instructed.

"And the sun under other sunflowers, which most of us will never see," the old man answered, springing upright to shake her hand with a smile.

"I left the packages on the porch," Alda said, rubbing her back. "My God, they were heavy."

"I thank you. I thank you very much, señorita. If you only knew how grateful we are to those who make such sacrifices," the old man said in a strong and lively voice, caressing her shoulder. "Did you bring toothpaste? We haven't had any for nearly a week, and our *compañeras* have been moaning because they've run out of flour and oil."

"Are there many of you?" Alda asked.

"Yes. Counting the children, fifteen. Most of them are off collecting wood. I stayed in the house with Buttons, standing guard upside down. As you can see, we have not been trained in the military."

The boy burst into laughter. "Nor in the monastery, either. No, señorita, Don José Miguel is more fun to be with than monks or soldiers."

The old man gave the boy a look before he told Alda, "We were concentrating on our exercises when you came up. We have to train to stay in condition." Seeing Alda's puzzlement, he added, "You knew we were clowns?"

Alda's mouth fell open. "Clowns? No, I didn't know. I mean, nobody . . ." Her voice trailed off even as she realized why the old man's smile and friendly eyes had warmed her.

"It's been fourteen months," the old man said, turning to shake his finger at Buttons like Chaplin making a point. "Fourteen months and ten days, to be exact, since the vulture and his hired assassins decided to kill all the clowns in the country, and those of us who managed to escape death had no other alternative than to seek refuge here. For how long is anybody's guess. But the important thing is that we are alive, that we can still see the sun rising high above the sunflowers, casting its light on other planets that most of us will never see." He gave Buttons a light shove. "Let's go get the groceries, little Buttons! And then we will give a guided tour of our house to this charming señorita, whose beauty shines like a star."

As he and Buttons carried the groceries to the kitchen, José Miguel said, "Thank God we didn't bring the circus animals too! Otherwise, you would have needed ten men to carry provisions. Imagine – in one week a bear eats forty kilos of carrots and several kilos of honey! A condor must be fed five kilos of meat a week or it starts losing its feathers and soon dies. Now the puma and the jaguar, who are very aristocratic animals, put away ten kilos of chicken each, and you wouldn't believe the lion's diet. He eats like a king!"

"I'll say!" Buttons said. Holding his nose, he added, "And stinks, too!"

"I miss them all," José Miguel said, shaking his head. "Even the filthy smell of them. Before the beginning of each show, all the performers assemble behind the curtain for the opening parade. The girls in glittering tights, the animal trainers in their shiny boots and fierce moustaches, the clowns painted all the colours of the rainbow, and the awful aroma of the lions swaying back and forth on their short leashes – ah, señorita, if you only knew what a beautiful sensation, what a wonderful moment that is! No matter how long you've been with the circus, your heart pounds as you wait for the curtain to rise. It's like being born again." He set a sack on the counter and helped Buttons with his. "But this is no time to become sentimental, not when we have visitors. Come," he urged, taking Alda's arm, "I'd like to show you the house, which used to be inhabited by the man who owned all the land around here. This used to be a huge hacienda which stretched from what is now the main street to the mountains."

Talking back and forth, Buttons and José Miguel led Alda through each room in the house, some containing once elegant but now dilapidated furniture. Afterwards they took her to a small park behind the house, next to a pond shaded by huge willows, under one of which stood a large metal cage full of birds with colourful feathers.

She stood entranced. "These are the most exotic birds I've ever seen in my life!" was all she could say.

"They are doves," José Miguel explained.

Alda's mouth dropped open for the second time that day. "Did you say doves?"

Buttons nodded enthusiastically. "Sure! He paints their feathers," he cried, pointing at José Miguel. "And when he gets bored, he washes the colour off, and paints them a different colour. But each one is always different."

Hearing voices in the kitchen, they returned to the house to find a number of people examining what Alda had brought them, chattering among themselves and oohing and aahing as they discovered sorely needed items.

"Stay for dinner," one of the women called to Alda.

José Miguel patted Alda on the cheek. "Better yet, stay for the night, and after dinner we'll put on a special performance just for you."

Alda accepted the invitation, feeling like a child who can't wait for Christmas morning to open her gifts. The laughter and camaraderie of these people buoyed her spirits as if she were riding around and around on a sparkling and musical merry-go-round.

After dinner, the conversation drifted, then turned to their companions who had been killed.

"They assassinated Don Pedro and Carmelita, who never did harm to anyone," a woman said. "Don Pedro performed as the Magician of Pakistan. The billboards always announced him as the unknown son of a notable prince of Baghdad. Carmelita, who could impersonate anyone, usually played the role of Madame Pompidoux."

Another woman said, "Don Pedro was fantastic! A real phenomenon, I tell you. He always appeared on stage wearing a turban and Turkish shoes, just like Aladdin. He outlined his eyes in heavy black paint and stood in the centre of the ring, staring at the crowd with a long face. Then he would put his hands on the crystal ball, a huge thing mounted on a two-legged table, creating an air of mystery and suspense. The people lapped it up. Meanwhile, Madame Pompidoux came into the limelight dressed in her elegant velvet dress and danced around the table, adding fantasy and magic to the scene."

"Yes," a voice recalled. "Then the Magician of Pakistan made some strange movements with his hands, do you remember? He approached the table making mysterious waving gestures with his hands, giving the crowd a sinister look, and suddenly out of the crystal ball sprang huge flowers which smacked him in the head."

Someone laughed. "And that's when the real show started!"

"Right," someone else interrupted. "Because he would hold his head as if it hurt and explain to the people that he didn't do traditional magic, but rather Pakistani hocus-pocus, which could be dangerous."

"And he had these long silk handkerchiefs," another person added. "They flew all over the place in his hands. Countless rabbits appeared from out of them. And Madame Pompidoux stumbled around the stage chasing after the rabbits."

Another woman began laughing. "Yes, and every time she bent over to pick up one of the bunnies, she showed her old-fashioned long panties with a big heart drawn in the middle."

"A green heart!" a man explained. "With a smiling mouth missing two teeth painted inside it!"

"Poor Carmelita," a woman's voice broke in. "She adored Don Pedro. A neighbour found their bodies after they'd been dead for several days. Don Pedro was sitting on his favourite red-velvet armchair, the one he'd bought at the flea market on San Diego Street. Carmelita was lying naked on the bed. God only knows what those bastards did to her before they cut her throat."

"And old Chirola," someone said. "Sometimes when I'm about to fall asleep, I see him again in the centre of the ring playing his trumpet, all dressed up in a purple suit with silvery stars that sparkled under the spotlights."

"And Cumparsita," said another voice, "who was not very talented, although he gave a good performance when he mimicked coaxing a cobra out of a basket with his flute."

"Yes, I remember that!" a woman cried. "As good as Chaplin, in my opinion."

José Miguel stood. "We'd better get into our costumes. This show will be in homage to all those comrades who have been taken from us." He smiled at Alda. "And, of course, to you as well, our beautiful provider."

"May I watch you paint your face?" Alda asked him in a hesitant, childlike voice.

"No!" a young man said. "That brings bad luck."

José Miguel cocked his head and gave the young man a look. "Our luck could not possibly be any worse, Pepe. So let's forget about superstition. It's all right, Alda. Come with me and you'll see how an old man can transform himself into a young-looking clown," he added, stretching out his arms and performing a graceful pirouette.

José Miguel made Alda wait in the bedroom. After a few minutes, he stumbled into the room in his huge patent-leather shoes. He was wearing a pair of short pants over striped stockings, which gave him the look of a young boy. In the lapel of his tuxedo jacket there was a red carnation that matched his drooping bow-tie.

"Come," he told her. "I want to show you all my junk." Going to a large chest of drawers where he kept several boxes along with brushes, sponges and odd-looking flasks, he said, "Here is the white paint for the face, which we get by mixing cream and zinc oxide. And this is the black paint we used to prepare by collecting soot from a cooking pot. Now, however, we live in modern times, and you can buy it already prepared at any pharmacy. The bright red is vermilion powder dissolved in liquid vaseline. As you can see, we only use three colours: white, black, and red – our flag, symbol of our territory, where there are no political divisions or closed frontiers. Costumes and some paint, that's all we need to put on a good show, plus our good-luck pig, which we will do without tonight."

Alda clapped her hands in amusement. "You have a lucky pig?"

"Before we begin painting our faces," José Miguel explained, "we take a lemon and stick four matches in it for legs. Then we draw a pair of eyes and bore a hole in its head with a knife and insert a lighted cigarette upside down. The smoke is supposed to attract a crowd. Woe to us if the cigarette goes out while we're doing our faces. It means that attendance will be very small, which is a real disgrace. It's sad to perform in an empty tent with ten or twelve people scattered among the low-priced seats. Anyway, look, the first thing you do is paint your whole face white . . ."

Alda watched José Miguel posturing in front of the mirror, covering his face with a white cream. His hands flitted here and there, deft as a flight of birds. When he finished, she noticed that the clown's eyes had acquired an expression of unusual innocence.

"See?" he said. "As if through an enchantment, all the marks life has carved on my kisser have been erased. No traces of suffering or joy, no wrinkles, you see? Only the unblemished face of a new-born child, despite the fact that I am sixty-five years old. It gives me great pleasure, because under this white mask I can see who I really am, my true essence, what I have been since the moment I was born, even though the years have altered me, damaged me, erased all traces of innocence. So, Alda, here I am, the true José Miguel, who has very little to do with the old man you met this afternoon, standing on his hands, upside down against a garden wall."

Alda frowned at her image in the mirror beside the clown's white face. "I wonder who I really am, José Miguel," she said, examining the wrinkles under her eyes with loathing, hating the two lines that trickled from the sides of her nose to the edges of her mouth.

"You are a blossom under the sun," José Miguel said with a smile of encouragement. "A beautiful and brave woman who puts her life in danger to protect those who need help."

Alda looked away and in a lowered voice said, "I am also a prostitute, José Miguel. The only other alternative I had in life was to become a maid."

"You made a wise choice," José Miguel said with conviction. "Lord, it must be so degrading to live in the house of strangers and serve those who will never stop looking down on you. Besides, I can think of a lot of jobs worse than making love."

"Me too," Alda replied. "In some ways, you know, it's not that different from trying to make people laugh."

José Miguel chuckled. "I see what you mean. Look what an important role we both play in this miserable world. Imagine a life without sex or laughter! That must be worse than death."

"Except that you'd die of boredom," Alda added as she laughed with José Miguel.

"Exactly!" he said. "You'd have to die to have fun. Because I'm certain there is some entertainment in the realm of death. St Peter must lose his keys once in a while. You can picture the scandal that would cause, angels everywhere, combing the heavens, while St Peter stands at the gate trying to explain why no one can come in just yet."

"And what about in hell, if someone turned the gas off," Alda exclaimed, unable to stop giggling.

"Well, we'd better hurry up," José Miguel said. "The others are probably about ready. Now, I will re-make this face, constructing a mockery to all the wrinkles in the world. Look here: two long, thick, black lines around my lips, which I now paint red." Alda could not stop smiling; even his voice made her laugh as he tried to speak without moving his lips. "Now, two red dots on the edges. Next, a red sun on each cheek, enormous suns, the colour of the real McCoy sinking into the sea at twilight. Now, my wig. Go and take your seat. The show is about to begin!"

Illuminated by kerosene lamps, men, women and children began their parade into the centre of the drawing-room, singing a melody from a Sousa march and disappearing one by one into the shadows behind the light. Several came stumbling and somersaulting forward to present funny skits in their falsetto voices. Wielding huge plastic combs and scissors, three clowns pantomimed an absurd battle, a drum-roll and cymbal accompanying each pratfall, the room with its old furniture a stage for skilled acrobats who faked clumsiness. Some walked on their hands; others did backflips and landed in awkward-looking but perfect splits; two women began fighting over a pan of spaghetti and ended up locked together in a human wheel that rolled back and forth, spewing curled paper spaghetti into the air like snow.

When the show ended, all of them sat at the table drinking tea before going to bed.

"José Miguel," one woman called out, "tell Alda our story."

"All right," he agreed. "But first turn off the lamp, because I get more inspiration from the darkness." He turned to Alda. "Let me begin by saying that we clowns do not belong to this world where people are constantly inventing scientific stuff and fighting wars. We don't have anything to do with progress; on the contrary, untold centuries go by and we remain the same: painted faces and simple souls. You, Alda dear, must be wondering why, and I am going to tell you the story which for centuries has been preserved by all the clowns of this world." He paused to gesture to a girl standing across from him. "Maria, honey, please bring me another cup of tea. Our story states that in the beginning everything was a space as solemn as the mouth of God, who later on with His silent breath created Adam and the first woman, Lilith. But very soon poor Lilith had to leave Paradise because, as you may know, she refused to put up with her husband. 'Your name is Adam, which means man made from clay,' she told him, 'so don't try to dominate me, because I too was made out of clay. You have no right to give me orders, inasmuch as you and I together share the light of the same moon and sun,' she added, before turning on her heels and leaving him alone in the garden. That is why God had to make another woman, this time out of Adam's rib, to keep him company amid all those animals and birds, which were not in his likeness and could never become a proper companion. How clever of the Creator to make a woman who was similar to Adam but not made of the same material, so that she would never feel the urge to rebel.

"You must remember from your Sunday-school classes that in the beginning was the space of forms. God had separated light and darkness to create day and night, making time itself his creation, circumscribed between dawn and twilight. After drawing the horizon over the waters, He divided the sky from the earth and the seas. So He gave us, to be more explicit, a space surrounded by limits: the sky above, the earth below; God Almighty up in heaven, and Adam, made in His likeness, down on earth. The birds, the fish and all the animals were put here so that man had his dominion over them, establishing a hierarchy and thereby fulfilling the expectations of God, who desired from man total obedience. On the other hand, Eve had been fabricated so that Adam was on top, both in word and flesh, in speech as well as copulation. Thus Paradise for her was a place of nothing but orders and commands, rules and prohibitions.

"It was then that the serpent showed up to speak to Eve. The serpent, with her infinite wisdom, had already come to the realization that Eve, as a woman, carried the seeds of rebellion, which is why, at the most propitious moment, she started extolling the sweetness of the apple. And when Eve – snake-bitten, so to speak – convinced Adam to take a bite of the forbidden fruit, Paradise burst into flames and violent lightning. In the midst of this turmoil, God named Sin as though it were another animal, and condemned Adam to earn his bread from the sweat of his brow, and decreed that Eve and her descendants would bring forth children in sorrow.

"But God did not know that His perfection was only human, and therefore subject to a margin of error. Which explains why He never suspected that, despite His clever craftsmanship, He had misplaced a small portion of primordial mud wherein light had not been separated from darkness.

"And there we were! At the precise moment when God pronounced sentence on Adam and Eve, causing Paradise to tremble, we clowns decided to emerge and populate the earth. Wearing our white faces and rainbow antennae, we squirted to the surface, and encountered a world created by a long-bearded old man which seemed to us a place of sadness, too orderly, and for each rule only two possible alternatives: punishment or reward. Festive and light-hearted, we danced to the river bank and cupped water in the palms of our hands to pour on the brown earth and ashes as we sang. Those were the first musical chords heard on this planet. It was then that, being true brothers and sisters, we started embracing each other, and as our hands were covered with wet earth and green grass and flower pollen, our gestures served to paint our bodies. Excited by all that colour, we transformed our eyes into unusual stars with the shape of inverted half moons or twinkling petals of carnations. 'We must invent laughter in the tragic world of the Law,' we all cried at once. And in a chorus of moving hands, we painted our lips in a big smile as white as the foam on the sea.

"Since then, dear Alda, clowns everywhere, men and women alike, have laughed their way through this black-and-white world where most people stand like unhappy pawns on the chessboard of power, stuck in a rut and waiting for permission to move."

The next day, Alda returned to the city, feeling different in body and soul. The heartfelt warmth of all those people persecuted by the dictator had left her with the sensation of having immersed herself in the healing waters of deep wisdom. And as if she had been baptized anew, she began to understand the world in terms of the evil forces inherent in power. It seemed to her now that her mother's violence arose from some emotional, oceanic depth, the currents of which drove her to desire total, exclusive control of her husband, who was constantly in other women's arms, whose idea of love was a succession of affairs which transgressed the sacred bonds of marriage. Or perhaps her father had not committed adultery as an act of personal freedom, but as a way to possess his wife by keeping her in a constant state of jealous fever. Staring at a poor hut on the road, Alda remembered that her father waited for his wife to beg before, with a man's air of superiority, he handed her the weekly allowance she needed to maintain the house.

If something like this can happen between two people, she thought, it must be even worse in the case of a whole country. She shivered as she recalled those moments when agonized screams penetrated the walls as she lay with Arreola. On entering or leaving the torture houses, she passed by closed doors, silent, as if no one inhabited the rooms. But during the time she had spent with Arreola, Alda occasionally made out muffled noises which resembled doves milling in a crowded coop and, on at least four occasions, strange, pain-filled shouts had pierced the day while Arreola laboured over her. Each time she had moaned louder, raising her anguished voice so that it might unite with the suffering of that unknown human being.

"Someone must put a stop to this shit," she told herself. Suddenly she heard once more Alicia reading that passage from the Bible on the day they had buried Deborah: "An enslaved people liberated by a woman's hand." She repeated the phrase several times, her eyes fixed on the green leaves shining from trees in the distance.

And that afternoon, amid the loud songs of Julieta, Alda read about Deborah, the prophetess, in one of the chapters from the Book of Judges. It recounted that the people of Israel had fallen under the power of the tyrant Jabin, King of Canaan, who had as General of his army a cruel man called Sisera. Devoid of freedom, forced to travel down the torturous avenues of enslavement, the Israelites suffered great torment under Sisera, being oppressed to such an extent that not even the taste of bread brought happiness to their hearts. At that time lived Deborah, a prophetess who judged and guided her people from a seat under a palm tree on Mount Ephraim. Bravery had disappeared during the darkness of oppression, but Deborah raised her head and her voice high, and in her vigour she became the mother of Israel because the Lord had chosen a new and miraculous way of making war, utilizing the bravery of a woman. Determined to save her people, Deborah sent for Barak, son of Abinoam, and commanded him to lead an army to Mount Tabor. She had decided to ambush Sisera in that place and force him to suffer defeat at the hands of a woman.

And Deborah's prophecy was fulfilled, although she did not meet the vanquished Sisera. When the evil General and his army were surprised by Barak's battalion, Sisera was horrified to see his soldiers falling before sharp Israeli knives, and he fled on foot. His flight led him to the tent of Jael, the wife of Heber the Kenite. "And Jael went out to meet Sisera," Alda said to herself, trying to memorize the lines, "and said unto him, 'Turn in, my lord, turn in to me; fear not.' And when he had turned in unto her into the tent, she covered him with a mantle. And he said unto her, 'Give me, I pray thee, a little water to drink, for I am thirsty.' And she opened a bottle of milk, and gave him drink, and covered him. Again he said unto her, 'Stand in the door of the tent, and it shall be, when any man doth come and enquire of thee, and say, "Is there any man here?" that thou shalt say, "No".' " Jael promised she would guard the entrance of the tent, but feeling compassion for the people of Israel and following the prophecy of a woman, she took a hammer and nail and went softly unto Sisera, and "smote the nail into his temples and drove it into the ground, for he was fast asleep and weary. So he died," Alda read, "gathering sleep with death."

The last paragraphs of that chapter detailed how forces from heaven had inspired Deborah to defeat tyranny, that the stars had led Jael to kill Sisera, that by piercing his temples she made freedom shine once more, as bright as the sun in the east. And Alda, listening to Julieta singing with a voice full of pain that their land had been stripped of God's kindness, imagined that the death of the Benefactor of the Republic could also occur through divine forces and the brave deeds of a woman.

Upon his return from the north, Alda found Arreola pensive, almost taciturn. He made love to her with intense passion, whispering repeatedly that he could not get her body out of his mind, then fell silent.

"You look worried," she said, kissing him.

"Not worried, no. It's just that one orders things so carefully and all of a sudden they take a different course, as if, like wilful children, they wanted to disobey."

She stroked his neck. "That's because you organize so many activities. It's incredible, really," she consoled him with that tone of admiration he liked so well.

"You're right. This afternoon, there's a meeting of the High Command where they will discuss my project to cordon off those streets around the shanty towns." He clamped his lips shut and grimaced. "Those subversive elements must be isolated."

"Will the Benefactor be at the meeting? How fantastic if he is there so that he can realize at last that you are the most valuable officer in the entire army."

"I don't think he plans to attend. He has been very busy of late because things get out of control and don't work out as planned. He's beginning to feel that people don't understand his lofty goals. As a result, yesterday he decided to call for a weekly gathering in his honour, to allow civilians the privilege of his presence. The first such conference will take place this Friday in front of the main balcony of his palace, and it wouldn't be a bad idea for you to show up, along with the other women from your barrio."

"But they are always so busy," Alda murmured as she nibbled his ear, stroking his penis as she felt her panic rising, trying to coax him into an erection which would soon make him forget this threatening idea.

But even though he grew hard, his one-track mind failed to swerve into sexuality. "There are many of you, eighty-four to be exact. At least that was the number computerized at the detention camp, and I doubt this total has changed much either way, since populations don't demonstrate severe fluctuations except during war or plague or other calamities. The gathering will start at four o'clock in the afternoon, and the guests will be advised to be there at three. You and your friends will stand in the first two lines, which I will reserve for you."

"Sensational," she moaned, fondling him in vain now. "It will be marvellous to listen to the Benefactor and see him in person while he speaks. The girls are going to be so excited! Thank you, my love, you're so generous," she said breathlessly, crawling up to straddle his body and holding a breast to his mouth.

And although the Colonel closed his eyes as he sucked her nipple, caressing her and then lifting her upon him, for the first time Alda sensed that he was growing tired of her. If she was going to act, it would have to be soon.

After consulting Doña Carolina, who gave her permission, Alda arranged a meeting with the other women living in the street of night to inform them that it was absolutely imperative for them to attend the dictator's rally.

"Girls," she told them, "we don't have any choice. Señora Leonora says that if we refuse to go, we not only run the risk of another military raid and a vacation in a detention camp, but also, and which would be worse, Arreola might suspect that some of us are working for the Resistance."

"Exactly!" Meche said angrily. "And we can't risk being taken prisoners because this time they will kill us all for sure!"

Patoja hit the table and brushed the hair from her face. "Let them kill us! I'm not going to pay my respects to that evil bastard, who should be burning in hell! If we go to that meeting, Deborah will turn in her grave and weep with shame!"

Julieta held up her hands. "I know, my special friends, that I don't belong to your, uh, trade union, but if you'll allow me an opinion, I think it's obvious that the Colonel wants us to go in order to give the impression that his boss is as popular as Julio Iglesias – and this is a good sign, because it means that people are starting to resist. Sooner or later, the oppressed rebel. This I know better than any of you, because I come from the north, my beloved land of interminable suffering and brave struggles. That is why, my sisters, we have to discuss this matter strictly as a political act."

A voice rose in sharp staccato. "Fuck off with your politics, Julieta! Whores have never had anything to do with politics!"

Julieta nodded in agreement. "That's how it was in the past, Adelita, but the forces of history alter people's lives whether they like it or not, rich or poor, maiden or whore."

"Definitely!" Alda broke in. "Absolutely!" She thought of how much her own life had changed since the time they had spent in the detention camp. "Julieta is right. All of us must go so that no one becomes suspicious. Only in this way will we be able to continue helping Señora Leonora and her comrades in the Resistance."

"Yes! You've hit the nail on the head!" Julieta said with an approving smile. "That's the right strategy."

Adela was still in a critical mood. "Here you are again with your damned strategies! For Julieta everything is strategies, have you noticed?"

"But Julieta is right, Adelita," Meche intervened. "Alda's plan for us to go is a strategy, like those plans they make in adventure movies."

Adela turned to her in scorn. "And this moron, always comparing everything with some damn matinée, my God!" She swung back on Julieta. "What a joke. Where did you come up with the idiotic idea that people change along with history? That's dumber than Meche!"

"People don't change," Julieta said. "And they don't get smarter. The evil grow old, wear out, and they can't fuck over people the way they used to. It doesn't matter generally, there's always a substitute waiting in the wings. The good rebel and are usually killed. That's history: wave after wave of the same water in which some bathe and others drown. But remember this: people die, not ideas."

On Friday afternoon the women of the street of night came out of their houses dressed in their best, least-seductive finery. Upon arriving at the front gate of the palace, Alda spoke to a guard and they were allowed to enter the grounds and form the two front lines below the balcony. They stood up straight and simulated an attitude of respect, ignoring the nearby soldiers who kept leering at them and laughing among themselves. At four o'clock sharp the conductor of the army band raised his baton, and the musicians' instruments broke into a strident military march which blared loudly out of speakers wired to the tree branches on either side of the plaza and bolted next to various high windows in the surrounding buildings. As the last notes rose through a crescendo and died, two tall and powerfully built soldiers (who had been standing at attention but examining the crowd beneath them during the band's performance) about-faced and opened the towering doors to the main balcony.

A trumpet pierced the afternoon with high, held notes as the Benefactor and his wife appeared, he wearing a white uniform with a bemedalled and starred red and blue sash across his chest, she dressed in a blue two-piece suit that tried but failed to complement her dumpy figure. Arm in arm, they walked to the rail with solemn, measured steps (their pace funereal, as if it were the prelude to a medieval minuet) whereupon the General raised his arms to the programmed roaring applause and smiled like a crocodile watching baby deer approach a waterhole. He stroked his white moustache self-consciously as he waited for the din to subside, noticing a fleet of school buses parked near the plaza and the schoolchildren waving flags and banners as their teachers had been advised to instruct them. He waited another half a minute, nodding his head left and right to acknowledge the cheering factory workers who had been given one new shoe to attend, the other to be handed out after the rally. Then he adjusted the microphone and cleared his throat several times to give them time to wind down. At last, when the crowd quieted, he removed a sheaf of papers from the inside pocket of his tunic, laid them on the podium, and began speaking in his high-pitched, belligerent voice.

"Fellow citizens," he said as though it were an accusation, "I have invited you here this afternoon to celebrate our victory over the forces of evil. During the last twelve years, I have often pointed out that to live in our Fatherland has become an exceptional privilege. Never could this be more true than today. Thanks to the arduous efforts of our noble security troops, our nation is the only spot in this hemisphere where order and progress truly flourish hand in hand, for the good of all citizens. Poverty and misery have all but disappeared . . ."

"Yeah," a whore said softly, "they starved to death."

". . . and crime is almost non-existent now that those outlaws who sought to make our land the prey of disorder have either been eliminated or exiled to other countries more tolerant of traitors . . ."

"Sure," a fat woman near Alda muttered. "He sent them to Argentina, where the military drugged them and threw them out of airplanes into the sea."

Alda gave her a furious look and whispered, "For God's sake, shut up! You want the soldiers to lock us up again?"

" . . . If you'll permit me to repeat myself, this country, which flourishes through order and progress, only smiles on those who are prepared to obey our laws and co-operate with our goals, to respect our will, which after all is the will of the people, and which has led our Fatherland to the enviable role of a strong and law-abiding nation . . ."

"Translation:" a whore chuckled, "eat shit and compliment the chef."

". . . But the light of the present must not be allowed to cloud our vision of the shadows of the past. Those who do not like our system are free to go. We would prefer that they leave; it would be in their best interests, for we do not intend to tolerate dissent. We must never forget that our country found itself beset with the terrible plague of communism, led by insidious Marxists who caused us to fall into a terrible darkness. We must never forget the constant and indiscriminate aggression of those leftists, real enemies of all that is good, who deserve our most intense repudiation. And we must never forget, my fellow citizens," he slammed his fist on the podium and winced with pain before bellowing, "we must never forget that the enemy is still with us!"

As the crowd roared to its feet, the woman near Alda said angrily, "That same old song and dance. *El enemigo todavía está con nosotros*. Number one on their hit parade. I'll tell you about that sorry line of shit. I had a customer last month, a *carabinero*, a policeman who went to the pharmacy for a prescription. As he was going in, he ran into two guys coming out who had just robbed the place. He pulled his gun on them and was about to shoot when one of the guys flashed a badge at him. Get this: it was the secret police, out robbing a store, to keep the people thinking that *el enemigo todavía está con nosotros*. What a pile of crap!"

". . . Our country has no desire to experience another odious adventure with communism. For this reason, my fellow countrymen, you who are gathered here to celebrate so many of our victories, we must remain alert, aware of the harmful past, and resolved to defend ourselves against the disease of Marxism. But have no fear of the future. Our military forces, inspired by divine providence, those soldiers who rescued us from chaos, have an iron will, forged in steel and dedicated to preserving our nation. Because light must always defeat darkness, just as the sun defeats the moon each morning to allow day to begin." He paused to acknowledge a brief burst of clapping and watched a number of officers and enlisted men rise to their feet, attempting to create a standing ovation out of polite applause. "A foreign journalist recently asked me if I felt satisfied with my work and my mission. I told him to look around, visit the towns and villages, drive down any street in Santiago and ask the people if they were happier with this administration than with the previous one . . ."

"Better tell him to duck when he asks, though," a whore said with a laugh.

". . . I explained to this reporter that I was merely a warrior, not unlike a gladiator fighting lions in the Coliseum, except that the other side was almost out of lions." He waited for the laughter, as his speechwriter had indicated in the margin, shrugging his shoulder for emphasis as he had seen Mussolini do in old film footage. "But aside from my duties as a gladiator, I have been, and will continue to be, the architect of our destiny, which lies on the path of peace in order, and order in tranquillity!" He punctuated this remark by slapping his fist into his open palm, and after a moment raised his hand to still the applause.

"It's time now to speak of the progress we have made." He turned a page carelessly and watched in amazement as it wafted upwards and sailed off the balcony like a paper plane. He turned red in embarrassment and had trouble getting started again. "It's, uh, about time we take a moment to, uh, list those achievements which, like street lamps installed by the electric company, illuminate our Fatherland from the Atacama to Tierra del Fuego, and which have been the beacon pointing the way to our future. To begin with, from the agrarian sector to the unions of retired workers, this country – under my direction – has taken giant steps in the re-distribution of land and cost-of-living adjustments to various pension funds . . ."

"The military got the pick of confiscated estates," Patoja, who was standing behind Meche, said contemptuously. "*Their* pensions were trebled."

". . . In the urban sector I issued several orders pursuant to rejuvenating our cities. My first directive was to implement the necessary arrangements to start new housing construction in hundreds of localities, so that the poor could become owners instead of tenants." He waited for the applause, scanning the crowd, recognizing several officers in plain clothes clapping wildly and urging their neighbours to join in. "My second directive was to rebuild the sewage systems. We will concentrate our efforts in the major cities at first, but in time our engineers will overhaul the sanitation problems in every town and village in our country . . ."

"Good idea," a whore with a deep voice pointed out. "We're living in shit up to our noses; maybe he can fix that while he's at it."

". . . In addition, one of my goals from the beginning was to install modern gymnasiums in all our schools, so that the sons of the Fatherland might grow up strong and healthy. Some months ago I even established a fund for scholarships to be awarded to our most outstanding students in gymnastics, and I have no doubt that within a very few years this programme will lead to our nation being distinguished by our own entrants in the Olympic Games!" The Benefactor flashed that savage smile of his at the cheering crowd. But he was tired of reading, bored with the upturned faces of so many people transported to his palace in military trucks, bribed or threatened to pay homage to him. He thumbed through the remaining pages, moving his lips as he counted. Enough, he decided. Time to cut to the chase. He hooked his wife's arm and pulled her to his side. She said a silent prayer as she realized that he was about to embark on one of his famous, usually tongue-tied, extemporaneous monologues that made him look so foolish and with imitations of which certain subversive nightclub comedians brought the house down.

"Before concluding this afternoon," the Benefactor asserted, "before we go our separate ways, it would be remiss if I failed to mention the invaluable moral support I have received from my adoring wife." His wife gave him a look and he stopped, realizing his error, then added, "Adorable wife, I mean. Because behind every king there is a queen, no? What would become of a man if he didn't have a woman to lie on, uh, to rely on? *Sí*, our masculine intelligence needs a feminine heart to establish and rekindle our humanity. Women were born to be mothers. There is no more sacred duty in this world than motherhood! And so, for all you mothers out there, I salute you!" His wife applauded as well, smiling up at him and praying that he would end it soon. "Remember the saying: a mother's love is an abyss too wide to be measured. Due to our mental superiority, we men are predestined to forge the new roads of civilization, whereas women, with their infinite capacity for love, must meanwhile with their fragile hands build the nest that we call our home. The principal role of the weaker sex is, and will for ever be, to provide men with a refuge, a soft pillow on which to rest after their daily battles . . ."

"Or in his case," Julieta said maliciously, "a nice fat set of sagging tits."

The Benefactor pointed a finger and let it track from right to left. "You women out there, do not forget for one instant that God sent you to this world to be the true angels of the house. Angels, *sí*, because women reflect the purity of the Virgin Mary, which is why all women should be put on a pedestal. The insurmountable genius August Comte wrote this, in French, of course, a long time ago, and I, in homage to his memorable words" – he stared with affection at the whores of the street of night standing below him – "I tell the women who have graced us with their presence this afternoon that they must continue to cultivate the radiant pearl of innocence and virtue which, even from this balcony, I see shining in the eyes of each of you." The Benefactor was moved; he wiped his eyes, held out his hands. "My fellow countrymen, before I leave you today, I want to assure you that I shall continue to advance towards my goal of reconstructing our nation until my last breath, if need be. And now, since my duties and obligations leave me little time for social gatherings, I must say goodbye, invoking the Lord Almighty, in whose name I proudly proclaim: LONG LIVE OUR FATHERLAND!"

Raising both arms high like Nixon, he waved to the crowd, rejoicing in the acclamation that seemed to confirm his leadership.

Filled with pride, he did an about-face and bumped squarely into his wife, who stumbled into an aide, knocking his hat off. Recovering himself, the Benefactor offered her his arm and, aiming at her cheek, kissed her ear as they left the balcony.

Elbowing and pushing their way out of the crowd, Alda and her companions left the square where many people, now that the secret service agents had momentarily forgotten them, milled around with serious, drawn faces, many showing grief and desperation, faces thin from hunger, faces staring at worn-out shoes, faces whose eyes registered impotence and anger and betrayal and a need to shout, faces with the look of hatred one sees in the eyes of caged animals in a zoo.

Alda and the others were walking past the Avenue of the Heroes when Julieta gave voice to their frustration and rage by saying, "I'm ashamed to admit that that monstrous buffoon is a member of my species. What he deserves," she announced to no one in particular, "what we should really do, is burn the bastard when we get home."

"For the love of God, Julieta," Meche complained, "what do you mean? How can we burn him when he's taking a nap in his bedroom surrounded by guards?"

"No stupid," Julieta said good-naturedly. "I'm talking about an exorcism?"

"An exor-what?" Patoja asked. "Shit, what a word!"

"Ah," Meche said contentedly. "I know what you're talking about. You mean like in church, when the priest drives out the devil."

"Give the girl a coconut," Julieta laughed. "The rest of you will have to wait until we get home. But listen, my beauties, before you put on your working uniforms, before the clients arrive, I want you to meet me at Deborah's tomb. We'll have the ceremony there, to cheer up our little Deborah. Bring all the dirty rags you can find. I'll take care of the rest."

The women arrived at Deborah's memorial. They had managed to fill several plastic bin bags with dirty dishcloths, dusters and old clothes. Julieta motioned for them to dump the mess into a metal barrel in which she had just stacked some kindling. Once the women had tossed their loads into the container, she made the sign of the cross and picked up a five-gallon can of gasoline. She poured the pungent liquid over the mound of rags, singing an incantation in a loud voice. Three times she raised her face to the heavens and lowered it. Then she struck a match and lit the gasoline. The bonfire burst into flames, leaping upwards and producing a cloud of dark smoke. Julieta ordered the women to be silent by touching a finger to her lips. Next, slapping her thigh three times with her left hand, she began a strange dance, hopping around the flames, whose heat had begun to melt the lipsticked insults against the dictator on the wall where Deborah's epitaph had been inscribed. Suddenly Julieta stopped, raising her arms high, her face contorted and red from the heat.

"Die!" she screamed. "Die once and for all, you devil from hell!" She lowered her head and sank to her knees, her voice falling to a whisper as she chanted, "Die . . . die . . . die . . ."

". . . Die," echoed the other women, their voices a low murmur.

At that moment they heard Deborah rejoicing, heard her laughter vibrating against the wall where lipstick grease dripped down like oddly shaped trails of menstrual blood.

Julieta rose slowly from the concrete, her eyes burning into the women, her breasts showing through the unbuttoned blouse, holding her stomach as though she were about to give birth. She smiled, turning to the flames, and put her hands on her hips before spitting on the fire, which miraculously began to die, going out gradually and leaving only a soft bed of smoking coals by the kerb.

"Clean up the ashes and wash the street with plenty of water, Patoja," Julieta said in a hoarse voice. She buttoned her blouse before turning around and walking away, her voice breaking into one of her favourite love songs. The women followed her, many of them looking dazed, some of them holding hands. The feeling of repugnance and defilement produced by the dictator had been purged from their souls.

From that afternoon on, every time the women of the street of night were forced to attend a rally for the Benefactor of the Republic, Julieta conducted the ritual of flames.

Apart from these episodic interruptions, the street remained as indolent as the bed of a sluggish river, flowing with the songs of Julieta, the hushed conversations of Meche and Roberto, the arguments and intimate chatter of Martina and Señora Rosa, and the clack-clack of Alda's heels as she left the house to meet Colonel Arreola.

Then one Wednesday afternoon as Jairo approached the corner where he customarily played his music grinder, Alda and Meche ran out of the house to greet him.

"Hey, *hombre*. Tell me, is there any hope for my broken heart?" Alda asked in a joking voice, using the coded phrase they had established on that first day Jairo had arrived in the street of night.

But Jairo looked worried. "Ay, Aldita – I'm afraid the fortune-telling will have to be postponed until next week."

Meche was troubled. "But why, Jairo? Is something wrong?"

Jairo shrugged his shoulders and said, "Roberto has been sick in bed for four days now, and they have decided to suspend all messages until he recovers."

"What's wrong with him?" Meche asked anxiously. "Is it serious?"

"No, Señorita Meche. Don't worry your pretty head. It's only a case of the flu, but even so, he won't be able to come this week." He gave Meche a look of fatherly affection, then exchanged a more sober glance with Alda. Taking a fortune card from his shirt pocket, he wrote several sentences and handed it to Meche. "Here.

The poor boy is so lonely . . . visit him, make him feel better. This is his address."

Meche ran back to the house to ask Doña Carolina's permission. Alda said goodbye to Jairo and then went to Meche's room, where she pulled her close and advised her to be discreet. Half an hour later Meche almost waltzed to the bus stop, feeling like a teenager on her own for the first time, heading for a meeting with a new beau.

She arrived at the address without incident and rang the bell, fluffing her hair while she waited. A young woman opened the door and looked at her with mistrust.

"Roberto lives in that room behind the main house," she told Meche, pointing to a side path. "Go around the garden and walk on in. We've left the door unlocked in case he needs something in the middle of the night."

With her heart racing, Meche opened the rustic wooden door and found herself in a dimly lit room with little adornment save a bookcase on her left, on one shelf of which there was the enlarged photograph of a young woman with light-coloured eyes who was smiling flirtatiously. In the corner down from the bookcase she saw a surprised Roberto trying to sit up in bed to greet her.

"No, don't move. You must conserve your strength. Don Jairo gave me your address, and I decided to come and keep you company for a while. Is that all right?"

He lay back, smiling weakly. "Of course it's okay. I've had a fever for four days running. God, how boring it is to be sick."

"True. When my grandma fell sick she always complained that lying in bed for too long a time made people wither like flowers." Her eyes fell on a pitcher and glass on the night table. "Would you like some water?"

"Yes, please. But sit down," he said, taking both of her hands in his.

She sat on the edge of the bed and stroked his cheeks with that tenderness that overflowed in her heart every time they were together. And for the first time they kissed long and deeply, without the accompanying background of raucous voices and female laughter that had up to now always punctuated their caresses.

Roberto ran a hand through her hair. "What time do you have to go back?"

Meche kissed his hand. "That's up to you. Doña Carolina told me to take all the time I wanted."

The look in his eyes was as soft and gentle as his hand on her hair. "I never told you that I spent seven months in a detention camp. The soldiers would sometimes jerk open our cell doors after midnight . . . they tied our hands and dragged us to the patio, beating us with clubs as we walked barefoot across concrete that had recently been hosed down, telling us we were going to be shot. They would blindfold our eyes, cursing us with insults about our parents, our sisters, the wives of the married men, and in the middle of these insults, they dragged us to the wall and slammed our backs against it. They even gave the order to shoot – ready, aim, fire! – but it was all a game of pretend, a game only they enjoyed, because they took pleasure in terrifying us. When they released me and I returned to my normal life, I found that I wasn't normal any more . . . I found that I could not fall asleep. It was impossible, because once my eyes closed, I lay there waiting for the soldiers to burst into my room and kick me out of bed. It was impossible, until I discovered that I could sleep if I left the radio on. Absurd, isn't it? But it's true, the voices of radio announcers, both men and women, were like a sedative, a tranquillizer; it was as if the ads for Escudo beer and Palmolive soap assured me that I was far away from that purgatory created by countrymen for countrymen. So, if it doesn't bother you too much to sleep with the radio on, you could spend the night here."

Meche accepted, wiping away her tears. They lay together for the next two hours, kissing and touching but going no further. Then Roberto turned on the radio and in a few minutes drifted off.

She waited for his breathing to assume that rhythm of deep sleep, then she sat up quietly and stared at the young woman in the photograph. Moonlight played on the stranger's features, and it occurred to Meche that Roberto's kisses had united her with this other woman, as if they were both somehow the same person; and suddenly the lips in the photograph seemed to be smiling, the light-coloured eyes staring at Meche with an expression of profound companionship, their message indisputably clear: we are one, I live in you, my love is yours, prolonged beyond death. Meche turned to caress Roberto's feverish back, remembering the texture on the tips of her fingers of the magnolias which grew in the cemetery next to her village. In a few moments, smiling and despite the radio, she slipped into a deep and dreamless slumber.

The following morning she surfaced through sleep hearing, as though under water, the harmony of a far-off women's choir while someone nibbled at her neck and strange but gentle hands explored her naked body. Opening her eyes, she saw Roberto, felt his lips cover hers, his body sliding against her, feverish but not from any illness, while the voice of a priest began the mass; her body hot now, too, like a lake in the rainforest during a summer shower; her lips in his hair, raising up over him to offer her naked breasts, which he took in his mouth like a starving infant; and for the first time she let her hands travel down his hard body, her fingers softly combing the dense foliage of his pubic hair before they folded like petals around his thick erection. With a moan, Roberto turned her on her back and drove into her deep and hard at the moment when the priest's monotonous Latin ceased and the choir lifted their voices into another hymn; riding her even harder now, frenzied, as if his passion were a source of pain, grunting not from love but from the lash, his body wild and plunging, his tears falling on her face, as if in grief instead of delight at the end of his long and self-imposed imprisonment; she taking his head in her hands to kiss his tears away, her eyes catching sight of his dead beloved, whispering in Roberto's ear: "We are both here to love you for ever, my darling." He stiffened and slammed into her one last time, exploding as she whispered over and over, "For ever . . . for ever . . . for ever . . ." And then it took her as an organ crashed into a series of chords and the choir voices rose distortedly over the loudspeakers of an unknown church; took her by surprise and carried her along like a tide, gasping for breath and groaning in unbelievable pleasure; pulling her along with him through a nest of heavy sea anemones and a cloud of kelp that soothed her burning body with silken tendrils; locked as one now, joined on this exquisite journey, rolling on the bed as if it were soft sand, still feasting on each other's lips as the brightly coloured lights went dim, falling as they fell into a lethargy of shared nothingness, the only kind of void where loneliness does not exist.

Roberto tightened his arms around her, breaking into a sudden fit of laughter. Meche realized that this was the first time she had seen him truly happy.

He raised up, arching his back, and grinned at her. "I hope you're aware that we made love throughout the entire mass."

"I know," she said, feeling a pang of sadness as he receded inside her. "It was the seven o'clock service. They always broadcast it." She hit him on the shoulder. "We are guilty of committing an act of sacrilege."

"You think so?" he asked as he kissed her. "How can so much love be sacrilegious, my darling?"

"I have a confession to make. I've loved you from the first moment I saw you."

"I felt the same way. But I didn't recognize my love at first, for so long I've been stumbling around like a man in a fog. I think I was crazy for a while. But not any more. Can you come back and stay the night with me?"

"I'll find a way," she promised him.

The first thing she did upon arriving back at her house was to go to Alda's room and tell her what had happened. She recounted every detail, her eyes alive with joy, which made her, Alda thought, even more beautiful.

"Christ, that's really wonderful, sweetie," Alda said. She embraced Meche, adding, "I'm truly happy for you. Now, let's go celebrate with Martina." She took her by the arm. "Because this definitely calls for a drink."

In Martina's room the three of them linked arms and made a toast to Meche and to each other, because this was their first moment of happiness since they had become friends.

"It's like magic to make love to someone you love, *huaina*," Martina said. "It's one of the few times God smiles on a woman." The old woman sighed and emptied her glass. "And though most of my life's been as bitter as a bad apple, He's smiled on me twice."

Alda filled her glass with rum. "You were pretty lucky, I'd say, Martina. My only true love left me and sailed off into the sunset for ever."

"Aldita!" Meche, already tipsy, blurted out. "Now I understand what you meant when you told us that night at the detention camp that losing your virginity was like being in a shower of fireworks!"

"More than that, baby," Alda assured her. "Explosions of colour like a rainbow of comets, jungle sounds and jungle heat, music crashing all around like huge waves, birds fluttering against you with silky feathers. Kiss my arse, love is a god-damned miracle!"

Martina licked her lips, the rum loosening her tongue. "Well, I don't know about the feathers, but the rest sounds familiar. Love hits everybody in different ways. For me, it was trees. Maybe because I spent so much of my girlhood in the south. I remember it was like walking in a forest full of big trees, giants, so high they blocked out the sun, and yet the shade was warm, not hot but comfortable, like the hide of a horse after a ride. But even bigger than the trees was that lost feeling of being empty as a graveyard and the hurt inside when fate took my sweethearts away. *Ay, Dios*. You should have seen my Juan Manuel . . . he was such a kind man, and he adored me, but of course that evil bastard had already put a curse on me after I ran away from him, and that was that. Pour me another shot, *huaina*," she told Alda, pointing at her glass. "I'm in the mood for talking." She made a face. "Shit, I forgot – you already know about what happened to Juan Manuel."

"But you never told us anything about your other lover, Señora Martina," Meche said.

"I've tried to forget him," Martina said. "Put it out of my mind. You see, he didn't die."

"Oh, shit," Alda exclaimed with remorse, "don't tell me it was that guy we had that fight about the first time we met!"

"Hell, no!" Martina said indignantly. "I didn't even like that little fart. But let's be honest: when I met him I was over the hill, and it flattered me to think he might be interested. I wasn't mad at you, Aldita, I was pissed off at old age. I wanted to hit my mirror, but I hit you instead." She drained the glass and lit a cigarette. "Shit, the booze is getting to me. Stick around, I may tell you my life story."

Alda and Meche laughed and embraced her like daughters. "Don't stop now," Alda urged her. "You're getting to the good part."

Martina dropped her cigarette and nearly lost her balance stamping it out. "What the hell! My mamma always said it's no use taking secrets to your grave. After Juan Manuel died I spent nearly three years of my life taking care of someone else's children in the main house of a hacienda in the south. The kids were cute, though, and I loved them dearly. Lord, the oldest must be fifty by now, but I'll wager he hasn't forgotten his old nanny, or the ghost stories I used to tell him by candlelight after I tucked him in. Then one day my boss's father showed up, come from somewhere in Europe, and before he'd unpacked his bags he was trying to get my drawers off – followed me around like a dog on heat, old and ugly and smelly, like that dirty prick the devil sent to me as a husband. So one night I just stuffed my things in a pillowcase and hit the road; actually, I followed the paths along the railroad tracks, wearing out my shoes and heading nowhere in particular. Man, I was a brave little filly in those days, when my legs were young and strong, and the rest of me wasn't bad either! I could have set up shop in a dozen villages, but something inside my heart told me to keep going. So I just wiggled my bottom at them and went on. I remember walking for two days without seeing so much as a shithouse. To make things worse, it was so hot you could've fried an egg on the rails."

"You must have been sweating like a sinner in church," Alda said innocently.

Martina wagged a finger at her. "It wasn't funny, *niña*. I was terrified of fainting and falling on the railroad tracks. Come to think of it, that would have been the best thing for me."

"*Ayayay*," Alda scolded her. "Don't be so melodramatic, Señora Martina." She pulled the cork from the rum and tossed it out of the window. "Here, have another drink."

Martina nodded, slurring her words as she said, "Yeah. A little more hair of the dog that bit me. I don't remember the last time I got plastered. Anyway, along with the heat, I was also starving to death. Weak as a worm. Then I saw the tents, up ahead quite a way. At first I thought I was going crazy, that the thirst and hunger had baked my brain. But they were real tents, I saw that as I came closer. They belonged to a group of gypsies, who took me in. Just like that. I guess they thought I was an outcast like them. Gypsies are good people, but very fussy when it comes to blood lines. Too damned fussy. But I didn't know that then. I spent the first night with the women, and the next day I met Danilo, the best-looking man I ever saw, tall and broad-shouldered, strong as an oak tree. When he made love to me – and he had the longest, thickest cock I ever felt, so hard I thought it was made of oak, too! – when he shoved that monster into me, I closed my eyes and saw all the stars in heaven, but it was like looking at them in an earthquake, only it was my arse and not the ground that was shaking; and, God forgive me, I felt like a beast being fucked in the Garden of Eden. But one day the oldest gypsy woman, the headman's wife or something, she took me to the pond where they washed clothes and told me I had to leave. Otherwise, she said, Danilo would be expelled from the tribe. 'If you truly love him, young lady, you will go, now,' the old bitch told me. This was over forty years ago, but I still remember her saying, 'We gypsies have to follow our customs and speak our own language, or our hearts will go dry. So if you don't want Danilo to die with grief, please leave right away.' So I picked up my pack and started down the road again, the one that led me here. In between, my life has been shit. Until I met the two of you, who have given me so much love."

Martina regarded Meche and Alda with half-closed eyes, weaving gently back and forth. Looking towards the kitchen, she said in a loud voice, "It's true I never had any cubs of my own, Señora Rosa, but you can see that these two girls are the same as daughters to me."

Alda took her arm and caressed her wispy, grey-white hair. "You'd better take a nap, Señora Martina. You'll have to start dinner in a couple of hours."

"Oh, shit! You're right, my girl. If I don't sleep off this rum, I'll be mixing things up arse over backwards, breading the fish with chilli beans."

She was still laughing as Alda covered her ancient body with a blanket. Meche stood at the foot of her bed, touched because Martina's wrinkled eyelids in their sunken dark orbits reminded her of two withered roses.

At twilight, Meche took a bath with some special herbs that Julieta sold her. She chose her lingerie as if she were preparing a trousseau for her wedding night. Buoyed with happiness, she walked to the bus stop carrying a bunch of white carnations and a paper box containing the dinner she was planning to serve Roberto.

Out of politeness, she knocked at the door to the main house and was startled to see the same woman open it, her face a mask of grief and her eyes red from crying.

"Señorita, *por Dios*!" the woman cried to Meche. "They've taken Roberto prisoner!"

Meche felt a stab of pain in her chest that left her short of breath and dizzy. "Who . . . who took him away?"

The woman threw up her hands. "Who do you think? They came around four o'clock. Dressed in civilian clothes. I stood by the window and watched them creeping through the garden, knocking down my plants and stepping on the flowers. I came out shouting after them, hoping to warn Roberto and give him time to get away, but he was too sick to move and they were all over him before I could get the words out of my mouth. They beat him as he lay in bed and dragged him out without allowing him to dress . . . with this cold, and him so sick. One of them slapped me when I told him Roberto hadn't done anything wrong. They threatened to come back for me if I didn't shut up, but, my God, señorita, Roberto lived out there for four years, and he was never a bother; always so loving and kind to our children. And my husband is so frightened! He says we'll be on their blacklist now, that we may have to go away before they return to take us. Trouble is, we've no place to go, we're poor; at least those with money can take a plane and escape from their claws. What a disaster, God protect us! Since the dictator came to power, señorita, I've felt such anguish, seen so much suffering, that I've come to wonder why we were born, only to be condemned to live in terror, fearing prison or torture or death squads climbing over the walls at night, fearing for our lives even when we sit down to eat what little food there is. Here in our barrio, the helicopters fly overhead like buzzards, three, four times a week, day and night, at night inspecting the street with searchlights; and the noise! The dogs go crazy, barking and bellowing as if our fear had infected them." Seeing Meche's tears, she embraced her. "Forgive me for running on. See if you can find a way to save Roberto, because we can't get involved

– we have to protect our children, if we can. That's why we haven't worked with the Resistance for over two years now."

Meche said goodbye and, still weeping, walked off in a daze. She went down streets well lit by those powerful street-lamps the dictator had ordered installed as part of his project to create the façade of progress; it was both cruel and ironic, she felt, that the lights illuminated old run-down houses, silent grey shapes that made her feel as dismal as if she were walking past a line of mortuaries. Further on, she came to a barrio without any street-lights whatsoever, dark and uninviting, where life was lived in perpetual shadow, a haunt of muggers and criminals of every kind, and she found herself wishing that one of the beasts that lived in this jungle would attack her and relieve her of this pain that was sewing stitches in her heart. She stumbled and stopped by a tree, leaning against it while she cried with her face raised to the night.

After a moment she noticed in the distance a series of tiny orange lights, flickering and weaving as though someone were sending messages with little torches. She looked at her hands and discovered that, absurdly, she was still clutching the carnations and the box of food. Dropping them at her feet, she went off towards the light. At the corner she came upon a scene she would never forget: a narrow street lined on both sides by candles placed intermittently along each kerb, their frail glow forming two boundaries, like the lights that demarcate an airport runway. "One candle for each of our dead, comrade," a young man whispered to Meche as he walked by, grazing her arm with his elbow. The pavements were full of people: men, women, children, crowded together like shoppers but quiet, speaking in whispers, their voices muffled but rising occasionally to pronounce words of protest against the dictator.

Meche did not return to the street of night until dawn. She came into the kitchen with a lost look in her eyes and stood by the sink, trembling. Alda left off dancing with a young suitor and ran to meet her. She bit her lips on hearing the news. Recognizing

Meche's exhaustion, she led her to Martina's room, where both women undressed the girl and put her to bed. They sat beside her, stroking her hair and arms until she recovered some strength and was able to speak.

"They are going to kill him and I won't even know where his grave is. They'll burn his body or throw it into the sea like they always do with rebels. Filthy bastards, they deny us everything, even the bones of our dead. That's all I've been able to think about since that lady told me they had arrested Roberto. I feel empty, drained of blood."

"Cheer up, Mechecita," Alda consoled her. "It's probably just a routine imprisonment. It happens all the time, like it did with us. The odds are they'll set him free in a couple of days."

"No!" Meche said furiously. "Stop treating me like a child! That's what you two have done since that night we met at the detention camp. But you're wrong; I'm not a naive simpleton, not at all, and I know perfectly well what's going to happen to Roberto, so stop trying to kid me. We all know that right now they are beating the shit out of him, interrogating him 'in seriousness', as they like to put it, punching that face I love so much, covering his lovely body with bruises, and there's not a god-damned thing anyone can do to help him!"

"We could pray," Martina said, wiping her eyes. "The three of us could kneel and ask God for help, my child. You're the one, *huainita*, who always says God protects us all."

"I don't believe any more!" Meche screamed into her pillow. "Not in God or the Virgin Mary or the saints, or the power of goodness. Goodness is too vulnerable. In this country, goodness is like a lamb surrounded by wolves."

Alda patted her head. "Be strong, honey. Come on, help me think. Tomorrow I have to see Arreola. Maybe I could talk to him."

"What for?" Meche demanded. "So that he'll discover that you're part of the Resistance too?"

"You could go and talk to Señora Leonora," Martina suggested. "Right now, tonight. She'd know what to do."

"You don't understand," Meche said in a dull voice. "No one in this world can help Roberto now."

Martina's face brightened. "Maybe Señora Rosa could come up with something! She has power over the living."

"But not over the dictator who runs this country," Meche said. "No, Señora Martina, the dead can't help us either. We have some other problems to worry about as well, Alda. If they make Roberto talk, they'll find out about us, and we'll both be arrested. What then?"

Martina made the sign of the cross. "Holy shit, you'd better beat it, girls. Find another city. Come on, get your stuff together and hit the road. The sooner the better."

Meche took her hand. "If we go, you go with us."

"What's the use of dragging these old bones along?" Martina said. "You're young, both of you, and you can change with the weather. I'm too old to change my spots. Remember, Alda, when we were on that train coming back from the prison camp? You said that the three of us were like the earth, the water and the moon – you meant our friendship was eternal, right? So I'll be with you wherever you go; every time the moon appears, that'll be me. But I want you to be somewhere safe where you can see the moon come up, okay?"

Alda, who had been sitting on the bed with her head in her hands, sat up and said, "It's not that simple, Martina. I don't expect you to know how things are – how could you, spending all your time in the kitchen? Look, this entire country has been turned into a huge jail, from north to south, surrounded by the steel fences that son of a bitch has ordered to be built, detention camps everywhere; shit, he's probably set one up in Antarctica for all I know, soldiers everywhere, in every village, checking papers, taking names, making lists—"

"Alda's right," Meche broke in. "Roberto told me that they now have all their data in computers linked from one end of the country to the other. They even have videos of suspected and known rebels and other troublemakers."

"So forget about escape. There isn't any escape for us. That's not the solution," Alda said in a dead voice, as if she were talking to herself. She jumped up and started pacing, slapping her thigh and muttering to herself. Martina was suddenly frightened. She cleared her throat and wiped her eyes with a corner of the blanket. She was about to say something when Alda suddenly stopped and stared out the window.

"That son of a bitch is going to get his, I promise," she vowed. "I'll be damned if I'm going to run off and hide like those clowns. Like fish out of water, and for what? To save their lives and continue their art. While that prick has the run of a palace. Plenty of food and running water, no worries about medicine or where his next meal is coming from. The cocksucker has perverted our lives, stolen our laughter, made us outlaws because we love our country, because we want our freedom back!" She stared at the window as if watching someone. "You filthy excuse for a human being, I hope you burn in hell, surrounded by all those who suffered and died at the hands of your fucking soldiers." She turned to Martina. 'Take care of Meche, Señora Martina. I have to go out." She slammed the door behind her and crossed the patio with firm, resounding steps.

Alda waited until 10 o'clock for the bus that would take her to the ranch where the clowns had taken shelter. A pregnant woman carrying several packages stopped beside her and regarded her with curious eyes.

Alda smiled at her and said, "Don't be alarmed, señora. Better days are coming."

The woman stepped back in surprise and took off quickly, looking back at Alda with suspicion.

When she reached the old ranch house hidden among the eucalyptus trees, the clowns came out to greet Alda with much hugging and kissing, even though their expressions were as sad as the depressed people she met constantly on the streets of the capital.

One of the women took her to the kitchen and made her a cup of coffee. She gave Alda a wry grin and said, "We've been so despondent lately that we hardly speak to each other. This house reminds me of a monastery; it's as if we share some kind of solitary confinement. The children rarely laugh any more. Thank God you came! Hey, Mario," she shouted into the drawing-room as she poured hot water into Alda's cup, "let's organize another show for Alda tonight."

"No, don't," Alda said, taking her arm. "Thank you, but I'm in a hell of a hurry, and I have to catch the four o'clock bus back to the city. Where's José Miguel?"

"Who knows? Down at the pond maybe. He keeps away from the house as much as possible. Leaves early in the morning and spends all day roaming around the grounds. His moods are so unpleasant that no one goes near him."

Alda set off across the patio, passing the cage where the doves roosted, their feathers shorn of paint now, and after a few minutes she came upon José Miguel sitting on a huge boulder shaded by tall pine trees.

"What the hell are you doing here?" he asked gruffly, trying to smile but ending up with a grimace.

"I came to see you, José Miguel," she said, sitting beside him. "And don't ask me why, because I don't really know. It just occurred to me. Are you all right?"

"No. I'm in a terrible state. All of us are going through a dreadful time. We used to be able to talk about the future, make jokes to cheer each other up. But now, we're like prisoners in an asylum: the men in a bad mood, always arguing; the women crying in the kitchen while they cook; and the children getting the worst of it from both ends. Ironic, isn't it? We who live to make children happy now send them screaming to their rooms." He scratched his chin. "I remember when we made everyone laugh, kids and grown-ups alike. Shit."

"You must be patient, José Miguel. This nightmare has to end some day. Things will change. We have to wait."

"Change, my arse! We've been telling each other that for years now. Sometimes I think we'd have been better off to be arrested and taken to one of those camps. Better to be dead than to be clowns who have no audience but themselves. It's strange: by profession we believe in hope, which is why we came to this run-down ranch, to continue our craft, to teach ourselves the old tricks and the new, because we were born to be clowns; it's all we know. It wouldn't be difficult to get a job working in construction, say, or sweeping the streets like those poor people on the minimum wage. All we'd have to do is put on a different disguise; our real faces, huh? But what is a clown without his painted face, without his art? A walking corpse, my princess, a dead man wandering among the living. It was a mistake to think that we could crawl into a hole and still keep the illusion of our former world alive. During the first months, we used to practise and rehearse every day, as if we'd brought the circus with us. How naive, eh? We can't strip off the environment that gives us our identity. We become non-entities, nothing . . ." José Miguel closed his eyes and saw himself for a moment at centre stage, surrounded by the laughing people, the crashing cymbals, and the phosphorescent glare of the spotlights. He turned to Alda with a sad face. "A tiger without his stripes isn't a tiger any more. And a circus without music and an excited audience isn't a circus. And therefore we do not exist either, Aldita. Imagine an author forced to write with invisible ink: mimicry without meaning. That's us."

She put an arm around his shoulder. "*Hombre*, get a grip on yourself. We aren't beaten yet."

He shook off her arm angrily. "There's no way out! Can't you see that? All we know is the circus. It's blood deep; no, deeper – we drank the circus from our mothers' milk, grew up in dressing-rooms, played with tiny tents our parents made for us as toys. I performed for the first time at the age of two, my father dressed as a woman and carrying me in his arms. They say I grabbed the buttons on his blouse and yanked until the two balls he wore for breasts fell out and started bouncing on the stage. I can stil see them rolling around, still hear the people screaming with laughter, and that was sixty-three years ago, which is how long I've been a clown, Alda, and I've never wanted to be anything else. But this is a different world. Here, people fight and torture and kill because they desire power and fame." He broke off to wipe the tears from his eyes. He then hid his face in his hands and said, "Let me be honest with you. This old clown would rather be dead than live in such a madhouse."

"Don't talk like that!" Alda flared. "Listen," she told him, gripping his arm and staring into his eyes, "do you know the story of the tyrant who died by the hand of a woman?"

"No," he replied, unable to take his eyes from hers.

"It's the tale of a woman called Jael, who gave shelter in her tent to a cruel tyrant ruling over the people of Israel. After he fell asleep she drove a nail through his temple and killed him."

"That's the kind of death all tyrants deserve," José Miguel said. "But why tell me?"

"Because since the first day I visited you and your friends, I haven't been able to get Jael out of my mind. That time we were looking at our faces in the mirror, remember? I realized I'll never know who I am. Maybe I was born to be a nobody, and that's why I became a whore, although I suspect that decent women, too, are born to be nobodies."

José Miguel nodded his understanding. "That's the fate of women in this world where Lilith was doomed to roam the earth in darkness in the form of a devilish Sin."

"Yes, I remember your story. But look, for many years I deceived myself, thinking that I didn't care about what happened to me. I even laughed at those men who pretended to be so important, even after we'd gone to bed. I discovered that all men are alike in bed, but when I started to work in the Resistance I felt, for the first time in my life, that I had some purpose, some destiny awaiting me, that it wasn't all an accident, that life wasn't a haphazard affair, that my parents truly loved each other when they made me, even though it's far more probable that my mother didn't even want to have sex that night, and my father must surely have done it out of a sense of duty rather than real passion – I mean, he was always in love with some other woman, so I imagine that he was bored while he was making love to my mother—"

"What the hell are you getting at, Alda?" José Miguel interrupted. He smiled for the first time. "You sound more pessimistic than I do."

"I'm sorry. I'm having trouble sorting out my thoughts. I just want to explain certain things to you, although I'm not sure why. Neither Meche nor Martina would understand what I'm talking about. Anyway, I keep thinking about Jael's story, her actions, which Deborah predicted, mainly because I've come to the conclusion, José Miguel, that even though fate designated me as a nobody, I have the right to change the outcome. I have the right to be someone who counts. Don't I?"

José Miguel cocked his head and looked at her as if seeing her for the first time. "And you want to be like Jael, is that what you're saying? Well, just don't forget that this isn't Israel. Nowadays, the military men don't ask a woman for shelter. On the contrary, they hate women because they fear them, fear them more than men. When they torture women, they become merciless as beasts."

"That doesn't scare me any more," Alda said. "Listen: I know I can kill the dictator. This Saturday we have to go to the inauguration of a new housing development. The arsehole has had twenty or twenty-five prefabricated houses built on the outskirts of the city for a few of the poor people he hasn't put in jail yet. He really enjoys these ceremonies. It gives him the opportunity to look like a real benefactor of the people. He and his top officers wear all their medals and spend most of their time posing for the cameras. I'm going to see Arreola this afternoon. I know I can convince him to let me present a big bouquet of flowers to that hyena. In front of all the TV cameras. Think of that!"

José Miguel almost fell off his perch on the boulder. "What the fuck's the matter with you? Kill him? Kill him in front of the cameras? Has Arreola been giving you drugs?"

Alda held up a hand. "Listen to me, dammit! Doña Carolina always keeps a pistol in her night table. She teaches all the girls to shoot, in case a customer or a thief attacks us, so of course I can kill him, and, most important of all, I could give my life to save our people."

José Miguel shook his head in amazement. "My God, you're serious."

Alda nodded. "I knew you'd understand. That's why I came to talk to you."

José Miguel took her hand, stroked it, looking off into the distance. "You know, our world, the circus, is so different: made up of wooden rings and hoops and circles of hay, bright lights and outlandish costumes. There are acrobats who leap into space without a care, men and women walking the tightrope, trapeze artists who are as graceful as birds – all defying the limits imposed by the world of men. It's really quite lovely. And all this time I've sat here on my butt, doing nothing but dreaming, hoping that one day our country could become as free as the circus, all of us on the high wire, every man, woman and child smiling into the lights. That would be something, wouldn't it? Imagine: the band plays the Blue Danube waltz while the white cranes of freedom, peace and joy soar overhead in unison, like true brothers and sisters – no, like human beings, no need for silly gender separations, just us, people, human beings united in joy, with or without the need to procreate, because heterosexual or homosexual, every minute would be like making love."

"It won't happen unless I hand that monster the bouquet of flowers," Alda suggested.

"Okay," José Miguel surrendered. "But don't be fooled by how stupid he appears. He's clever as a fox when it comes to watching his arse. You need a better plan."

"So," Alda agreed. "Explain what I have to do."

"You need a distraction, something that will cause him to lower his guard. Some interference that will catch his bodyguards' attention. You'll be frightened, nervous, and if everybody is looking at you, they'll shoot you down before the flowers hit the pavement, or someone at the last second will spot the gun and jump on you."

"But how can I create a diversion?"

"Easy. You need a bystander, a poor old man from the barrio with a huge moustache who has come to pay his respects to the Benefactor of the Republic. A tall old man who, at the moment you hold out the flowers with the grateful smile of a dutiful daughter, will suddenly begin to perform a series of artful and astonishing somersaults off to one side, catching everyone's attention, just as he has always done at the end of every show."

Alda frowned. "But José Miguel, they'd kill you too."

He smiled. "Ah. Can't you picture it: to die in the middle of a string of somersaults. What an end for a clown! Now that's the kind of death I have dreamed about."

"Now you sound like the crazy one. I'm not going to let you risk your life."

"Please, let me help," he said in a soft voice. "It will be better than dying here alone among the boulders, which is what I see in store for me unless some miracle occurs. Besides, I wouldn't be the first José Miguel who died for his country. Not at all. When they asked José Miguel Carrera what his last wish was as he stood before the firing squad, he asked for a piece of water melon grown in his own far-off country. Remember that from your history books? And after he was dead, a woman who loved him kissed him on the mouth and, like someone cutting flowers from a garden recently watered by rain, she snipped off several locks of his hair and embroidered them into a small tapestry which now lies under glass in the national museum. Let's suppose for the moment that I was going to be killed. Do you think I might be granted a last wish?"

Alda laughed at him. "Well, supposing it were in my power to grant such a request, I'd say yes, of course." Her eyes twinkled with merriment. "What would your last wish be?"

José Miguel took her by the shoulders. "To make love to you . . . under these trees, as an offering to nature before taking leave of her."

Something inside Alda melted as she looked at his face, which suddenly seemed to her the profile of a saint who, like St Francis, had come to the world to dispense joy and laughter. Excepting João, who had guided her into the pure territory of love free from the inhibitions of any law, no man had ever proposed sex as an act of offering to nature, the kind of germination which endured despite ambition and ignorance and violence among men. Such men had set her on the road to prostitution in the need to pervert pleasure and by their desire to soil her body by reducing it to the status of a commodity, while in nature it was a temple, not subject to any price.

And, at that moment, she came to the realization that the impulse to give affection to the army of men who had lain with her had been due to her feeling that sexual pleasure was intertwined with the harmonic chords that underpin the universe. She could not move, so strong was her emotion, her instinct that in the arms of José Miguel she would spin off into the constellation of all creation; and so she was still, liberated, unshackled from all those former gestures of seductions she had once perfected when sex was a commercial contract. She was in some way purified, a priestess awaiting a supplicant's ritual, her eyes fixed on the tall green trees which fused into the horizon like a green pathway to the blue sky. And she knew she was about to cross the threshold into an unknown region.

José Miguel rose, his face on fire with a fervour that was at once sensual and spiritual. He lifted her to her feet and slowly bent her backwards against the warm rock, his shining eyes glowing in the sunlight. He kissed her, lifting her dress and caressing her body inch by inch, his mouth climbing her body, seeking purchase in each crevice, pausing at the corner of her thighs to rest and drink, ascending slowly to the dark foliage under her armpits before following the stream between her breasts which trickled down her stomach and met its source in the thick bushes of her pubis.

Arching, bent like a bow, Alda felt herself merging with the blue sky in this moment of ecstasy as his tongue continued on that most primitive of journeys, rising over the hills of her flesh and slipping its way into the heated cave which lay at the juncture of her thighs. And for the first time in her life, Alda found herself willingly engaged in a burnt offering of herself to the spirit of the true God, who remained untouched by the foul stratagems of men. She closed her eyes and heard the silence that accompanied the first creation, saying to herself that such silence is the sacred aura surrounding all females who give birth in the deep forests. She knelt over José Miguel, kissing him passionately, and both of them remained entwined while the sun burned its way across the world.

Taking advantage of the fact that Meche had fallen asleep after drinking the herb teas she had been forcing her to drink over the last two days, Martina went into the kitchen to discuss her unhappiness with Señora Rosa.

"Things will get worse, *huaina*," the old woman said. "You'd better come with me."

"What's all this – get worse?" Martina said in a rising voice. "Didn't you tell me you'd come from the other world to help?"

"That I did. And I've given you a lot of good advice. Don't be ungrateful, because God will get you. It's just that one needs a ton of witchcraft to defeat the *wecufu*. Many battles must be fought. Even you should know that it's not easy to do away with evil; you need patience to beat the devil, you have to be like a drop of water which eats through rock. It's not a matter of a few days, Martina, my God! And, like you, I'm no spring chicken any more, my power is limited."

"But how the hell can things get worse?" Martina broke in with alarm.

"Hush now, girl! Stop asking questions. You're as curious as a cat. It's a fault you've had since you were a kid."

"Look, Señora Rosa, let's put all the cards on the table. You can't tell fortunes to a gypsy, right? I only want to know one fact, and don't lie to me, because these days Alda roars in and out of the house like a flooding river. Tell me true. Are they going to kill Alda?"

"That girl will never die," Rosa assured her. "She will bloom anew every spring, like the blossoms on the almond trees," the old woman said like a prophetess.

"God, you're a stubborn woman. Quit playing tricks; get to the point."

"But I've already answered you, child. Listen, grab some flour and start making those biscuits that melt in the mouth."

"I won't fix a damn thing for you," Martina said furiously. She turned to leave the kitchen but stopped at the moment Señora Rosa cried out in pain, as if she'd been mortally wounded.

Martina took a step back to the counter, her voice full of concern. "What's wrong, Señora Rosa, for the love of God?"

The old woman's voice quivered. "Don't leave me, *huaina*. I don't want to be alone. Stay with me for a little while longer."

Feeling sorry and a bit guilty, Martina leaned over the burner and saw Rosa's face. It was full of pain. "You still want some biscuits?" she asked in a sweet voice.

"Yes, now. Get the flour and this time be sure you don't put too much salt in the water," the old lady said weakly.

Martina felt a spasm of strange anguish in her heart. She put four handsful of flour on the wooden counter, forming a small mound, in the centre of which she scooped out a hollow, the mound now resembling a snow-covered volcano with its peak blown off. Smiling at Señora Rosa, who watched her with half-closed eyes, she heated the lard and salty water and poured them slowly into the crater, the mound gradually becoming soft as silk, sticking to her palms as she kneaded the dough. When Rosa's sigh gently stirred the burner's flames, Martina felt a sharp pain in her chest. Her legs went wobbly, and her face fell into the dough before she collapsed on the floor. In those moments before she lost consciousness, lying with her upturned face as white as a lily floating on a pond, Martina saw her beloved Juan Manuel open his arms in invitation beside the clay baking oven and, with a smile and a feeling of lightness that redeemed all her life-long suffering, she saw herself rise to walk with him through the doorway of death.

Doña Carolina closed the house so that they could mourn Martina's passing. Tacked to the doors and tied around the balconies were black ribbons announcing that the routine of sexual pleasure had been interrupted by death's abrupt arrival. At twilight the grieving women gathered in the big parlour, each dressed in black; the house was silent and colourless, devoid of music and merriment, drab as the unpainted faces of the guests, all women of the street of night wearing veils of black Chantilly lace, who entered Doña Carolina's house, walked to Martina's coffin to kiss her forehead, and then took their seats in complete silence.

When everyone had arrived, Doña Carolina came slowly down the stairs dressed from head to toe in a tunic made of black velvet and wearing a tiara of jasmine flowers that adorned her tightly braided hair. She went to the head of the coffin and rested one hand against Martina's cheek. Facing the assembled women, she began the elegy.

"We worship our dead by ourselves, outside the church which condemns us, whose rituals we have replaced with our own. Death has chosen to embrace you, dear Martina, gathering to himself your body, which was sacred because it allowed you to earn your bread. In this house your hands were those of an angel, preparing our food three times a day, giving us the gift of God in the form of vegetables and meat in dishes that not even Adam and Eve enjoyed in the Garden of Eden." She paused and patted Martina's cheek.

"I will miss your *congrio frito*," Adela testified, "with its golden crust and juicy white meat. No one could prepare fish like you, Martina."

"Nor could anyone match your delicious *sopaipillas*," a voice blurted out.

"And your egg soufflé with parsley and black pepper," said another.

In a tearful voice, a woman cried out, "My lips will never forget the red juice of your roast beef stuffed with garlic, green peppers and carrots."

"And the tender chicken breasts you covered with onion slices will always be in my memory," someone said in a trembling contralto.

Doña Carolina looked up from Martina and willed the group to silence with her eyes before continuing. "Blessed art thou among whores, who in your youth gave joyful shelter to so many men between your thighs. Honoured among patrons of our holy craft, you knew how to lead each man who entered your bed through multiple paths of pleasure, leaving him so exalted that he paid without complaint, praising the priceless movements of your hips."

Before she could go on, the voices rose around the room: "Priceless hips, and priceless breasts, by God!"; "And your black eyes bewitched so many hearts."

Doña Carolina raised a hand, waited, went on: "Many were the fruits of your pussy, which sweetened the lives of those who spent so much time coming in and out of your room and your body. For the body is a holy sepulchre! And godly as well, for the Lord is present, too, when men and women roll among the sheets." She opened her mouth but a few women could not contain themselves.

"You tamed so many cocks in your life, dear Martina!"

"Thick as an elephant's trunk!"

"Long and thin as a cigar!"

"Or those unwilling little members that refused to rise, that you played like an expert with your nimble fingers and their magic music, until the little fellows stood up like bedposts!"

Doña Carolina motioned to Alda and Meche, her acolytes, who crossed the room in silence and stopped at the record player, where Alda slipped a record on to the turntable. As the first notes of a bolero filled the parlour, the guests left their seats to dance, by themselves, each alone with an imaginary lover, placing their cheeks against invisible cheeks, the wind from the open windows tossing aside their veils long enough for them to receive make-believe kisses. They danced like this until the melody ended and Doña Carolina resumed her elegy.

"Death rejoices as he penetrates your body, and joyful art thou upon receiving him, for Death is masculine, the only lover who never abandons his mistress. Once inside you, he stays put, for ever."

"Day and night, insatiable, a dream lover crazy for your honeyed tunnel," a woman interrupted.

"Mad about the smell of oregano on your skin!"

"Caressing you and kissing your nipples until the end of time!"

Doña Carolina raised both arms as if she were a bird about to take flight. "We are gathered here tonight," she said, looking at Martina, "to make a covenant with Death. Let us proceed," she added, nodding to Alda, who set the needle on another record.

Now it was a rumba, the beat of tropical drums. The women bent their heads and swayed to the music, moving their hips and legs and whispering erotic incantations. When the melody saxophoned to an end, the women took their seats and fell silent. Alda and Meche passed among them with two red trays edged in bronze on which were laid out little pieces of cake and shot glasses filled with *aguardiente*.

Holding the wedges of cake aloft, they recited in one voice: "This is your body, Martina." They washed the cake down with grappa, closing their eyes.

"For you will need sustenance on your long journey," Doña Carolina intoned, removing her tunic, under which she wore only black knickers. Bending over Martina, she held in turn each naked breast to the dead woman's lips. Outside the wind whipped down the street of night, sweeping into the parlour, causing the candle flames to dance, and carrying Deborah's lament, now loud and flowing with the wind, around the room.

Doña Carolina stood by the coffin while Alda and Meche removed the tiara and unbraided her hair, combing and fluffing it with their fingers. No longer weeping, her eyes shone with excitement. "Now," she ordered, "everyone must go to her room and wait for the lover Martina will send us from the other side. Tonight it will be an adolescent, with golden skin and auburn hair, who will fold his wings and enter our beds, where we will initiate him into the art of lovemaking."

The next morning, Alda went to Meche's room carrying a small package and found the girl sitting in her nightgown with a forlorn expression.

"Don't cry, sweetheart. Roberto will be saved. The whole country will be saved, my dear Meche! One day when you least expect it, he'll knock at the door, just at sunset, and you'll be together again. Trust me."

But Meche just sat there, her eyes on a crucifix mounted over her bed.

Alda sat beside her and took her hand. "Meche, listen, I want you to promise me something."

Meche finally turned, acknowledging Alda's presence. "What did you say? A promise?"

"Yes. I want you to swear that, whatever happens, you'll take good care of yourself. That you'll eat every day and exercise to keep up your strength, so that when Roberto returns he'll find you even more beautiful. Promise?"

"Okay," Meche said listlessly.

Alda cuffed her lightly on the head. "Come on! Stop moping and get off your arse. Sitting around like this will make you fat, and then Roberto will slam the door in your face. Now, look, I need another favour. I won't be able to attend Señora Martina's funeral this afternoon."

Meche's eyes came to life. "You can't be serious. What could be more important than Martina's burial?"

"I'm sorry, baby. I feel like shit about it. But I have something very important that can't wait."

"Call Señora Leonora and explain. She'll understand."

"It's not her."

Now Meche took her arm, her grip surprisingly strong. "You're going to see Arreola, that filthy murderer! You choose to wrap your legs around an assassin rather than to bury one of your best friends? What's the matter with you?"

Alda lowered her eyes. "I don't have time to explain, Meche. Please believe me, this is an appointment I can't refuse." She looked up, forcing a smile, and laid the package between them, opening it to reveal a flower with red waxy petals. "So, this *copihue* is from the forests of the south, like Martina. After they lower her into the grave, throw it on top of the coffin, and tell her that I loved her the way only women can love each other." She paused to fight back the tears, then brightened again. "It's incredible, you know, that those military pricks will never know that they brought the three of us together, that despite the cruelty and hatred, we found each other and became friends. Odd, how God blesses you, huh?"

Meche laid her head on Alda's shoulder, unable to speak.

Alda stroked her hair. "I love you the same way, my little girl. It fills my heart."

"Mine too, Aldita. Like the sound of bells in church. But I feel so bad, so dead inside . . ."

"Knock off this shit about death!" Alda said sharply. "Remember, you promised to take care of yourself. And a promise is a promise, right?"

Meche lowered her face to Alda's lap and wept. "I'll try. I really will. But I hurt inside so, I can hardly bear it."

Idly examining one of Meche's blonde curls, Alda said, "Any suffering is bearable, sugar. All you have to do is imagine that you're a beggar who tosses his pain in his pack each morning before setting out to face the day. Sooner or later Roberto will come back, and both of you will be happy for ever. Now, let's see a smile," she said, laughing a bit too loud. "I have to go now, honey. I can't be late for this one. Don't forget to toss the flower in before the first shovel of dirt, okay? And take care of yourself, whatever happens, you hear?"

Running her fingers through Meche's hair, Alda looked at her tear-stained face as if trying to memorize each feature. She held Meche in her arms for a few moments longer, then stood up and went to the door, where she turned to wave goodbye.

She cried as she dressed, wondering if there was any story in the Bible about a woman who abandoned her daughter to keep an encounter with death.

Some hours later, she joined the crowd of people in the street, elbowing her way to the cordon of policemen who formed a human fence in front of the podium. Hard-looking men, they stared suspiciously at Alda, then roamed her body with their eyes as she stretched and craned her neck to locate José Miguel. It was only when the TV camera crew came back-pedalling down the street that she noticed on her left an old man wearing a faded green sweater who waved to her and twisted one end of his enormous moustache.

"Here he comes," someone shouted through a bullhorn, and many soldiers dressed in civilian clothes began applauding and whistling, smiling and waving small banners at the cameras and the bright lights that swung back and forth to illustrate another approving crowd of ordinary citizens.

She heard the stamp of boots from down the street before she saw Arreola in full military dress, goose-stepping as he led the guard of honour. In front of them came two squads of soldiers hoisting banners and a regimental flag. The procession came to a halt, boots slamming in unison on the pavement, in front of the speaker's stand. Arreola did an about-face and walked over to Alda, motioning the policemen to step away and taking her by the elbow. He led her to the head of the ranks, where she stood beside him, clutching to her chest the pistol hidden in the big bouquet of chrysanthemums. She smiled nervously at Arreola and watched José Miguel moving to her left. At that moment the Benefactor marched into view, and the crowd broke into even wilder applause and acclamations. The dictator, surrounded by his personal bodyguards, stepped on to the podium, where he adjusted the microphone and gazed around at the people, who gradually fell silent.

"Citizens," he squeaked, "I come before you this afternoon to inaugurate yet another new housing complex, one of hundreds of such residential glories my government has constructed, our goal being that all of our people who lack shelter shall have a roof over their heads as long as they are obedient citizens in our brave and admirable Fatherland!" He waited for the applause to subside, recognizing one animated captain dressed like a construction worker. "I dislike being redundant, but I would like you to bear in mind that, thanks to my Herculean will, poverty has been eradicated from our nation. With that in mind, allow me to join in the celebration," he said, raising two gloved fists into the air as he shouted, "Long live our Fatherland!"

"*Viva*!" the crowd roared.

"*Viva* the Benefactor of the Republic," another officer dressed as a commoner shouted in a gruff voice.

"*Viva*!" the crowd agreed.

Another voice rose above the throng: "Long live the Great Defender of our Land!"

"*Viva*!" the crowd responded.

The dictator seemed to rise on the balls of his feet, resembling Mussolini in the films he watched at least once a week. He slashed the air with one hand, like a bandleader stopping the music, and stared down at Alda, who stared back in some confusion until she felt Arreola's hand on her back, shoving her forward and whispering, "Now, the flowers!"

Taking a deep breath, she stepped forward until she stood just below the dictator. She was beginning to extend the bouquet to his reaching hands, her finger tightening on the trigger, when José Miguel vaulted out between the policemen and did a perfect forward somersault, to the absolute astonishment of everyone present, including the Benefactor's bodyguard, who for a second thought José Miguel was part of the afternoon's entertainment.

"Oh, shit, a clown. I hate those parasites," the dictator cried out in rage. "Shoot him!" he ordered, leaning over to shove one of his bodyguards into action just as Alda pulled the trigger. The bullet struck a colonel standing behind the Benefactor. As the wounded man fell backwards, Alda was dragged to the pavement by four soldiers from the honour guard, who stripped the gun from her hands and began kicking and beating her. She heard shots as she passed out. The last thing she saw was José Miguel's body jerking as the bullets hit him.

She was unconscious when an officer of the Intelligence Service took Arreola firmly by the arm and said, "You're under arrest, Colonel. We've been keeping an eye on you and the whore for several months now, though I must confess I never thought it would lead to this."

"Take him to our headquarters," an old General barked, "and shoot him at once!"

"No," the Benefactor said in a shaky voice, mopping his face with a handkerchief. "Not that. Lock him in an office and leave a loaded pistol on the table."

The intelligence officer came to attention and saluted. He pointed at Alda. "What would you like me to do with this traitor?"

The Benefactor spat in Alda's direction. "Take her to the centre of the square and assemble the people. One bullet, in the head," he ordered, then started for his limousine between two flanks of bodyguards who kept step with him, threatening the crowd with their eyes, which stared at the shocked faces with contempt.

They carried Alda to the middle of the square, where she regained consciousness lying on her stomach as two soldiers were tying her hands behind her back. Then one of them slipped a black blindfold over her eyes and lifted her into a sitting position. The hell with this, Alda thought; I'm not going to be shot sitting down, and I damn well won't let these bastards yank me to my feet. She stood up shakily and planted her feet, lifting her head and thrusting her breasts out as she had done that morning in the detention camp when she had sung a tango to Arreola. But now she no longer identified with the words; no more was she a "doll", or a "toy of passion", for she had come to inhabit regions far removed from those of a simple prostitute who strutted her way through the transcendental transgressions of morality with all the awareness of a mummy. She rejected the tango, with its silly "flower of sin" image, attributed to whores; she knew the people would not allow her memory to wither away so easily. Though blinded, she knew she was surrounded by a silent crowd; she could smell their fear, feel it in the air, and her entire body rebelled at this final perversion, her need to revolt deepening and erupting as she stood on her toes and shouted, "Down with the damned tyrant!"

She heard the wave of murmurs as someone hit her in the face with a rifle butt and hard hands slammed her against a wall. Its surface was wet, sandy, and she remembered João kissing her as the sun was fading over the horizon, its last violet rays going dim on the surface of the sea, whose gentle waves caressed the beach of black volcanic sand. She saw a succession of images that flashed before her like a deck of cards being shuffled: herself at four embracing her father and balanced on his shoes, the brown ones she shined every Saturday to make him happy, the two of them moving forwards and backwards in the game she loved to play, both of them laughing; then, she was a year or two older and wearing her favourite light-blue nightgown and falling asleep next to her mother who smelled like the round box of face powder she kept in the first drawer of her dresser; next it was an afternoon and she was clutching Martina and laughing at one of the old lady's jokes, smelling the odour of tobacco on her bosom, feeling the tender loving weight of Martina's hands on her hair, hands like dark and wrinkled parchment as they flew among the pots and pans; then she was kneeling at Meche's feet to pin the hem on that white dress they had bought together, which she had stitched up after taking careful measurements, staring up at Meche's face from time to time and feeling maternal as the young girl smiled down at her with eyes as blue as the early morning sky; now she was sitting at an opened window in the street of night, profiling her breasts that strained against a low-cut red dress; and then a white silk summer blouse; and then a blue winter outfit which had shrunk the first time she washed it . . . The cards ruffled faster now, and she could barely see herself wearing other clothes of different styles and colours, with square and vertical low-cuts that amounted to little more than the ornamental trimming for the dark coronas of her breasts, the sensuous weapons she had rubbed against Arreola's lips.

At the moment she felt the cold pistol barrel against her temple, Alda remembered Deborah, which in Hebrew meant bee, who was given that name because she was intelligent, vigorous and diligent, and her honey was the sweet taste of freedom. And then it seemed she heard the effervescent buzz from the hive as well as a distant melody, and then a group of clowns came into view, waving at her with their large white handkerchiefs that fluttered like birds, the clowns smiling with tenderness and she smiling back just as the bullet entered her brain, the explosion itself lost as she was lost in the deafening roar of a flight of helicopters swinging low over the recently inaugurated housing complex.

Sitting at the desk, Colonel Arreola fondled the pistol. For a brief moment he remembered his wife and children, and he congratulated himself for having left all his family business in order. The notarized will stipulated that two-thirds of his assets were to be shared by his two sons, the remaining third going to his wife and his daughter. His notes, the records kept so assiduously for all these years, were also in perfect order, amounting to no fewer than one hundred and forty pages typed on eight-and-a-half- by eleven-and-a-half-inch paper. He had left instructions for his wife to have his papers published in case he died serving the Fatherland in an encounter with subversive elements.

His thoughts drifted to an afternoon in childhood when his grandmother sat him on her lap and asked him what he wished for the most in all the world. "That all the people and all the things around me never disobey or lose sight of their place in the world," he had answered solemnly. The old woman had laughed loudly, hugging him, celebrating his precocious remark. "You want the world to run like a Swiss clock, huh?" she asked, kissing his cheek. Then she wagged her finger at him, her voice serious as she told him, "Women are always on the margins of order, my child. You'll discover that when you're grown, when you're a big man, after you get married." His wife, Arreola reflected, had always obeyed him, helping him to maintain an immaculate and respectable home. It had been the other woman, that whore, that bitch, who had betrayed him – he who had always displayed tact and intelligence, associating exclusively with loyal women.

During his youth his father had forced him to attend an opera, insisting that he needed a certain acquaintance with culture. He went reluctantly, slumped in his seat in a bad mood, listening to the boring arias of dwarfs and giants and maidens who struggled to possess a ring. Somewhere in the middle of the thing, however, the violence had excited him. He sat up straight, engrossed in what he now considered an admirable spectacle. When Brunhilde jumped on the back of a horse to die with her beloved on a huge burning pyre, Arreola swore with absolute conviction that henceforth he would only grant allegiance to women who demonstrated heroic fidelity. Now he cursed himself, he who had always been recognized for planning things so carefully, which was why he had felt so comfortable at the Military Academy, where everything was just so, the way it was *meant* to be, right or wrong, good or bad, without the infection of any contradictions or problematics (a word he hated so intensely, a word the Marxists, before the glorious advent of the Benefactor, used to spit at you out of the corners of their mouths, trying to masquerade as intellectuals). And when he marched in parade, goose-stepping proudly in his best uniform to the music of a military band, he had always felt so fortunate to belong to such a secure world, one without absurdities, without ambiguity or contradiction, where the contrary factors of problematics did not exist because God and the Fatherland offered only two options, clean and shiny as the barrel of a polished weapon: victory or death.

A wave of anger swept over him, the sudden realization that he was going to die without struggle, not on a battlefield in hand-to-hand combat, but in an empty office where the door was locked. He slammed a fist on the desk, the idea occurring to him that the only hand-to-hand action he had engaged in, loosely speaking, had been with Alda, the traitor, who had led him to an ignominious death, the worst an officer could imagine. But of course he himself bore the blame for allowing those vandals, his instincts, to invade his superior mind. Yes, he deserved such a dishonourable end. He closed his eyes to ward off the image of her naked body, rubbing against him and purring like a cat on heat, whispering, her legs outspread like wings, giving voice to a symphony of repugnant moans.

Beside himself, all self-control abandoned, Arreola laid down the pistol and gripped himself with both hands, squeezing his erection hard, muttering, "You fucking whore, you fucking whore," before he began furiously punching his own penis, again and again until he hit a testicle and screamed in pain. Rubbing himself gently where it hurt and once more smelling Alda's dark, electric skin which gave off a heavy aroma of lilacs, he leaned back in the chair, stroking himself, immersed in a pleasure so intense he nearly fainted, his fist pumping him to the pinnacle of power; then, feeling the semen on his hands, he looked down to see the front of his trousers stained with a ropy grey substance like snot, and in self-disgust he sprang to his feet, picked up the pistol and came to attention, stuck the barrel into his mouth until it came to rest against his palate, and pulled the trigger.

That same afternoon, the women of the street of night met in front of Deborah's memorial to give Alda a symbolic burial. Holding aloft a lighted candle in one hand, they stood with their heads down until Patoja appeared wearing a black veil and carrying a can of red paint. She raised an arm to still their crying and then climbed a stepladder to deliver the ritual words, after which she intended to end the ceremony by printing an epitaph for Alda on the wall behind her.

But at that moment three black cars came around the corner and proceeded slowly down the street of night. As they came abreast of the women, the men inside opened fire and there was instant chaos: screams and curses and the sickening whump of bullets striking human flesh; the women flinging themselves on to the pavement and trying to crawl for some cover, dragging the wounded and the dead with them. Only Meche remained standing. It seemed strange to the assassins that anyone, especially a young and pretty blonde with such a sad smile, would step forward and walk towards the guns, as if wishing for the death that a second later spun her around and dropped her like a bloody bird . . .

. . . a bloody swallow in the street of night in the land where the flow of time ran forwards and backwards, as in a voice which had long ago resounded in the place where the world ends, emerging clearly over the din of an earlier event: "I am not a martyr. I was not born to be a martyr. I am a social reformer who is fulfilling the mission of defending the people," said the voice, belonging to a man named Salvador Allende, "but those who intend to repress history by ignoring the will of the people must be aware that, while I do not come as a martyr, I shall continue with my mission without one step backwards . . . I will vacate the presidential palace only when my democratically elected term expires," the speaker declared while a wave of determined miners applauded and the hope of justice seemed alive on that far-off afternoon in a city in the north. And minutes before his death, while other machine-guns chattered in the distance, Allende's voice rang out once more, under siege in the presidential palace during the last hours of the *coup d'état* by tanks and special troops and undergoing bombardment from military war planes; rang out over the radios, transmitted across the city from a pirate station, the only one that would broadcast his words that day; rang out to declare that social reform could not be stopped by force, with tanks or under threats from criminals; that this grey and sour moment in history would one day itself be erased by other human beings advancing down the wide avenues of solidarity.

And meanwhile in the street of night the present had indeed exploded, burst into fragments and splinters of its former self, and from that moment the voices of the future began to ring out, voices which rose on the wind and wafted through the night air like sirens that could be heard a long way off, as far away as the Benefactor's bedroom, whose eyebrows had grown thick with the passing of the years, forming a dark shroud for his brooding and sunken eyes, until it seemed that their hard and inhuman pupils were permanently soiled with the black filth of death.

"He'll be deposed!" the crowd would soon be shouting over and over, their laughter igniting passers-by and cars filled with equally hopeful citizens, the street of night and the streets of the nation filling with laughter, trumpets and car horns, a chorale of expectant voices that united in harmony throughout the country like spring rain. In the days to come, men, women and children would sing with joy in the spirit of that future solidarity Allende had earlier predicted, singing out an invitation for all to cross the bridge of history and enjoy the rainbow signalling the end of that desolate storm which had engulfed the land; singing out to announce the rebirth of the *dulce patria*, the sweet land.

"He'll be deposed!"

"He's going to fall!"

"His days are numbered!"

"The dictatorship is over, folks!!"

Singing out in jubilation as they came down La Alameda, the principal avenue of the capital, to form the throng escorting the newly elected presidential candidate, a civilian who walked and waved to the crowds alongside and those leaning out of tall buildings to toss confetti on him and his entourage.

"Thank God that at last we'll have a president chosen by the people," cried a young woman journalist who during the sixteen-year dictatorship had written her columns under the strict eye of military censorship. She laughed with a colleague and clicked the record button on her tape recorder to preserve the roar of the people who shouted chorus after chorus of one simple word: "Freedom".

Which had not yet arrived in the street of night, lying now in darkness like the entire nation, where that late afternoon the women bustled here and there to attend to their wounded companions after the assassins sped off. Handling her scissors skilfully, Julieta cut bandages from white bed-sheets and dressed the torn legs and arms of women who had been carried to the pavement. As she worked, Julieta thought of Alda's sacrifice, and how she had offered herself like so many of her countrymen and women. "These deaths shall not be in vain!" she shouted as Adela handed her another bottle of iodine and went off weeping to find more sheets. "Making history is hard work, my sweet comrades," Julieta said to those around her, pouring iodine into a slight hip wound, smiling to herself, thinking that history was a river whose current carried evil and good along on its journey through time, giving equal passage to hope as well as despair, but that despite its uneven and seemingly impartial tides, one quality always surfaced no matter how many miles and years flowed between its banks, and this was the eternal drive of human beings to resist injustice, as powerful and enduring as the sea itself.